THE
QUANTUM
DECEPTION

PRAISE FOR *QUANTUM DECEPTION*

"The realistic cyber espionage and high-stakes politics make for one killer story."
    -R. C. Hancock, author of *An Uncommon Blue*

"Welcome to the world of cyber terrorism. A world where foreign governments and their agents create America's worst technological nightmare. Undetectable and seemingly unstoppable malware threatens US financial collapse. Only a brilliant mind and the world's fastest computer stand in the way. Denver Acey's *Quantum Deception* will have you turning pages in light speed wondering if the NSA, FBI, and the US Secret Service can stop the attack in time. Fast-paced cyber warfare with a deliciously sinister plot."
    —Joel Narlock, author of *Drone Games*

"A fun, fast-paced novel. I found the technical plot both intriguing and thought provoking. Well worth the read!"
    —Bill Bodine, software architect

"*The Quantum Deception* is terrifyingly realistic. Acey creates a world of suspense full of lovable characters and some you love to hate. At the end I was left wanting more."
    —Marilee Jackson, author of *Midnight Runner*

"I loved the suspense and action in this technically realistic adventure. Anyone who knows about IT will enjoy this book. Acey's writing is thought provoking, considering all the news about cyber attacks."
    —Beck Locey, software engineer

DENVER ACEY

THE QUANTUM DECEPTION

BONNEVILLE BOOKS ™

An Imprint of Cedar Fort, Inc.
Springville, Utah

ISBN 13: 978-1-4621-1617-1

Published by Bonneville Books, an imprint of Cedar Fort, Inc.
2373 W. 700 S., Springville, UT 84663
Distributed by Cedar Fort, Inc., www.cedarfort.com

LIBRARY OF CONGRESS CATALOGING-IN-PUBLICATION DATA

Acey, Denver.
  Quantum deception / By Denver Acey.
    pages ; cm
  ISBN 978-1-4621-1617-1 (softcover : acid-free paper)
  1. Hackers--Fiction. 2. Computer viruses--Fiction. I. Title.
  PS3601.C488Q365 2015
  813'.6--dc23
                          2014033447

Cover design by Michelle May
Cover design © 2015 by Lyle Mortimer
Edited and typeset by Melissa J. Caldwell

Printed in the United States of America

10 9 8 7 6 5 4 3 2 1

To my wife, family, and friends.
Your support and encouragement made this book possible.

APRIL 24, SALT LAKE CITY, UTAH

The water was frigid, but she was prepared. A black neoprene dry suit covered her entire body, including her head, as she rhythmically bobbed up and down in the water on the moonless night. Only a small snorkel tube and some gentle ripples in the water revealed her presence. Swimming in the canal for almost an hour, she was just starting to feel fatigued. But Reina had conditioned her mind and body for this type of strenuous activity, and despite being submerged in the forty–five–degree water, she was confident that she would succeed. Her mission required secrecy and anonymity—two of her best talents.

She heard the roar of jet engines overhead, indicating that she was almost at the drop-off location. Reina had never played a round of golf in her life, but she was intimately familiar with the layout of Wingpointe Golf Course. Using satellite images posted on the Internet, she memorized the terrain of the golf course when planning her attack. Reina never understood why Salt Lake City had built the golf course immediately next to the international airport, but it made her mission easier.

Reina arrived at the exit spot ten minutes later. The twenty-two-year-old climbed out of the canal stealthily, her youthful and athletic body blending into the darkness. She maneuvered along the berms of the golf course until she reached the first fairway. Hidden in the thick cattails behind the putting green, she found her package. She didn't know who had left it there, nor did she care. Reina understood that such questions were inconsequential.

The dark April night didn't hinder her efforts as she opened the container and skillfully assembled the shoulder-fired, surface-to-air missile. This particular weapon was a North Korean model. It was similar to the other "fire-and-forget" SAMs she had trained with in her youth. In just a manner of seconds, she had the rocket staged and ready to go. Reina checked her diving watch—12:08 a.m. The midnight flight was scheduled to leave momentarily.

With its proximity to Salt Lake International Airport, the golf course was the perfect location to implement her terrorist attack. Reina had an unobstructed view of the airplanes as they taxied out onto the runway. She patiently hid in the cattails, watching for the color and insignia of the commercial airliner she wanted. At 12:24 a.m., her target came into view.

Flight 2512 was the nonstop, red-eye from Salt Lake City to Washington, DC. The flight was only half full, which didn't bother the crew or the 126 passengers on board.

The 757 throttled to full power as it lifted off and ascended over Wingpointe Golf Course. Reina stepped out of the cattails and positioned her petite frame in a sand bunker. She aimed the shoulder-fired missile at the plane, and the infrared sensor quickly locked on to the turbine engine as the only significant heat source in the cold night sky. The rocket soared out in a white flash and raced toward its target, exploding just behind the starboard engine. The pilots of the 757 never had a chance. Despite their best efforts, the damaged airplane quickly lost altitude as it veered sharply to the west and plowed into the snowcapped Oquirrh Mountains.

Reina didn't pause to admire her achievement. As soon as she fired the missile, she began her retreat. Reina knew that anyone within a half-mile radius had likely seen the bright flash of light, and she wanted to be clear of the area when the police arrived. Sprinting back toward the canal, she threw herself and the spent rocket tube into the icy water. The discarded cylinder sank to the muddy bottom as Reina began the hour-long swim away from the airport.

• ———— •

DRAPER, UTAH

The pager chirped loudly on the nightstand, waking Tanner Stone out of his deep sleep. It took a moment for him to clear his mind as he focused on the alarm clock and saw that it was after midnight. It was times like this that the thirty-three-year-old wished he had a company cell phone, but those were strictly prohibited. Due to the top-secret nature of his job, a one-way pager was the only electronic communication device authorized by his employer.

Tanner checked his pager and immediately recognized the phone number for his boss, Helen Ripplinger. Grabbing the cordless phone next to the nightstand, Tanner stumbled into the bathroom and closed the door, taking care not to wake his wife. Megan Stone had never complained about her husband's occasional late night interruptions. Megan, who was also part of an on-call rotation at her job as a database administrator, understood, like every information technology professional, that modern computer systems needed constant babysitting.

"Tanner, thank goodness you called," Helen Ripplinger answered. The emotion in her voice was tangible. She continued hastily, not giving her employee a chance to respond. "Turn on your TV. There's been a terrible accident."

APRIL 24, SALT LAKE INTERNATIONAL AIRPORT, UTAH

The specialized police unit at Salt Lake International Airport was the first to arrive on the scene. Even though Wingpointe Golf Course was technically off their property, the airport police quickly responded after the control tower had reported a bright light just before Flight 2512 went down. A call from the tower also went out to the local law enforcement agencies. Before long, police cruisers from the Salt Lake City Police Department began filling the area.

"Give me an update!" a sergeant shouted, trying to bring order to the group of police officers gathering by the golf course clubhouse. A local news crew was also crowding the scene, probing for information.

"I've got an eyewitness who says there was a flash of light in this area followed by an explosion," shouted a deputy from the airport police unit.

Another voice rose out of the commotion. "A freight handler over at the cargo terminal said she heard a loud swooshing sound

4

before the plane went down." He pointed toward the FedEx terminal adjacent to the golf course.

More police cars and news reporters arrived, adding to the chaos. The lights and sirens, coupled with the thumping sound of TV helicopters overhead, caused sensory vertigo for the police officer trying to calm the situation. Then, unexpectedly, he felt a strong hand on his back. Looking over his shoulder, the sergeant recognized the familiar and stern face of Special Agent Derek Cannon from the local branch of the Federal Bureau of Investigation.

"Let me take a crack at it," the fifty-year-old FBI veteran said. The police sergeant nodded his head in reply, willingly handing control of the frenzied situation over to the FBI.

Derek stepped forward and addressed the disorderly group. At six feet eight inches tall and 260 pounds, Derek was an intimidating presence who commanded immediate respect. Ironically, most people recognized Derek not from his service in the FBI but from his former college basketball days as a power-forward for Syracuse University.

"Okay, everyone, gather around. I'm Special Agent Derek Cannon of the FBI. This is Special Agent Sara Heywood," he said. He gestured to his petite, younger partner standing next to him. Both agents were dressed in casual clothes, but they couldn't have been more different. Agent Cannon was a powerful, athletic African American, who might have played in the NBA if he hadn't ruptured his Achilles tendon during his senior year at college. On the other hand, Agent Heywood was a twenty-eight-year-old Caucasian, just five feet three inches tall, and weighing a fraction over one hundred pounds.

"I want two groups formed here," Derek said. His voice boomed over the crowd as he pointed with his hands. "On my left, I want anyone who has information from the eyewitnesses. On my right, I want everyone else to coordinate with Agent Heywood and search the area for clues."

Derek didn't need to elaborate or motivate. Everyone felt the gravity of the situation.

APRIL 24, DRAPER, UTAH

Tanner was fully awake now. The emotion he heard in his supervisor's voice forced him to be alert. With phone in hand, he left the bathroom and stumbled toward the television sitting on top of the dresser. He heard his wife stirring in bed as he turned on the TV, but he didn't bother muting the sound. Focusing on the screen, Tanner saw the breaking news logo from a local TV affiliate, announcing the airplane crash. A pit immediately formed in his stomach. He fought to ignore obvious questions forming in his mind.

"That was supposed to be my flight, wasn't it?" Tanner asked over the phone.

"Yes. It went down shortly after takeoff," Helen answered. Her normally charming voice was sterile and numb. "The police are searching for survivors, but the crash site is on the face of the Oquirrh Mountains. Only helicopters can get up there right now because of the steep terrain."

Tanner sat on the edge of his bed, running his free hand

through his matted brown hair. He felt like the wind had just been knocked out of him. He was supposed to be on that plane with his coworker Bryan Morrison, but an unplanned visit to the hospital forced Tanner to cancel his trip at the last minute.

Nobody spoke for a while, and the prolonged silence on the phone became unbearable. Finally, Helen ended the awkward moment. "Tanner, it's not your fault that the plane went down."

Tanner's head spun as conflicting emotions swelled inside of him. He was ecstatic to be alive, yet he felt responsible that Bryan and all those innocent people had died on that tragic flight. Despite his boss's assurance, Tanner felt like he was drowning in guilt.

"Honey, what's going on?" Megan asked. She sat up in bed, wondering why her husband was watching TV in the middle of the night.

Tanner ignored his wife's question. "What caused it?" he asked over the phone. Already, his analytical mind was assessing the situation.

"I'm not sure," Helen said. "The details are still coming in."

"Do we have any intel from our group?" Tanner asked.

"I can't discuss that on an unsecured line, but I'm calling the team together," she answered.

"I'll be at work within the hour," Tanner said. He hung up the phone. His wife was sitting beside him now, watching the live feed of the crash site as it was broadcasted from the news helicopter.

"That was Bryan's flight," Tanner whispered. With an audible gasp, Megan immediately understood the repercussions of her husband's words. She leaned in and gave him a long embrace.

"Was that Helen on the phone?" Megan asked.

"Yes, she's calling everyone together."

"You'd better get dressed," Megan said empathetically. She took a hair elastic off her wrist and pulled her blonde curls back in a ponytail. She knew she wouldn't be going back to sleep anytime soon.

Tanner quickly showered before putting on a pair of jeans and a Polo shirt. He listened to the news updates while getting dressed. From the varied reports and video footage of the crash site, he understood the chance of survivors was slim. Numbness again encompassed Tanner as he thought about how close he had come to death. If it weren't for his wife's contractions, which suddenly stopped when they finally made it to the hospital, he would have been on that flight to Washington, DC.

"Is there anything I can do?" Megan asked. She could see the concern and worry in her husband's blue eyes.

"Not right now, but I'll call you later," Tanner said. He grabbed his jacket out of the hall closet and put it on.

"Good luck," Megan said. She reached up to give Tanner a hug and a kiss. She was taller than average for most women, but Megan's pregnant belly made it difficult to wrap her arms completely around her husband.

Tanner said good-bye and went out the door. He drove down the hill from his home in Draper, Utah. He momentarily stopped at a convenience store, surprising the late night clerk who was reading a vampire novel on the early Monday morning. Tanner wasn't as young as when he started in the information technology field years ago, and he couldn't pull an all-nighter without something to help keep him awake. His drink of choice had always been Mountain Dew, even before he found the LDS religion seven years ago. Tanner quickly paid the cashier for his forty-four ounces of quick energy and got back into his Honda Civic. He missed the Toyota 4Runner he owned when he lived in Albuquerque, New Mexico, but the Civic was a more practical car for his life now.

Ten minutes later, Tanner turned off Redwood Road toward the entrance to Camp Williams. Located on the south side of the Salt Lake Valley, Camp Williams was the primary training site for the Utah National Guard, but Tanner wasn't affiliated with the National Guard. His employer was only a tenant on the military base.

Tanner handed his photo ID to the armed guard, who seemed surprised to have another civilian coming to work at the early hour. "Good morning, Mr. Stone," he said.

Tanner still wasn't comfortable with his last name. Compliments of the FBI, Tanner had received a new identity when he relocated to Utah last year. It was easier for Megan to adjust to a new last name because she had legally changed it when she married Tanner just before leaving New Mexico. However, Tanner still sometimes mistakenly wrote his last name as Zane instead of Stone.

"Thank you," the guard said. He handed the ID badge back to the driver. Tanner rolled up his window and followed the deserted road toward an ominous-looking building on the hillside.

The 1.5 billion dollar facility was officially called the Community Comprehensive National Cybersecurity Initiative Data Center, but for the 107 National Security Agency employees who worked there, they simply referred to it as the Utah Spy Center. The super-secret building began operation last fall, and it was sold to the public as a one-million-square-foot data center designed to house thousands of computer servers. Few people, however, actually knew the facility only had one primary computer system with the ability to eavesdrop on billions of phone calls, faxes, emails, and text messages from all across the world.

Tanner parked his car in the nearly empty lot and walked toward the entrance of the modern-looking building. He took his blue National Security Agency identification badge and scanned a card reader mounted next to the door. This was the first and easiest of three checkpoints, or access control terminals. The green light on the card reader signaled Tanner's authorization to enter the lobby. Inside, another uniformed guard stood ready at the second security checkpoint.

"It's a little early to come into work, isn't it?" the muscular guard joked. Even though he recognized Tanner by sight, the security officer still instructed Tanner to put all of his belongings on a plastic tray. Tanner purposely packed light, making sure to leave his personal cell phone in the car because unnecessary clutter always slowed down the screening process.

The guard watched as Tanner placed his car keys, pager, wallet, and fountain drink on the tray before sending everything through a machine. Similar to X-ray equipment found at major airports, this device wasn't looking for illegal weapons but prohibited communication gadgets. While his personal belongings went through the scanner, Tanner swiped his ID badge and entered a PIN on a keypad next to the scanner. This two-factor authentication method, using a combination of something Tanner owned plus something that he knew, provided extra security from unauthorized access into the ultra-secure building. A pleasant, computer-generated voice announced, "Tanner Stone, systems analyst, level five." Tanner stepped through the turnstile and showed his ID badge to the guard.

"Yeah, it's early, but the boss called us in. You heard the news, I imagine?" Tanner asked as he collected his belongings.

"Yes. That's terrible about the plane crash," the security officer responded. He shook his head sadly as he opened the door for Tanner.

The interior of the NSA spy complex was divided into two sections. One part was an administrative area with standard office cubicles, and the other was a state-of-the-art data center. Tanner again scanned his ID badge and entered his PIN at a locked door, granting him access into the administrative area. He went straight toward Helen Ripplinger's office, only to find it empty with a yellow sticky note posted on the door—"We're in the conference room." Tanner turned ninety degrees and headed down another hall toward his team's common meeting area. Inside the spacious conference room, Tanner found his boss and two other coworkers watching the news of the plane crash on a large LCD TV.

"Tanner, I'm so glad you're here," Helen said. At age fifty-eight, Helen was nearly twenty years older than any of the systems analysts on her team.

"What's the word from the crash site?" Tanner asked. He stopped his six-foot-two-inch frame just short of the doorway. He didn't dare enter the room just yet, sensing bad news ahead.

"There are no survivors," Helen said. Her face was ashen with disbelief.

Tanner thought that he would have been more analytical about the situation, especially in front of his peers, but his confidence quickly faded. As an only child, Tanner had often thought of Bryan Morrison as his older brother. The reality of the moment was overwhelming. Sensing Tanner's loss, Helen walked over and gave her employee a comforting embrace as he silently wept for his friend.

APRIL 24, SALT LAKE INTERNATIONAL AIRPORT, UTAH

Special Agent Cannon didn't jump to any conclusions. As a seasoned FBI investigator, he was supposed to consider every possibility, but even a fool could connect the dots tonight. Derek studied the security video captured by the closed−circuit TV camera on top of the golf course clubhouse. Even though he couldn't clearly identify the perpetrator from the recording, it was obvious that he had fired a missile of some sort. Right now a swarm of cops, FBI agents, and FAA officials were scouring the area along the fairway for more evidence.

Derek regrettably knew this day would come. Ever since September 11, most agents in the FBI had quietly recognized the fact that it was only a matter of time before a terrorist brought down an airliner with a surface-to-air missile. SAMs were surprisingly easy to obtain on the black market, compliments of countries like China and North Korea pawning their military hardware. The SAM was becoming almost as pervasive among terrorist groups as the Russian AK-47 rifle. Derek shuddered about where his thoughts went next. *How long would it be until a terrorist group got ahold of a crude nuclear device?*

A voice called out over the radio. "Derek, you better come take a look at this." It was Special Agent Sara Heywood's Louisiana drawl, bringing Derek out of his thoughts. Sara was coordinating the search effort out on the golf course for evidence.

"On my way," Derek said. As he jetted out of the hastily established command center toward the practice green, Derek mistakenly thought it was already morning. Floodlights from news crews and police cars lit up the area, creating an artificial daylight. Ignoring the shouts from the press quarantined out in the parking lot, Derek grabbed a golf cart and sped off toward the fifth hole where he saw Agent Heywood in a dark blue FBI jacket.

"Check this out," Sara shouted, before the golf cart even came to a complete stop. Leading her senior partner over toward the sand trap, she pointed out scorch marks on the high side of the bunker.

"Looks like the rocket was launched from here," Derek said. The warm air from his lungs condensed in the cold morning darkness. The area where he was standing corresponded to the approximate location of the missile's origin on the surveillance video. "Let's get the lab folks over here and see if they can identify any type of residue."

"Already on it," Sara said. Derek was impressed with Sara's innate ability to conduct an investigation. Salt Lake City was her second assignment out of the FBI Academy, and even though she was almost half his age, Derek saw unlimited potential for Sara in the FBI.

"Now look at this," Sara continued. She directed Derek over toward the south side of the putting green. "See this group of cattails here? They're all smashed down. I bet our perp hid in here, waiting for the chance to strike."

Just then, a police officer yelled out as he ran toward the two FBI agents in a sprint. "I found a container in the weeds by the canal," he said, trying to catch his breath. Agent Cannon and

Agent Heywood quickly followed the patrol officer back toward the canal. Shining their flashlights on the object, the group stared at the olive-green box on the ground. As Derek examined the foreign writing on the military-looking SAM container, he realized that his fears were now confirmed.

"Get the county dive team out here. I want this canal searched ASAP!" he ordered.

———•———

NSA DATA CENTER, UTAH

Tanner was still in shock as he walked with Helen down the aisle of gray cubicles that were abandoned at the early morning hour. The two NSA employees went to find a "clean room"—a specialized conference room guaranteed to be free of any electronic surveillance equipment. Their upcoming conversation had to be confidential.

Stepping into the windowless room, Helen flipped on two switches before closing the door. One switch turned on the overhead fluorescent lights, and the other switch activated the electromagnetic countermeasures to jam any eavesdropping devices. Even though this room and the entire spy facility were swept daily for illegal surveillance equipment, paranoia was a cultural belief at the NSA.

"First of all, how's your wife?" Helen asked as she gracefully sat down in a conference room chair. Even at this early morning hour, her artificially colored brown hair and makeup were impeccable.

"She's fine. It was a false alarm," Tanner said. "Her contractions stopped at the hospital. The doctor sent us home but told Megan to take it easy for several days. We're still a month out from her due date."

"You're not traveling to DC or anywhere until Megan has that baby. I would hate for you to miss the birth of your first child," Helen stated resolutely before changing subjects. "Tanner, I want you to take the lead on this investigation. I need you to pull from your unique experience and see if you can find anything unusual on the Internet about this plane crash."

Before Tanner was hired at the NSA, he had hacked into thousands of computer networks across the globe. He made millions of dollars from his illegal activities before he suddenly abandoned computer hacking, reformed his ways, and joined the LDS Church. Becoming a Mormon was a change that he had never anticipated.

Tanner gazed thoughtfully at his boss before responding. "Are you thinking that Bryan and I stumbled onto something that we shouldn't have?"

"I'm not sure what I think right now, but suppose that you had died with Bryan on that flight tonight. If you were an enemy of the United States, what would your death have accomplished?"

APRIL 24, NSA DATA CENTER, UTAH

It was almost 3:00 a.m. Monday morning, and the remaining members of the Quantum Computing team were now all gathered in the conference room at the NSA data center. The five systems analysts and their leader, Helen, decided there wasn't any point in watching more of the news coverage. For the past hour, all the talking heads on TV had been speculating about a terrorist attack. Every news channel was showing the same amateur cell phone footage that was inadvertently taken by a traveler at Salt Lake International Airport. The video was low quality and grainy, but the two-second clip effectively showed an explosion immediately before Flight 2512 went down. The recording had been posted on the Internet, and it already had over three million hits.

"I'm sorry to drag you out of bed at such an early hour, but I figured none of us would go back to sleep," Helen began. "We lost a dear friend tonight, and Bryan's death will severely affect our team." She looked out over her diverse team. Even though they were physically located in Utah, Tanner was the only Mormon in the close-knit group. Everyone else had relocated from different regions around the country to work at the new NSA spy complex.

"To begin, I think you should all know why Bryan was on that flight in the first place," Helen said. She always felt it was more important to be a mentor than a boss, and she had compartmentalized her employees into three, two-person teams to encourage collaboration. Each unit focused on a region of the globe, with Tanner and Bryan monitoring Internet communication coming out of Asia. "Tanner, tell the rest of the team what you and Bryan were working on and the reason for the last-minute trip to DC," she said.

Tanner cleared his voice, speaking from his chair at the large conference room table. "Well, Bryan and I had two areas we had been working on the past several months. Our first objective was intercepting any communications coming out of Iran regarding the nuclear plant in Bushehr. We specifically tried to estimate the damage that this new Flame computer virus has done on their secret atomic program."

The other analysts around the table nodded in understanding. While the NSA wanted to claim credit for the highly sophisticated computer virus, which was a close cousin to the previous Stuxnet virus, the new malware was most likely an Israeli creation. Nobody wanted to see a nuclear-enabled Iran, but Israel definitely had the most to lose from another nuclear nation in the region. Even though they had little evidence, there was an unspoken understanding among most NSA analysts that Israel had created both designer viruses to thwart Iran's secret nuclear ambition.

The Flame virus was an especially sly piece of malware. In just a few short months, computer geeks across the globe quickly declared it the most devious computer malware ever created. Designed for remote surveillance, Flame was an eavesdropping virus that specifically recorded audio, screenshots, and keyboard activity on infected computers. It even had the ability to turn an infected computer into a Bluetooth beacon that would skim information from nearby

Bluetooth-enabled devices. One thing was for certain—whoever had created the Flame virus was already a rock star in the computer-hacking community.

Tanner continued his update. "We really haven't seen anything fresh from Iran in the past couple of weeks. It's still the same story over there. The Iranians are convinced that we created Flame to thwart their nuclear program, and they continue to blame Israel for assassinating some of their chief nuclear scientists."

"What about China?" Helen asked. She was referring to the information that Tanner and Bryan had recently gleaned from the secretive country.

"We've been keeping a close eye on China and its cyber-warfare program against the United States. China's leaders keep denying their involvement, but Bryan and I recently discovered some interesting Internet chatter between Beijing and Shaoxing. It was just a lot of background noise at first, but we decided to capture the data and dig deep. Then, just last week, we hit critical mass when we figured out that China has a new type of computer virus that can specifically target our banks and financial institutions. That was the reason for our trip back to Washington. Bryan and I were scheduled to brief the Electronic Crimes Task Force at the Secret Service in just a few hours. I missed the flight because my wife started having contractions, but it ended up being a false alarm," Tanner said.

For a few awkward moments, silence filled the conference room. Then Helen, sensing the sorrow of her team, spoke with consolation. "Bryan's loss is painful for all of us. He was a critical component of the quantum computing project, and one of the brightest people I've ever met." The compliment from Helen was sincere and significant. Rumors floated around the NSA that she had once scored 158 on an IQ test. "Nevertheless, there's nothing we can do to bring Bryan back. We can honor him best by determining who was behind the attack," she said. "The Brass back at Fort Meade has asked us to poke around and see what we can find on the Internet. I've assigned Tanner to take the lead on this analysis. Let's get to work," Helen said with resolve.

Her handpicked team nodded their heads. If anyone could scour the Internet and find information about the terrorist attack, it was the analysts in this conference room.

• —————— •

SALT LAKE INTERNATIONAL AIRPORT, UTAH

Three hours had passed since Flight 2512 went down, and the area around the Salt Lake International Airport was still a chaotic mess. The Special Agent in Charge, or SAC, of the FBI's Salt Lake City office had arrived on the scene, but he decided to remain in the background and let Special Agents Cannon and Heywood manage the investigation. They were doing a fabulous job, and they had already determined several key facts—the major one being the spent missile tube at the bottom of the canal. From this piece of evidence, the FBI had solid proof it was a North Korean, surface-to-air missile that had brought down the aircraft. Unfortunately, the FBI still lacked any substantial clues to positively identify the terrorist.

With the commotion of the crime scene and the recent focus on the North Korean missile tube, the size of the terrorist's shoe print in the sand trap was overlooked. It wasn't until Sara Heywood sat down for a break on the edge of the frost-covered bunker that she noticed it.

"Derek, come over here for a second," Sara said. She got up and gingerly stepped around the sand trap.

"What's up?" Derek replied as he came over from speaking with a group of FAA officials.

"Look at this." Sara hovered her foot over the shoe print in the white sand. Her size-six shoe was basically the same length.

Derek hesitated and then realized what Sara was highlighting. He had been focusing on the pattern of the shoe print in the sand, not the size of it.

"Are you kidding me?" Derek asked himself as much as anyone else in the area. Racing back to the clubhouse, both Derek and Sara reviewed the only footage they had of the suspect. Fortunately, the security video from the clubhouse had since been transferred to a laptop, which allowed the FBI agents to isolate individual frames. Watching the suspect emerge from the cattails, Derek paused the video and zoomed in the maximum amount. Despite the grainy picture on the monitor, both agents saw the faint contour of a woman's figure against the dimly lit background.

APRIL 24, SALT LAKE CITY, UTAH

Twelve miles south of Salt Lake International Airport, Reina watched the news coverage of the plane crash from the comfort of her living room. She had made the retreat back to her stylish apartment without any trouble. Now, sipping a cup of herbal tea before going to bed, she was absolutely convinced that she had accomplished her mission.

Reina didn't know who the specific targets were on Flight 2512. Nevertheless, by bringing down the entire aircraft, she was confident the police would immediately conclude this was a terrorist attack instead of a specialized assassination. That was the reason why she had purposely left the SAM container hidden in the bushes. The Americans would spend months trying to find a link to some random terrorist group instead of focusing on the murder of two particular individuals. It was a clever charade, and one of Reina's finest masterpieces.

Reina turned off the TV and walked toward the kitchen. Her muscles were sore from the vigorous swim, but it was nothing that she couldn't handle. She was vigilant in her workout routines, and her physical prowess was noticeable. When she wasn't running or swimming, she was lifting weights or practicing kung fu. Her body was a weapon, and Reina took care of it like a hunter who cherished his favorite gun.

Reina was also beautiful. With long black hair, soft brown eyes, and an olive-complexion, she was constantly approached by all sorts of men—despite her scar. Even after three surgeries, the doctors couldn't completely erase the faint, white line that ran the length of her face on the right side. The disfigurement was a constant reminder of her traumatic childhood in Mexico.

Sitting at her kitchen table, Reina logged into her laptop and checked her anonymous email account. It was the primary method of communication she used with the others in her group. Email was such a simple and wonderful technique for any criminal organization to secretly conduct business. With billions of electronic messages flowing across the Internet, Reina knew it was practically impossible for anyone to isolate her random email from all the others.

She found a new message from Rey, her partner in crime. He complimented her on a job well done, saying it was one of the most brilliant she had ever planned. Their superior would definitely be proud. After highlighting a few more details of their grand operation, Rey instructed Reina to get some sleep. She would leave for Boise, Idaho, in the morning.

APRIL 24, NSA DATA CENTER, UTAH

Tanner and two of his teammates stopped at the security checkpoint to the "Chamber" at the Utah Spy Center. They were about to enter one of the most protected rooms in all of the NSA. Inside was a one−of−a−kind supercomputer that officially didn't exist.

Tanner started the precise authorization process to gain access to the Chamber. First, he scanned his NSA badge and entered his unique PIN on a keypad. Then, he placed his palm on a hand scanner and repeated his name for the voice authorization system. The door popped open, allowing Tanner to enter the "man-trap." The man-trap was a small area just before a second set of double doors that prevented anyone from tailgating Tanner into the data center. Inside the man-trap, Tanner waited while his peers followed the same authorization process for themselves. Once inside the man-trap, all three analysts held their ID badges up to a camera and waited for a guard, who was monitoring from a remote location, to visually confirm their identities before opening the interior door. Nobody was allowed to enter the Chamber alone.

Done with the tedious entrance process, Tanner and his teammates found themselves in a small operations center. Two computer workstations sat on a solid desk in the middle of the room. Large monitors were mounted on the adjacent wall, displaying graphs and other real-time information about the data center's operation. One wall of the control room was a thick glass partition that went from the floor to the ceiling. The transparent divider separated the control room from a larger area that housed a top-secret computer simply called "QC."

QC was short for "quantum computer," and it was the nickname Tanner and his teammates had given their novel machine. QC was the NSA's ultimate weapon in intelligence gathering. Created by the scientists at Los Alamos National Labs, QC was a computer built on the principles of quantum physics. It didn't use silicon microprocessors found in traditional computers. Instead, QC had a prototype, man-made diamond at its core. Dozens of green lasers manipulated the atoms inside the 500-carat diamond to form qubits, the fundamental component of the quantum computer. QC was fast—blazingly fast—and it could perform 340 trillion, trillion, trillion, calculations at once. That was more computing power than every other computer on the planet combined! To unleash its phenomenal power, QC required enormous amounts of electricity. That was the reason why the NSA built the dedicated spy facility for the massive computer system in Utah. It was strategically located to draw its 100-megawatt power needs from the hydroelectric dams along the Colorado River. Helen and her team of systems analysts were the only ones with code word authorization to operate QC. As a result, they each had a top-secret/SCI clearance, which required a massive background investigation and a yearly polygraph test. The QC team programmed the supercomputer to consume and analyze massive amounts of digital information taken from the Internet. Those seemingly innocent pieces of data, when linked together, became of vital interest to the NSA.

Founded in 1949, the NSA was divided into two organizations—the Signals Intelligence Directorate (SID) and Information Assurance Directorate (IAD). Helen's team worked for the SID, collecting and analyzing foreign communications, or transactions, on the Internet. Shortly after Flight 2512 went down, the admiral over the entire NSA personally called Helen and informed her that the president of the United States had issued Executive Order 13224, authorizing Helen's team to begin eavesdropping on all domestic Internet transactions.

"Okay, where do we start?" Sydney Littlefield asked. She excitedly approached the console to the supercomputer and sat down in a chair. Recently out of college, Sydney was twenty-six years old and the youngest member of the team. She was still getting her feet wet at the NSA.

"We modify our normal program routines to include all the domain names and IP addresses registered in the United States," Tanner said. "Then, we tweak those scripts to capture and analyze domestic Internet transactions, like emails, blogs, chat rooms, or instant messages for specific keywords."

"What keywords?" asked Rachel York. She was the other NSA analyst who had entered into the room with Tanner and Sydney. Rachel was one of two PhDs on the QC team. Quiet and more reserved than the others, she was a genius when it came to math.

Tanner replied to Rachel's question. "We look for anything that mentions Flight 2512, Salt Lake City, terrorists, and other things like that," he said, suddenly realizing that they were looking for a digital needle in a cyber-haystack.

―――――――

SALT LAKE INTERNATIONAL AIRPORT, UTAH

Derek rested for a moment in the golf course clubhouse, unsure of the next step in his investigation. It was almost sunrise, and the airport had finally reopened. The governor's office had called out the National Guard to provide security and extra crowd control, but the disarray was still evident. Thousands of travelers had their flights delayed or canceled, and now they all scrambled to get on the first available plane. Fortunately, the FAA hadn't closed other airports around the country like they did after the terrorist attacks of September 11.

The FBI investigation had settled down a bit from the frantic pace of just a few hours ago. The suspect in the terrorist attack was definitely a female, but Derek didn't want to disclose that critical piece of information to the public just yet. He wasn't even sure how the suspect had managed to get to the crime scene, but he suspected that she might have come via the canal. The FBI also knew it was a North Korean SAM that was launched from the golf course, but there wasn't any point in tracking down the weapon because all the identification marks on the SAM container had been intentionally destroyed.

"The NTSB just found the black box," Sara reported, hanging up her cell phone. Derek thought about the irony of Sara's statement. Few people knew that the flight recorder box mandated by the National Transportation Safety Board was actually bright orange-red, not black.

"I'm not sure what additional information we'll get from that. I can guarantee it was the missile that caused the crash," Derek said. He took a stale doughnut off the snack bar counter and bit into it. He was dragging from lack of sleep.

"At least the airport is open. Hopefully we can get some of the crowds to disperse and go on with their lives," Sara said.

Derek nodded in simple acknowledgement. He could only hope Sara was right.

APRIL 24, NSA DATA CENTER, UTAH

Tanner and his teammates worked into the early morning hours. QC was operating at full speed, scouring the Internet and generating mounds of data for further analysis. No other computer system in the world could even attempt what QC was doing, and until last year, Tanner him—self wouldn't have believed it. By leveraging the principles of quan—tum physics, QC was literally eavesdropping on the entire Internet, yet the difficult work still remained. QC could generate trillions of bytes of data by finding patterns and matches, but turning that data into useful information required old—fashioned human analysis.

With the quantum computer humming along, Tanner decided it was a good time for a break. He left his two coworkers in the Chamber and went back to his desk. Grabbing the handset on the "black" (or unsecured) phone, Tanner dialed his home number. Megan answered on the second ring.

"I hope I didn't wake you," Tanner said with a yawn. He had run out of Mountain Dew and needed a refill.

"No, I was watching TV in bed and wondering if you were going to call." Megan's voice was smooth and comforting. It was exactly what Tanner needed after such a frenzied night.

"You've probably figured out that Bryan didn't make it," Tanner said gloomily.

"Yes, it's horrible," Megan said. "What's going to happen to his wife and kids?"

Tanner had been so focused on his work that he hadn't pondered on the fate of the Morrison family. "I'm not sure. Helen is going over later this morning to check in with the family. It's a terrible loss for everyone."

"Tanner, all the news channels are saying it was a terrorist attack," Megan said. Her voice was filled with trepidation. "Do you know anything more about it?"

"I can't say," Tanner replied. It was his canned response for whenever Megan asked him about the details of his top-secret work. "But I agree with the news reports. It does look like a deliberate attack."

"Should I be worried? I remember September 11 like it was yesterday."

"I know. We'll just have to see what other information comes out," Tanner said. He deliberately changed the subject. "Are you working today?"

Megan was a database administrator for a financial company. She had a nice setup where she telecommuted from Utah to her job in Albuquerque. It was a good arrangement for both the employer and the employee.

"I feel good enough to do some work, and sitting down in front of a computer isn't too strenuous," Megan said.

"Remember what the doctor said. Take it easy," Tanner cautioned. He wasn't sure if he was ready to be a father, and it made him anxious to know that he didn't have a lot of time left to prepare for the birth of his first child.

"I will. I love you," Megan said.

"Love you too. I'll call you later," Tanner said. He had barely hung up the phone when Helen stepped into his cubical.

"I'm starving. Let's go grab a bite at the break room," she said in a hushed voiced.

Normally the entire QC team made the trip to the break room together, but Tanner could tell by Helen's actions this was meant to be a private meeting. Passing through an access door, they entered the main hallway that led toward the small cafeteria. Even though it was just before 7:00 a.m., the building was busy with people. Many employees came in early to be on the same time schedule as their peers back at NSA headquarters in Fort Meade, Maryland.

Helen bought a muffin, yogurt, and a coffee from the small snack counter in the break room, while Tanner opted for a doughnut and another Mountain Dew. The two took a seat in the farthest corner, away from a group of people watching CNN on a large TV.

"Tanner, I just got a call from the admiral," Helen said, referring to the director over all of the NSA. "He said you need to tread lightly and follow some common sense, but to consider your investigation the highest priority of the NSA right now."

Tanner almost choked on his food. He hadn't even completed his two-year anniversary as an employee at the NSA, and now his boss was giving him free reign on the world's fastest computer. It was a lot to swallow.

"Why me? I'm just a systems analyst," Tanner said.

"The admiral knows about your unique past and the excellent work you did in Albuquerque. He was impressed," Helen said.

Tanner was stunned. "Who told him?"

Helen took a bite of her muffin and smiled. "This is the Director of the NSA we're talking about. He can get information when he wants it, even if a judge sealed your case."

Helen was referring to a bizarre incident in Tanner's past. Two years ago, he was kidnapped by a group of cyber-terrorists in New Mexico. The cunning criminals forced him to hack into Los Alamos National Labs and steal classified information. But Tanner outwitted his kidnappers and escaped before surrendering himself to the FBI. Unfortunately, the FBI hadn't fully resolved the case, but Tanner got a plea deal in exchange for his willingness to help. The federal judge involved in the trial sealed the case, and only Helen and a handful of other people knew the true details of Tanner's secret past.

Helen pressed on, encouraging her best employee. "You have a unique blend of analytic skills and street smarts that are invaluable in an investigation like this."

Tanner paused at Helen's use of words. "Do you know that's what my dad told me when I was younger? He often said that I was full of street smarts."

"Well, he must have been extremely observant," Helen said. She gave Tanner a motherly smile. Tanner reminded Helen of herself, back when she first entered the doors of the NSA many years ago. She felt it was her duty to cultivate Tanner's untapped potential. "You have QC and the rest of the team at your disposal. Follow your instincts. I trust you."

Tanner still seemed uneasy with his new assignment. "You might trust me, but do I trust myself? You're asking me to do stuff that will undoubtedly push the limits of privacy. With all the recent leaks, the NSA isn't very popular with the public right now."

Helen knew exactly what Tanner was implying. The NSA had a huge black eye from the Snowden scandal. The bad press loomed over everything the NSA did. "I understand, but we don't work in black-and-white here. The NSA has, and always will, operate in gray areas. That's the nature of our business, and it's how we catch the criminals."

Tanner took a deep breath. Spy-craft was messy, with ethical boundaries blurred beyond recognition. "I'll do my best." It was all that he could say.

"One more thing," Helen said as she finished her breakfast. "There's a telepresence meeting at 2:00 p.m. with the guys from the Secret Service that Bryan was supposed to brief. Help them out where you can, but don't let them distract you from your top priority."

"Great," Tanner said with a sigh. He already felt like it was up to him to make sense of this terrorist attack, and now he had to brief a couple of agents from the Secret Service's Electronics Crime Task Force. The day was getting crazier by the moment.

———•———

Reina hadn't been to Idaho before, and she wondered what it would be like. After just a few hours of sleep, she packed her clothes and "tools" before heading north on Interstate-15 in a black Dodge Charger. Having just crossed over the border into Idaho, she was now driving along a desolate section of Interstate-84. Strangely, the high desert landscape of the Mountain West reminded her of the time she had visited northern China with her guardian-uncle, Yang Dao. Even though she was raised by her uncle, Reina wasn't Chinese by birth.

Reina was born in Ciudad Juarez, Mexico, just across the border from El Paso, Texas. She was the youngest child of unique parents—a Mexican mother and a Chinese father. Her father had moved from China to work at a *maquiladora*, or Mexican factory, which made parts for a car company. He met Reina's mother at work, and they quickly married and started a family. Reina's early family life was humble but happy until tragedy struck in cruel fashion.

Ever since she was a child, Ciudad Juarez was a hotbed of violence. Two rival drug cartels, the Juarez and Sinaloa, engaged in daily battles to control the lucrative drug route into the United States. The violence and crime in Ciudad Juarez is off the charts, mimicking Chicago's turmoil during the Prohibition Years.

A crude car bomb, meant for a rival drug lord, prematurely detonated as Reina's family walked by on their way to Catholic Mass one Sunday morning. The indiscriminate explosion killed Reina's parents and seriously injured her older brother in the process.

With no family around to care for them, Reina and her older brother had few options for survival. In that lawless city, there were only two ways for a thirteen- and ten-year-old to make money—drugs and prostitution. Fortunately, Reina and her brother didn't have to resort to either of the repulsive choices. Just after their parents' funeral, a mysterious uncle came to Mexico and took the two siblings back to live with him in China. Yang Dao had a special calling for his niece the moment she stepped off the plane over twelve years ago. He sent her off to a private academy in Nanchang, China, about ten hours southwest of Shanghai. There she was schooled in academics and assassination. Linguists taught her how to speak Chinese, English, and French, while coaching her on how to blend into different cultures. From other specialists throughout China, Reina learned how to kill with both her bare hands and weapons, like the "tools" she had packed in her car. Reina had been trained her entire life to perform her duties without guilt, and taught to believe that every assignment was for the collective good of the People's Republic of China.

Reina's thoughts came back to the moment. She had another job to do. This particular hit was a man who had failed her uncle two years ago. Reina wanted to please her uncle, and for her, this assignment was personal.

APRIL 24, NSA DATA CENTER, UTAH

At the Utah Data Center, Tanner found solace in an empty conference room. He had been working all night and needed a quick nap to get his second wind. He woke up just before 2:00 p.m. and headed off to the break room to get a quick snack. When he arrived, he saw a large group of people gathered in front of the TV. Something bad had happened.

"What's going on?" Tanner asked Melvin Otterson, his peer on the QC team. Mel was tall and skinny, with a balding head, a cynical attitude, and a weakness for cigarettes. He was crotchety in every sense of the word, but somehow Tanner managed to get along with him.

"The stock market crashed today. The worse drop ever," Mel said. At forty-six, Mel was the oldest analyst on the QC team. He had a master's degree in both mathematics and economics. Tanner thought that was an odd combination, but Mel often showed Tanner how effective mathematics was in predicting the economy.

"Wow. How bad is it?" Tanner asked.

Mel turned from the television and looked at Tanner. "Most of the finance guys expected a drop in the Dow Jones as a result of the terrorist attack, but nobody predicted it would be this bad. Almost 30 percent of the market vanished today."

Tanner knew enough about economics to understand that the financial markets didn't reflect reality, but the perception of reality. In a way, it was a self-fulfilling prophecy. If investors felt the economy was going bad, it didn't matter if their feelings were justified or not because their selling could create a bear market. "Aren't there some kind of safeguards in place to prevent massive losses like this?" Tanner asked.

"Yeah, when the market drops 10 percent, trading stops for an hour to let investors cool off and stop panic trading. That happened around 10:30 a.m. The market reopened an hour later and it looked like things had calmed down, but . . . ," Mel said. He let his thoughts trail off elsewhere.

Tanner could tell there was more to the story. "And?" he asked.

"Some crazy trades happened again and the market quickly dropped another 10 percent, triggering the second pause in trading. When the market opened up again, everyone cashed in. It dropped the last 10 percent in almost an instant. They closed the market for the rest of the day as a precaution," Mel said.

"This hasn't happened before, has it?" Tanner asked.

"No," Mel sharply replied. "But the markets have been very skittish the past year, so who really knows if this is abnormal or not. I think a drop in the 10 percent range would have been more appropriate," he said.

Tanner's pager suddenly vibrated, and he checked the caller ID. It was from a close friend in Albuquerque. "Mel, I'll see you at our afternoon meeting. I've got to take this call," Tanner said.

He walked back to his cubical in the administrative area. Preparing for his conversation, he chose the "gray" phone instead of the black phone. He wasn't sure why everyone referred to the secure telephone as the "gray" phone, because it was actually a beige color. Nevertheless, this specific device was cleared for confidential and classified communication, and that was something that Tanner wanted as he placed his call to New Mexico.

"Hi, Tanner," a female voice answered. It was the Special Agent in Charge, Nicole Green, of the FBI's field office in Albuquerque.

"Thanks for getting back to me, Red," Tanner said. He called Nicole by her nickname, a reference to her bright red hair. Only a few close associates dared to refer to Nicole by her nickname, but Tanner had definitely earned the right.

Nicole was the FBI agent who had headed up the investigation into Tanner's kidnapping two years ago. Tanner was the primary witness in a cyber-terrorist plot that almost succeeded in stealing the classified blueprints for the exact quantum computer now located in the Utah data center. Nicole helped Tanner relocate to Salt Lake City with a new identity and a new life. She even got him the job at the NSA. Nicole and Tanner kept in touch often, calling each other with any updates in Tanner's kidnapping case, or to ask for special interagency favors.

"How are you holding up?" Nicole asked. She had spoken to Tanner earlier that morning, and he had told her his personal connection with Flight 2512.

"It's crazy up here. I'm going on just a couple hours of sleep," Tanner said. "We're trying to see if there's any connection between the terrorist attack and some interesting information that we recently discovered here at the NSA."

Nicole knew not to ask Tanner any specific details about his job. She understood the NSA's unofficial acronym was "Never Say Anything" for a reason. "Well, I've got the seating chart from Flight 2512," she responded. Tanner had asked her earlier if she could do some research to help answer a question. She continued, "But the answer isn't going to give you a warm fuzzy. Bryan was the only government official on that flight."

"Thanks, Red. I appreciate your help."

There was a long pause. "Why do you want this information?" Nicole finally asked. After that deadly shoot-out on top of a remote mountain peak two years ago, Nicole had learned to appreciate Tanner's instincts.

"I can't tell you anything right now, but we'll keep in touch," Tanner said.

"Listen, the primary FBI agent on this case is Derek Cannon. I know him well. We worked together in Houston. He's the one that gave me the seating chart. If you want, I'll see if he's interested in contacting you," Nicole said.

"Okay. Set something up for tomorrow, but keep it discrete," Tanner said.

"I will. Give Megan a hug for me," Nicole said before hanging up. After all Nicole had done for Tanner and his wife, she was considered part of the family.

Tanner left his cubical and headed over to the telepresence conference room for the two o'clock meeting. As he approached the door, he could see two men in dark suits on the other side of the virtual conference room table. *Great, now I've got the Secret Service to deal with.*

The telepresence room was a secure, high-tech studio that provided significantly more features than just normal video conferencing. The room had a large table with chairs on one side and several LCD TVs on the opposite wall. Using high-definition cameras and audio equipment, the setup created the illusion of having all the participants in the same room. It was a stunning and surreal arrangement.

"Tanner, come in and let me introduce you," Helen said. She pointed to the older man on the large television screen first. "This is Agent Todd Payne."

Tanner figured Todd Payne was approaching fifty because he had shades of gray beginning to show on the temples of his brown, crew-cut hair. He carried some extra weight, but Tanner could tell that Todd still had a muscular build. "Weren't you scheduled to come out and do the briefing with Bryan?" asked Agent Payne over the video conferencing system.

"I was, but a last-second family emergency made me cancel my plans," Tanner said. He took his seat at the table.

"And this is Agent Adam Crawford," Helen said. She pointed toward a taller man in his mid-twenties. Adam appeared much younger than his aging partner.

"We're sorry to call at such a bad time. We know about your team's loss," Agent Crawford offered sincerely.

Tanner noticed that both men wore blue-colored ID badges on their suit coats, signifying they were cleared members of the intelligence community.

"The rest of my team should be here momentarily," Helen said.

Tanner felt uneasy being in the same virtual room as the two agents. The NSA and Secret Service were often at odds with each other when it came to stewardship of digital crimes. In addition to their roles in guarding the president and investigating counterfeiting, the Secret Service was also given the responsibility to investigate cyber crimes. Agent Todd Payne and Agent Adam Crawford were both specialists in cyber crime.

When the rest of the QC team arrived, Tanner rubbed his bloodshot eyes and started his briefing. "As part of the NSA's normal eavesdropping activities on the Chinese military, we also listen in for other information about their economy or government in general. We were recently looking for solid clues to determine if China was behind a cyber-attack on a corporate website here in the United States when Bryan and I stumbled across something very fascinating. I can't go into the details on how we got our information, but we believe that the Chinese are working on a new computer virus that has the ability to exclusively target our financial institutions."

Agents Payne and Crawford listened with interest. Tanner continued, "We've identified a fifty-one-year-old individual named Tang Ju-Long that we believe is heading up the computer virus work in China. Unfortunately, Tang is a very common surname, and it took us some time to track down this particular individual. It wasn't until this past week that we found the right guy," Tanner said. "Tang Ju-Long has an interesting background, starting with a degree in computer science from Berkley."

"Is he a US citizen?" asked Tanner's teammate, Chad Blake. Chad was a lanky African American who was originally from Dallas. Slightly younger than Tanner, Chad was the other PhD on the QC team. He got his degree in physics, and he was responsible for calibrating the dozens of lasers that controlled the quantum diamond embedded in QC.

"No, he was a foreign national, studying in the United States. He listed South Korea as his home country," Tanner replied. "After graduating in 1986, Tang Ju-Long worked at a microchip company in Silicon Valley. Then, in 1991, he went back to South Korea and disappeared. We think he moved to China shortly thereafter."

"How sure are you about this?" asked Agent Crawford via the telepresence equipment.

"Confident enough to schedule a midnight flight to come out and brief your organization," Tanner said. "Bryan and I had prepared a more detailed presentation, but this is the core of the information."

Agent Payne sat back in his chair and took a breath. So this was why the NSA asked for a last-minute meeting with the Secret Service. The information on Tang Ju-Long was appealing, but Todd wasn't entirely convinced. He was from a small town in Missouri, and he had a "show me" type of personality.

"We haven't heard anything about Tang Ju-Long, and we've got intelligence from the CIA on the ground over there," Todd said.

Helen spoke up with a calm and resolute voice. "Agent Payne, everyone on my team does their due diligence in verifying any information during analysis. I completely trust Tanner. If he says that Tang Ju-Long is the architect behind some sort of novel computer virus coming out of Asia, I'm convinced."

"Well, I'm not. I can't take Tanner's word at face value. I need to see the information myself," Todd replied.

"That's a difficult request because I won't let Tanner travel anywhere until his wife has their baby. If you want to see our data, we'll need you to come out to Utah," Helen said through the telepresence monitors.

"That's doable. We can book a flight and get there by tomorrow," said Agent Crawford. The two groups spoke for a few minutes longer before ending the short meeting.

As the NSA analysts headed out of the telepresence conference room, Helen gently took Tanner by the arm. "I know you're not happy about having the Secret Service involved in this, but let's try and work together. After September 11, everyone in the intelligence community realized it's better if we share information instead of hoarding it."

"I know, but I don't like people dismissing our data before they've even looked at it." He shook his head, expressing his frustration and annoyance.

Helen changed the subject. "Do we have anything from QC? I imagine you haven't had a lot of time to work with her today."

"I'm going to let her run the programs all night. I'll come in early tomorrow to see what she found. Hopefully we'll get something useful," Tanner said with a tired smile.

"We will. QC's never failed us before, and she won't now."

"There's something else I need to tell you, but I wanted to wait until we were alone," Tanner said. He shut the door to the conference room. "Just before our meeting with the Secret Service, I got off the phone with Nicole in Albuquerque. She had the seating chart for Flight 2512. Bryan was the only government official on the airplane," Tanner said.

Helen took a thoughtful breath as she considered Tanner's statement. "That strengthens the theory that someone might have specifically targeted the flight to keep the information from getting to the Secret Service."

"If that's the case, we can't dismiss the attack as just an isolated terrorist event," Tanner said.

———•———

BOISE, IDAHO

Reina arrived in Boise, Idaho, just before dinnertime. She checked into a pleasant hotel near the middle of town and registered under the pseudonym of Maria Lopez. It was an easy process with her fake ID, credit card, and flawless English. The young lady at the registration desk didn't even give Reina a second glance.

Usually, Reina preferred to take a day to survey her surroundings before taking care of business, but she wouldn't have time for that tonight. Her target's presence in Boise was short-lived, and she had to act quickly before he fell off the grid again, just like he had done in Reno and Portland. Reina's target was a criminal named Jeff Kessler. Jeff was hired by Reina's uncle two years ago to manage a group of cyber-terrorists as they hacked into Los Alamos National Laboratory. Unfortunately, the project failed catastrophically, and Jeff escaped before Yang Dao had the chance to eliminate him for his stupidity. Since that time, Jeff had been on the run, trying to stay ahead of the Chinese, who wanted retaliation and their two million dollars back. However, Reina knew it wasn't so much about the money as the payback. Yang Dao wanted to send a strong message to the other shady conspirators that he employed. He didn't accept failure.

After getting settled into her hotel room, Reina unpacked her clothes and her tools. She always referred to her weapons as tools, just like her instructors had done back in China. Besides a unique assortment of handguns, knives, and explosives, she also had specialty tools that worked in more subtle ways. Finished unpacking her suitcase, Reina booted up her laptop and checked her anonymous email account. She decided to send a message to Rey. Though she preferred to use Chinese or Spanish to craft her messages, she always communicated in English as instructed by her uncle. Yang Dao had insisted that all the members of his spy team use English in an effort to disguise themselves as Americans.

Reina's digital message was brief, mentioning that she was in Boise. She would accomplish her hit tonight, building on her previous success in bringing down Flight 2512. Satisfied with her note, Reina encrypted the email using the common AES encryption algorithm before routing it through cyberspace.

About 350 miles away in the Salt Lake Valley, QC encountered the email and quickly decrypted the note. Inside the message, the supercomputer identified the keywords "plane," "Salt Lake," and "missile." Following her programmed search routine, QC made a copy of the entire message before re-encrypting it and sending the message to its final destination.

APRIL 25, DRAPER, UTAH

The alarm clock buzzed the same annoying way it had for years. Tanner hit the snooze button, buying another nine minutes of valuable rest. He didn't want to break the warm embrace he had with his wife. For the moment Tanner lay still, listening to Megan's quiet breathing while he gently twisted her long, blonde curls with his finger. He wondered if their baby girl would also have curly hair.

Family was important to Tanner, and he often felt there was something more to a family than just earthly relationships. The primary reason he had joined the Mormon Church was because the religion's focus on eternal families. It was comforting and natural to him.

Summoning all his willpower, Tanner stopped pondering the eternities and finally dragged his body out of bed at 5:09 a.m. It was an hour earlier than his normal wake-up time, but he wanted to get into work and check on the results from QC before the morning briefing. When Tanner got out of the shower, he was surprised to see his wife awake. He had tried to be extra quiet, but apparently he wasn't successful.

"Sorry to bother you," Tanner said as he got dressed. "Go back to sleep if you can."

"No, I want to get up and have breakfast with you. I probably won't see you until late tonight," Megan said. She got out of bed and put on her pink silk robe.

"I'm sorry about the crazy work schedule. I guess the bad guys don't keep normal business hours," Tanner said.

"It's okay. You're making the world a safer place for our child," Megan said. She patted her pregnant torso.

Tanner enjoyed a quick breakfast of cereal, toast, and juice with his wife. They chatted about trivial matters, like the weather or what was happening in their ward—the basic congregational unit in the Mormon religion. Tanner liked the loose and carefree talk because it was a welcome reprieve from his top-secret communications at work.

Sometimes Tanner wished he could core dump his memory, purging his brain of all the secrets he had learned at the NSA. *Cops must feel the same way.* Tanner wondered how police officers kept from becoming jaded in their daily work. From the stuff he learned at the work, Tanner knew firsthand that there were bad people who wanted to harm others.

As Tanner grabbed his jacket out of the hall closet, his mind drifted back to when he was single in New Mexico. He used to have a bass guitar, and he often played it to relax after a stressful day. But his guitar had been destroyed during his escape from his kidnappers, and he hadn't found the time to get a replacement. Tanner longed to play the guitar again, but with the move to Utah and a baby on the way, he found himself busier than ever.

Megan interrupted Tanner's thoughts, bringing him back to the present. "I love you," she said.

"I love you too." Tanner disabled the alarm system before giving his wife a prolonged kiss good-bye. "Page me if you need me. I'll try to call around lunch."

"I will. Have a good day," Megan said.

Watching from the garage door, Megan waited while her husband got into the car and drove away. She knew Tanner's job was often hard on him. He was always going full speed, analyzing and processing the world around him. It was the unique trait that made him such a good NSA analyst and, before that, an astute computer hacker. Unfortunately, it was also the characteristic that never allowed him to fully unwind when he was at home.

───•───•───

NSA DATA CENTER, UTAH

Tanner arrived at work just before 6:00 a.m. He dropped off the doughnuts he had bought on the way to work in the conference room and immediately went to find Rachel York. He had asked her yesterday if she would be willing to come in early and check on QC with him.

"Hey, are you ready to go into the Chamber?" Tanner asked.

Rachel had received her PhD from the Massachusetts Institute of Technology five years ago, and she was smarter than words could describe. She specialized in quantum algorithms, an emerging study of mathematics that focused on intricate equations. Rachel created the complex mathematical routines that QC executed to find patterns and similarities in digital messages.

"You bet," she said. Tanner and Rachel endured the tedious authentication process to get into the Chamber, and soon they were sitting at the main control center for QC.

"Let's see what she found," Tanner said. He logged in and retrieved a high-level summary of all the information QC had processed during the past twenty-four hours. The list was enormous with over twenty-three million results.

"Whoa, that's a ton of stuff," Rachel said, looking over Tanner's shoulder at the computer console.

Tanner acknowledged Rachel's comment by saying, "If you

took all the data that's stored on the Internet and put a number to it, you'd have several zettabytes of data. That's the equivalent of a trillion gigabytes of information—more data than if you stored every word that has ever been spoken since the beginning of time," Tanner said. "I guess that's the downside of being able to eavesdrop on the entire Internet. There's so much data in cyberspace that the initial search results are often overwhelming."

"That's where I can help."

"Exactly," Tanner said. "Your mathematical equations will sort through this enormous amount of data and hopefully give us something useful in return."

Rachel's computer routine employed a brilliant piece of code to search the massive, unordered list of data found by QC. As Tanner watched Rachel execute her program, he wondered if her name would ever be mentioned in the same sentence as Grover, Shor, or Simon—great pioneers who blazed the trail in quantum mathematics. Unfortunately, Rachel worked for the NSA, and the public would never know about her mathematical accomplishments. The highest recognition that Rachel could ever get was a lifetime patent exception, reserved for the brightest minds at the NSA.

Two hours later, Tanner and Rachel joined the rest of the QC team and the two Secret Service agents from the Electronics Crime Task Force for the morning meeting.

"I hope you all got a decent night's rest, because we're going to need our best effort today," Helen said, addressing the group seated around the table. Helen was a legend in the covert intelligence community. She had built a highly successful career, swimming against the current of mainstream wisdom, always looking for an outlying theme. "As you know, I don't believe in coincidences. Salt Lake City isn't a prime terrorist objective. So let's assume that Flight 2512 was targeted for a specific reason, maybe something that involves the information that Tanner and Bryan had recently uncovered about China."

"Whoa. Are you suggesting foul play?" asked Agent Payne.

"I'm not sure yet, but Tanner is working on an interesting theory that might have some merit," Helen said. She signaled toward Tanner to expound on his idea.

Tanner finished his doughnut and spoke to the group, choosing his words carefully. "Now, this is just a theory, but it's possible that someone found out about our discovery of this new computer virus and—"

"Intentionally shot down Flight 2512 to keep the information from getting out," interrupted Agent Crawford. "That's a huge assumption."

"It is a big assumption, and it's unnerving because it means we might have a leak," Helen said. "Tanner, who else knew about the last minute trip to DC?"

"Well, my wife knew I was going, but of course she didn't know why. I imagine that Bryan's family was in the same situation. The only other person at the NSA who knew the details of our trip was you," Tanner said, directing his hand toward his boss.

Helen didn't flinch or shudder at the statement. She demanded that her team never withhold anything from her. She always wanted to hear the truth, even if a theory was implicating her of wrongdoing.

"I can't even dream up a scenario where Helen would want to leak classified information," Rachel said for the rest of the QC team. "It's unfathomable."

"I appreciate the vote of confidence, Rachel," Helen said. "I think most of you have known me long enough to realize I don't play those games. Nevertheless, if any of you have doubts, share your opinion now."

Nobody said anything. Helen grew up during the Cold War era. She loved America, and her loyalty to the United States was absolute.

"Okay, who else knew about the trip?" Helen asked. She was confident that the leak wasn't from the NSA but somewhere else in the government.

"Just some folks at the Secret Service, I guess," Tanner said.

"It wasn't us. We're tighter than the NSA," replied Agent Payne, annoyed that a computer analyst from the NSA questioned the integrity of his organization.

Tanner could feel the tension starting to rise in the room, and he took a calming breath. "The only people at the NSA who know about our findings on the Chinese virus are in this room, and all of them found out about it *after* the plane crash," Tanner declared. "Every file and document on the project is tagged and logged. We would have a record of any unauthorized access."

"And all of our communication with other agencies is done over the gray phone," Mel Otterson said, referring to the secure and encrypted phone on every NSA employee's desk.

"That's right. So nobody can eavesdrop on our communication that way," Tanner said. "If there's a leak, it probably came from the Secret Service."

"Don't question our loyalty!" exploded Agent Payne. "The Secret Service is the most devoted organization in the world. We make Marines look insubordinate." His face was turning red with anger.

Everyone froze at the sudden outburst. Tanner had heard the egos of Secret Service agents were enormous. It made sense, seeing that some of them anticipated the moment they might take a bullet for the president of the United States. Still, the outburst seemed forced and excessive. "Well, where do you think the leak came from?" Tanner asked.

"There isn't a leak. You're trying too hard to connect dots that aren't even there," Agent Payne said. "The plane crash was an isolated and separate event that unfortunately involved your coworker." Todd's dismissive attitude about the death of their close friend, by calling the terrorist attack a "plane crash" was a verbal slap in the face to the QC team. The NSA analysts struggled to maintain their cool.

"That doesn't make sense. Why Utah?" asked Rachel. "Most terrorists don't even know that Salt Lake City exists. The probability of a random terrorist attack here is so low that I have a hard time even calculating it," she said, drawing on her education in mathematics.

"Not so. This was the site of the 2002 Winter Olympics, and it got a lot of international exposure from that," replied Agent Crawford. "Maybe someone was familiar with the area from the Olympics."

"Okay, everyone. Calm down," Helen said, using her civil personality to stop the bickering between sibling agencies. "Like Tanner said, this is just a theory."

The two sides paused and took a second to cool off. Agent Payne stood up and walked to the other side of the room, grabbing another doughnut. Maybe he had pushed back too hard on the NSA folks. Still, he didn't like accusations thrown across the table without any solid facts to back them up.

"Okay, maybe I overacted a bit," Agent Payne said as he sat back down. "But the real reason for our meeting today isn't about Flight 2512. We're supposed to be talking about the information you found on this new computer virus from China. I want to see the data for myself. When can I do that?"

Helen charted a new direction for the group, hoping to let cooler heads prevail. "Let's take a break while Tanner and I get our documents organized. We'll reconvene in twenty minutes."

Tanner left the conference room and headed straight for the restroom feeling flustered and upset. Who were these jerks from the Secret Service to come into his office and question his work?

The door to the restroom opened up as Tanner was washing his hands. It was Agent Crawford.

"It got a little tense in there, eh?" he casually said.

He walked toward Tanner with a slight, almost imperceptible limp. "You'll have to excuse my partner. He treats everyone that way. He's a hothead."

"Yeah, I guess so," Tanner mumbled. "What did you do to your leg?"

"Oh, that's an old injury from years ago. It only flares up in the cold weather, but it was enough to keep me off the presidential protection detail. That's how I got stuck working in electronic crimes," he said. "Just so you know, I don't always agree with Todd. But he's the senior guy, so I have to defer to him. I do think your theory on the terrorist attack is unrealistic, but I guess we should at least consider it."

Tanner was grateful for Agent Crawford's support. If Tanner couldn't convince Agent Payne to look for a leak in the Secret Service, maybe his partner could.

APRIL 25, BOISE, IDAHO

Reina returned to her hotel at 8:30 the same morning. She had just finished her ten–mile run and felt refreshed. With her task done, she now prepared to go back to Utah.

Her hit last night went flawlessly. Using the tip from her contact, it wasn't difficult for Reina to track down Jeff Kessler. Jeff was living at a cheap apartment complex on the south side of town. Reina discreetly followed Jeff around the city for a couple of hours as he went about his trivial activities, completely unaware that he was squandering the last hours of his life. When she finally approached the overweight and balding thirty-four-year-old at his favorite dive on Eighth Street, she knew it was going to be an easy job.

Reina flirted with her target for two hours in the crowded and dimly lit bar. Switching back to her Spanish accent, she put Jeff as ease. Because Jeff was on the lookout for a Chinese thug and not a beautiful Hispanic woman, he completely let down his guard.

Reina ordered copious amounts of drinks, ensuring that Jeff was sufficiently intoxicated by the time they left around midnight. Jeff eagerly anticipated where his evening with the beautiful woman might end up, but he didn't live long enough to find out.

Reina helped Jeff into the passenger seat of her car where he slouched drunkenly. She took advantage of his inebriated state and jabbed him in the thigh with a syringe full of concentrated oxytocin, a drug normally used to induce labor in pregnant women. However, the massive quantity of oxytocin that Reina gave Jeff resulted in a rapid overdose. Jeff complained about the unexpected poke in his leg, but he was so inebriated that he didn't fight back and soon forgot the whole ordeal.

As Reina drove the car away from the bar, Jeff thought it was strange that she knew where to go. He didn't remember giving her directions to his apartment, but it was hard for him to know for sure because he had a massive headache. Then, without warning, Jeff screamed in pain as all the muscles in his body contracted involuntarily. Jeff pleaded for help, but Reina ignored her passenger's slurred speech, a sign that the tissues in his brain were already beginning to swell.

Jeff was experiencing the beginning stages of hyponatremia, or low sodium levels in his blood. Furthermore, oxytocin was an antidiuretic, and given in the enormous dosage that Jeff had just received, it intensified the hyponatremia and caused a strange medical condition called water intoxication. Jeff didn't know it, but he was drowning, literally dying from having too much water in his body.

As the electrolytes in Jeff's system continued to fluctuate, the cells in his lungs began filling with fluid, restricting his ability to breathe. The tissues in his brain continued swelling. which, in turn, caused Jeff to seize. Reina casually drove around Boise, ignoring her tortured passenger, waiting for him to die. Eventually Jeff's body went limp as it succumbed to its fate. Satisfied that Jeff had paid dearly for his failure, Reina quickly disposed of his dead body in a dumpster before returning back to her hotel for the night.

NSA DATA CENTER, UTAH

Back in the Salt Lake Valley, it was just before 9:00 a.m. The QC team and the Secret Service agents had regrouped in the conference room. Tanner and Helen brought in several large folders containing copies of memos and various data printouts. The information described what the NSA knew about Tang Ju-Long and the details on the unique "Dragon Virus," as the analysts now called it. The folders were spread out across the large conference room table with Agent Todd Payne and Agent Adam Crawford hovering over the information like eagles preparing to go in for an attack.

"I'm having trouble following your analysis," Agent Crawford said as he turned another page in the folder, "but I can see—"

Just then the door to the conference room flung open, and Mel stormed in. "You gotta check this out!" he said. He turned on the TV and flipped the channel to CNN. "The Chinese just dropped an economic bomb. They announced they will no longer buy US Treasuries," he exclaimed excitedly.

"What does that mean?" asked Chad from the other side of the table. Chad was the scientist on the team, and he already had several lifetime patents for his work tuning the lasers that powered QC. Unfortunately, his knowledge of economics was slim compared to his brilliance in physics and optics.

Mel launched into a mini-lecture of economic theory without any prodding. "We all know the national debt is out of control. It's been skyrocketing ever since World War II, yet the government continues to spend money it doesn't have. So, the government funds its debt by issuing more and more bonds, which are basically IOUs with interest. For the past decade, the Chinese have heavily invested in these bonds. They hold over one trillion dollars of our debt. After the terrorist attack on Flight 2512 and the drop in the stock market yesterday, China decided it was too risky to keep buying our debt. They announced a moratorium about thirty minutes ago."

Tanner had taken several economics classes back in college, and

Denver Acey

he had a solid understanding of how the economy worked. "That's a powerful statement. They're basically saying they don't have confidence in our ability to repay our debt."

"Exactly!" Mel said, shuffling around like a little child. "Their announcement spooked everyone, and the financial markets immediately tanked. The president quickly ordered the stock markets closed for the rest of the week!"

"Can he do that?" asked Sydney.

"Yes. There's a law that gives him the power to do that. Apparently he didn't want another round of sell-offs like we had yesterday. The stock market already lost thirty percent of its value. That's catastrophic!" Mel said. "If the government can't find anyone to buy its debt, we risk defaulting like those countries in Europe did. We all know how messy that was."

The QC team and the Secret Service agents listened to the emerging news with deep interest.

A wave of economic panic was apparently spreading across the world as other countries unexpectedly followed China's lead. Russia and Brazil also announced a halt to buying US securities. Those two countries only held about 150 billion dollars in US debt, a relatively small amount compared to China's one trillion in US bonds. Nevertheless, the fact that other nations were losing confidence in the US government was monumental.

"In the long run, China's decision doesn't make sense," Mel said as he listened to the news reports, fidgeting with his fingers. As a former smoker, he still craved something to put in mouth. He habitually grabbed a ballpoint pen on the table and began gnawing on it nervously.

"How's that?" asked Rachel.

"China is heavily invested in America. It's in their best interest to see our country thrive. If we default on our debt, it will hurt China more than anybody else because they won't get their money back. Besides that, they're heavily invested in US corporations. When the stock market goes down, they also lose money that way," Mel said. He twirled the pen around in his mouth.

"Maybe they just got tired of keeping us on financial life support," countered Agent Crawford.

"Or, with another major attack on US soil, maybe China thinks the terrorists are gaining a foothold in America," Helen said.

"How would this decision help them?" Mel asked rhetorically. "The fact that they own so much of our debt makes us inseparable."

"There's something else," Tanner said. "It seems everything we buy now is made in China. We're their biggest consumer, especially in electronics like computers and smartphones. If our economy collapses, it hurts China because we can't buy their products."

"That's what I'm saying. A weakened US economy will only hurt China," Mel said.

The group of NSA analysts and Secret Service agents watched the live feed of the news for a few minutes in silence before Tanner asked an odd question. "Mel, what's the chance that this whole economic mess was deliberately crafted?"

"What? Like the announcement of China not buying any more of our debt?"

"Go back to yesterday. What's the chance that China deliberately brought down Flight 2512 to spook our economy, and give them an excuse to stop buying our debt?"

The other people in the room turned to Tanner, wondering what he was thinking.

"I guess that's a possibility, but a single attack on an airplane is minor compared to the shocking announcement they made today. China didn't do anything this drastic after September 11, and four planes were attacked back then," Mel said.

Tanner paused a moment as he organized his racing thoughts. "Let's say the terrorist attack was just the catalyst to get the whole thing going. Could China have done anything else to further encourage a drop in the stock market?"

"That's an interesting scenario," Mel said. He sat down and tapped the blue-and-white pen on the table as he thought. "China brings down an airliner to cause fear and panic in the financial markets. Then, they do a mass sell-off of their US assets, saying it's justified because of the terrorist attack. Nobody would blame them for suddenly dumping their stocks, but their actions would only increase the cycle of fear and cause the markets to plummet even further. Then, seeing that the markets have collapsed, China would be justified in their announcement of not buying any more of our debt."

Tanner nodded his head slowly. "Yeah, something like that," he said. The silence in the room from the other analysts accentuated the fear that Tanner might be onto something.

"Let me do some research and see which sell-offs occurred right before the big drop in the market," Mel said. "I guess it's possible that a large nation-state could manipulate stocks in such a manner. However, even if China purposely did that, it still doesn't answer the bigger question of *why*. The Chinese are only shooting themselves in the foot by weakening our economy."

"Unless China's goal is to cause so much economic chaos in the US that we're too preoccupied dealing with the mess to monitor what's going on in the rest of the world," Tanner said.

APRIL 25, ZHEJIANG PROVINCE, CHINA

The yellow city lights danced across the black, rolling hills like fireflies. *Another moonless April night,* Major General Yang Dao acknowledged as he looked out of his office window on the fourth floor. Located in the Chinese city of Shaoxing, about two hours south of Shanghai, the general's office was in an inconspicuous concrete building that bustled with activity twenty–four hours a day. The secret and secure facility housed the members of China's First Technical Reconnaissance Bureau—a division of Chinese computer programmers who constantly searched for new ways to hack into computer networks across the globe.

Yang Dao turned from the window and returned to the immaculate mahogany desk in the corner of his spacious office. For the past five years, Yang Dao had supervised the cyber-warfare operation of the People's Army with great success. The major general was the driving force behind China's triumphant electronic spying program that pilfered digital secrets from all over the world—especially from the United States. With stolen corporate trademarks and patents, Yang Dao's division of computer hackers had helped modernize China's economy in ways that would have normally taken centuries to accomplish.

Yang Dao sat down at his desk in the quiet office and rubbed his fingers through his short black-and-gray hair. From his source planted deep inside the US government, Yang Dao knew that the Americans had gained some knowledge of the novel computer virus developed by his military unit. Fortunately, the Americans didn't know that the virus had already infiltrated their networks, and it was ready to execute its code on computers all over the United States. But Yang Dao's plan to kill the two NSA analysts who had discovered the virus only partially succeeded, leaving one of the men alive. With luck, that small setback would soon be resolved. The major general felt confident his plan would move forward uninhibited once his niece took care of business.

NSA DATA CENTER, UTAH

Tanner was frustrated. He was wasting his valuable time in meetings and babysitting Secret Service agents. He should be spending his energy with QC, doing analysis on the information the supercomputer had gathered off the Internet. It was already noon on Tuesday, and Tanner hadn't even been back into the Chamber to see how Rachel's program was doing. For all he knew, QC might have already pinpointed who was behind the terrorist attack.

Hurry up and wait. It was one of the things he disliked most about his job. Despite the fact that he got to play on the fastest computer in the world, working for the government meant that everything else moved slowly. Like the other agencies in the intelligence community, the NSA wasn't immune to the roadblocks caused by federal bureaucracy. Tanner naïvely thought that the events of September 11 would have been a catalyst to get the intelligence community to move along, but instead it just added another layer of bureaucracy called the Department of Homeland Security.

Tanner left the Secret Service agents and headed off to another room for a conference call with the Federal Bureau of Investigations. Unfortunately, the FBI didn't have a telepresence room like the NSA had. Helen was waiting for Tanner in the conference room, eating her lunch in a well-mannered way. Tanner had often wondered if his boss attended some kind of charm school in her youth. With her elegance and refined manners, Tanner thought Helen could easily blend in with high society.

"Tanner, where's your food?" Helen asked in a concerned tone as she gracefully cut up her chicken salad.

"I didn't have time to get it. I've been running from meeting to meeting today," he said. He sat down next to the gray Polycom phone system, opposite of his boss. The phone in the middle of the table was similar to millions of models in other conference rooms around the country, except this one encrypted conversations for secure communication.

Helen spoke into the Polycom, beginning the meeting. "Tanner just arrived, so I think we can start now. On the phone we have Special Agent Derek Cannon and Special Agent Sara Heywood of the local FBI office," Helen said. "Thank you for your time. I know you're very busy."

Helen quickly explained Tanner's role in the discovery of a new computer virus coming out of China, and how the malware seemed to target financial computer systems in the United States. She then related how the information about the virus might be related to the terrorist attack on Flight 2512. Agents Cannon and Heywood listened intently, interrupting occasionally to clarify the information from the NSA.

"What about the folks from the Secret Service?" Agent Cannon asked. "Do they buy into your theory that someone might have targeted Flight 2512 in an attempt to keep the information from getting to them?"

"They aren't saying either way," Tanner said. "I think they're more concerned about the virus itself, not who shot down the airliner. I guess they figure that investigating the terrorist attack is the FBI's responsibility."

Tanner and Helen could hear the two FBI agents quietly discussing something on the other side of the phone call. After a moment, Agent Cannon spoke out. "Tanner, you said that you are running a routine right now that will search the Internet for any information about the terrorist attack. What exactly are you doing?"

"I can't go into the specifics because our equipment and search algorithms are classified, but basically we have the unique ability to sniff all the traffic flowing across the Internet. We're looking for keywords and phrases and then flagging the results for further analysis."

"Is that domestic or foreign Internet communication you're monitoring?" asked Agent Heywood.

Tanner immediately knew what Agent Heywood was really asking. The NSA wasn't supposed to be eavesdropping on any domestic communications, and certainly any FBI employee would be miffed at having someone playing spy on their turf. Tanner quickly looked at his boss for acknowledgment about whether he should answer the question.

Helen quickly jumped in and provided cover for her employee. "We've been authorized to listen in on all Internet traffic, both domestic and foreign, as established in Executive Order 13224," she said.

The FBI agents didn't say anything in response. Either they were digesting what Helen had just revealed, or they were thinking of a reason why the NSA might have broken the law. After a few moments of silence, Agent Cannon spoke again. "I'm concerned about the scope of your authorization. It sounds like you might be treading into waters of questionable legality."

"I understand your concern," Helen said, "but that's not how my team works. We do everything by the book, and only after we've been authorized. If you'd like, I can put you in touch with the Director of the NSA, and he'll confirm the authorization."

Agent Cannon decided it wasn't the right time for a conversation on privacy rights. "I'll look into the executive order later on. In the meantime, if you find anything else that fits into our investigation, will you please let us know?"

"We will," Helen said.

"One more thing," he said before ending the call. "Let's assume your theory is correct about a terrorist bringing down Flight 2512 to kill the investigation into the Dragon Virus. If so, I wonder if the people who killed Bryan know that Tanner is still alive."

They said their good-byes and Helen disconnected the phone call with the FBI. She stared at Tanner with a concerned expression. "Agent Cannon brought up an interesting point, but the way he said it made me think he knew more than he was letting on. Of course, he's not going to reveal the details of the investigation, but it sounds like the FBI has already considered the possibility of other motives for the attack on Flight 2512."

"What do I do in the meantime to be safe?" Tanner asked.

"Remain vigilant, I guess," replied Helen.

"Great. It's not like I'm already paranoid enough, working here all the time," Tanner said. He shook his head in frustration, knowing there wasn't much else he could do.

"Let's let the FBI think about what we just told them, and we'll follow up tomorrow. In the meantime, I have one more call I want you to be here for," Helen said. She quickly punched in an internal extension on the speakerphone. "This is the number for the Malware Analysis and Response Team back at Fort Meade. There are two guys over at MART who are specialists on computer malware. I forwarded your notes about the Dragon Virus to them this morning. Let's see if they have anything to confirm our suspicions."

The phone rang just once before being answered by a youthfully giddy voice on the other end. "You got Slammer on the line," he said.

"Hi, this is Helen Ripplinger at the Utah Spy Center. I've got Tanner Stone on the phone with me." Helen looked over at Tanner, who was mouthing the name "Slammer" back to his boss.

Helen quickly hit the mute button and answered Tanner's question. "His real name is Arthur Dawson, but he prefers to go by his computer alias," Helen said with a smile. "These guys are brilliant, but also eccentric. Just go along with it and try not to laugh."

Tanner immediately conjured up images of twenty-year-olds sitting in a dark room at NSA headquarters, surrounded with empty soda cans and crumpled up fast food wrappers. It was an amusing image, but Tanner knew the NSA hired the brightest minds, which often meant employing some unconventional characters.

Slammer quickly continued. "It's nice to meet you, Tanner. Hold on one second while I get Viper on the line."

After a moment, another young and animated voice joined Slammer on the phone. "Yo, this is some crazy stuff you sent us," said Viper. "It sounds like Chairman Mao and his buddies are up to their old tricks again."

"What can you tell us about the virus?" asked Helen.

"Well, we haven't seen anything on the Net about this specific virus, but that's not abnormal. We know the People's Republic has a massive computer espionage program run by their military," Viper said.

"The PRC has an entire division of hackers," Slammer jumped in, "devoted to spreading hate and discontent across the Internet."

Viper again picked up the conversation. "We're running a few scripts against some not-so-public IPs that we know originate in China. We're trying to get a whiff of what this virus is all about."

Tanner wondered where the NSA had found these two characters. Slammer and Viper acted like twins, even to the point of finishing each other's sentences.

Slammer quickly spoke again. "Since this is a completely new virus, we can't scan for any known signatures. We'll have to use a heuristic algorithm to sniff out parts of the code. But if the virus is using polymorphic tools to rewrite itself after infecting a system, it will be very difficult to get a trace on it."

The computer buzzwords the MART team used didn't make

much sense to Helen, but Tanner nodded in understanding. She was grateful to have someone with hacking skills on her team.

"Will you give me a call as soon as you find something out?" Tanner asked the two analysts on the MART.

"Will do. We've already geared up for a long night, and the pizza is on its way. This is going be sweet, man!" Slammer shouted out before saying good-bye.

"Where did we dig up those guys?" Tanner asked after the call ended.

"We found them a couple years ago at Defcon. They won the capture-the-flag event," Helen said. Defcon was the annual conference in Las Vegas where hackers gathered from all over the world to demonstrate their shady skills. "It took some negotiation and a fat paycheck to get them to sign on with the NSA, but they are worth every penny. They're the ones who discovered Thrasher last year," she said. She was referring to the computer worm that took down scores of Fortune 500 websites. "By the way, they're brothers if you're wondering. That explains their camaraderie."

APRIL 25, NSA DATA CENTER, UTAH

It was almost 2:00 p.m., and Tanner needed to check on the Secret Service agents. Agents Payne and Crawford were in a conference room, looking over Tanner's notes with Mel keeping them company. Unfortunately, Mel had a limited knowledge of the Dragon Virus, and by the time Tanner arrived, the two agents were thoroughly confused by the inadequate explanations.

"Tanner, I'm glad you're here. These guys have a lot of questions, and I'm ready for a break," Mel said. He got up and left the room.

"How's it going?" Tanner asked as he took a chair at the conference room table. He was glad to see there was still a tray of snacks left over from breakfast. The warm orange juice and crusty doughnut weren't very good, but they helped pacify Tanner's hunger pains.

"Now that I've had time to digest your notes, I'd say you have some solid points about this Dragon Virus," Agent Crawford said genuinely.

"Tell me why you think so," Tanner said. He employed one of

the tricks he often used with his peers. If another person could adequately and concisely explain Tanner's theory back to him, it was well crafted and documented.

"Well, according to your notes, your first hint of this virus was back at the beginning of February. You intercepted and translated a Chinese email going between Beijing and Shaoxing. The original communication was short, but it mentioned the initial penetration test on an American financial institution."

"Yeah, but that's not uncommon," Tanner said. "The Chinese scan our networks on a daily basis." Although it wasn't public knowledge, the analysts at the NSA knew that over 70 percent of all hacking attempts against the United States originated in the People's Republic of China, with the former Soviet Union coming in second.

"Okay, but the following week, you witnessed a huge spike in the Internet traffic from Beijing to a specific network switch in Shaoxing," Agent Crawford said.

"Maybe that was just a homesick sergeant in Beijing, trying to keep in contact with his mother," Tanner said with a laugh.

Agent Crawford flipped through some more papers on the large table, ignoring Tanner's joke. "Then, around the first week of March, you isolated the email traffic to a network switch and a specific IP address ending in 144. That IP was assigned to a computer in a large facility on the hillside of Shaoxing. According to your documents, that building belongs to the First Technical Reconnaissance Bureau. That's China's loose equivalent to the NSA."

"Go on," Tanner encouraged.

Until this point, Agent Payne had remained quiet, listening to Tanner and Agent Crawford play out their little game. He spoke up now, suddenly finding himself defending the same theory that, just yesterday, he had quickly dismissed. "Here's the intriguing part. Somehow, and I'm not sure how you did it, you managed to correlate that IP address to a voice-over-IP phone in that same building. You were then able to track every time a phone call was made back to Beijing. Given that most the calls were all made around 7:00

p.m. their time, I'd say you picked up on a daily conference call between Beijing and Shaoxing," Agent Payne said. "But to isolate a specific VOIP phone extension, you'd need some kind of hidden access to the switches on that specific Chinese network."

Tanner didn't confirm nor deny Agent Payne's assumption. Tanner just played his best poker face and let the speculation go unanswered.

The agent continued vetting Tanner's analysis. "Once you isolated the VOIP phone with the 7121 extension, you identified a bunch of outgoing calls from Shaoxing to the industrial city of Shenzhen. From the first of March to the end of March, you recorded sixty-six phone calls from Shaoxing to Shenzhen. In every instance, the calls were made to the exact same number."

"Those calls were in Mandarin Chinese, and we don't have any recordings of what they said," Tanner argued, playing devil's advocate.

"That's true, but you know the destination of the calls was in Shenzhen. It's to a computer firm that is managed by Tang Ju-Long, the foreign national who received his degree from Berkley before disappearing back to the Far East."

Tanner smiled. With a lot of notes and a little prodding, the two Secret Service agents had come to roughly the same conclusion as the NSA.

"There's still something missing," Agent Payne said as he leaned back in his chair. "You've traced the communications going from Beijing to their military's hacking group in Shaoxing. You've also traced phone calls going from Shaoxing to Tang Ju-Long in Shenzhen. So it definitely looks like there's a connection between the main government, the Army's elite hacking unit, and Tang Ju-Long. Unfortunately, we don't know the exact nature of the calls. For all we know, they were planning a birthday party," Agent Payne said. The skepticism had returned to his voice.

"Did you read this?" Tanner asked. He leaned over and flipped to the bottom of the stack of papers. He pulled out a translated page from the Chinese IT magazine *ChinaByte*. "It's an article written last year about information technology in China, and the advances they've made into antivirus detection systems. The article quotes Tang Ju-Long and his company's work on developing a new antivirus algorithm. If you read the translated text closely, it casually mentions the contract work he's done with a private party in Shaoxing."

Agent Payne took a moment to read the article before responding. "Okay, so he's probably developing an antivirus system for the Chinese government. That doesn't mean he's creating new viruses, let alone this specific Dragon Virus that has the ability to target our financial institutions."

"No, but this does," Tanner said. Reaching into the manila folder that he had brought into the room with him, Tanner pulled out a single sheet of paper. The words "Top Secret" were stamped in bright red ink across the top and bottom of the page.

The Secret Service agents weren't fazed by the classified document that Tanner handed them. They each had seen their fair share of restricted material, but this document was completely different. Instead of plain English, it contained lines of computer code.

"What's this?" asked Agent Payne.

"They're lines of source code we stole off a computer that belongs to Tang Ju-Long," Tanner said. He didn't mention that the NSA had used an undisclosed bug in the OpenSSL protocol to gain access to Tang-Ju Long's personal files. "From my notes scribbled at the bottom, you can follow the logic of the programming routine."

Agent Payne wasn't a computer geek, but Agent Crawford had some IT background. After reading Tanner's translation of the source code, he fully understood that it was indeed a virus program.

"How did you get this?" he asked. "This is amazing."

"Let's just say we have unique tools here at the NSA for eavesdropping on all sorts of digital communication," Tanner said.

"This looks like the beginning section of a virus routine, but the execution phase explaining what the virus actually does is missing," Agent Crawford said.

"That's the crazy part. It's not missing," Tanner said. "This *is* the entire program. Basically, this program stages the virus and gets it ready for further instructions."

"Instructions for what?" asked Agent Crawford.

"We don't know. We have a couple of our guys at NSA headquarters looking over it right now," Tanner said. "It could be anything from starting a keylogger to wiping out an entire database, but there's something else that's more troubling," Tanner continued. "In every virus routine I've ever seen, the beginning section of the code always contains information on how the virus should propagate itself. That's the first thing a virus does. It copies itself and infects other computer systems. This specific virus from China doesn't do that. It's like the virus already assumes it has infected millions of other computer systems."

"Now that's scary," Agent Crawford said. "It's a logic bomb, waiting to detonate."

"Can't we just scan our computer systems for these specific lines of code to see if we're already infected?" asked Agent Payne.

"We've tried, at least at a fundamental level. But the virus is either obscured down in some part of the operating system, or hidden in another way we can't detect it. We're waiting to hear back from our virus experts to see if they have any insight," Tanner said.

"So, I guess we're kind of stuck until then," Agent Payne said. "Do you have anything else we should be looking at?"

Tanner shook his head. "No, that's it for right now." He took a breath and changed directions. "Why don't you guys call it a day? I've got some other stuff I have to do that will keep me busy until dinnertime."

"That's a great idea. I can only stare at notes and documents for so long," Agent Crawford said. "Let's pick it up tomorrow. Maybe we'll have some more information from your antivirus folks by then."

Tanner escorted the two Secret Service agents out of the building, and then he quickly walked back to his desk. He called his wife before heading into the Chamber.

"Hey, Wifey," Tanner said, using his nickname for Megan. "How's your day going?"

"Good. Not much happening on my end. I've just been running some database upgrades."

"How's the baby doing?"

"She's been kicking and flopping around like crazy. I think she wants out," Megan said with a laugh. They still hadn't chosen a baby name. They had a solid list of five or six choices, but they couldn't quite decide which one seemed to fit best.

"I'm hoping to be home for dinner, about six or seven," Tanner said. "I've been super busy, and I got a couple of things I have to finish up before I leave."

"Don't forget about our doctor appointment tomorrow morning at eight," Megan said. Tanner had accompanied his wife to every one of her pregnancy appointments, and at week thirty-six, he wasn't about to break his streak.

"I won't. Love you."

"Love ya too. See ya around seven," Megan said.

Tanner took a quick second to lean back in his office chair and rest his tired eyes. He was often jealous of his wife and her comfortable working arrangement. Tanner felt that he would be more productive telecommuting from home where he didn't have to spend half his day in meetings.

Tanner glanced at his watch—3:42 p.m. It was getting late, and he hadn't done any real work. Fortunately, he still had time to do something useful besides occupying a chair in a conference room. He jumped up and hurried off to the Chamber. Hopefully Rachel and Sidney had some success to report.

It took longer than usual for Tanner to complete the authorization process to enter the secure data center. Since he was alone, Tanner had to wait for both Rachel and Sidney to come out and escort him back inside.

The three systems analysts walked back over to the operations desk for the supercomputer and sat down. The quiet and relaxing hum of the supercomputer on the other side of the glass wall beckoned Tanner to go to sleep. "I'm glad you're finally here," Rachel said.

"Same story as usual. I've been in meetings all day," Tanner said. He vigorously shook his head, attempting to stay awake. "Tell me what you've found."

"Well, the work started out a little slow because we had some issues with the lasers," Sidney said, referring to the green-colored lasers that powered QC. "Chad worked on it all morning, and we finally got QC running full speed again just after lunch."

Rachel continued the report. "When you and I kicked off my algorithms this morning, we already had twenty-three million results that mentioned anything about a terrorist attack or Flight 2512. With all the recent emails, blogs, and news articles about the crash, our hit count kept increasing. Around 11:00 a.m., we had over forty-four million results," Rachel said. "We didn't think our original approach was working, so Sidney and I started over with a revised program and algorithm. This new routine excludes anything that can be traced back to a legitimate news agency or article. Stripping out all that data, we quickly dropped our hit results to under three million."

"That's great, but it's still a lot of hay to find a needle in," Tanner said.

"Right, but we spent all afternoon refining our queries and whittling down the results," Sidney said. "Of course, we're making a lot of assumptions on what to filter out, but we finally got the count down to around forty thousand emails and web chat postings that needed further investigation."

"Okay, now that's more manageable," Tanner said.

"Wait, we're not done yet," Rachel interjected. "We decided to sort those forty thousand hits by date and time. We figured the emails and chats which happened closest to the time of the terrorist attack would be more valuable than later on when the Net filled up with news reports and conspiracy theories."

"And . . . ," Tanner said. He could see that his teammates were waiting to deliver the punch line.

"Pay dirt," Sidney announced with a smile. "We found several fascinating emails, but this one in particular gave us the chills. It was encrypted with AES, which makes the contents even more intriguing." She handed a printout of the message to Tanner. The email was brief and gripping:

> *Rey,*
> *I just checked into my hotel in Boise. It wasn't a long trip from Salt Lake. I'm ready for my hit tonight. It won't be as spectacular as a missile shooting a plane out of the sky, but you know this job has sentimental value for me.*
> *Love,*
> *Reina*

Tanner read the note again, carefully digesting each word. He couldn't believe it—a single email that specifically talked about who had attacked Flight 2512. "What did the other emails say?" he asked.

"Nothing as clear-cut as this. They were mostly conspiracy emails going back and forth on websites devoted to political unrest. This is by far the best one we found," Rachel said.

"*Reina* is Spanish for queen," Tanner said, remembering his Spanish from high school. "Was the email originally in Spanish?"

"No, it was in English, but it was encrypted to make it more secure. In the end, it wasn't anything QC couldn't handle," Rachel said.

"It seems the name *Reina* is some sort of code name because she's been emailing another person named Rey. That's Spanish for *king*," Tanner said. He paused a moment to gather his thoughts. "So it looks like we're dealing with someone of Hispanic descent, or at least someone who's comfortable speaking Spanish," he concluded. "I want to start a capture on the Internet for any emails from this Reina character. Also, put a trace on the destination email address for Rey. Maybe he'll email someone else who is part of their group."

"Why don't we just go after the email server that hosts these accounts and see who the users are?" asked Sidney.

"That's a legal issue. We can passively sniff data going back and forth on the Internet, but we can't deliberately crack the email accounts belonging to a domestic hosting company. That requires a search warrant, and that means we need to get the FBI involved," Tanner said. "Good work, you two. Stay here and see what else you can gather while I go show this to Helen."

Tanner left the Chamber and quickly headed toward his boss's desk. Helen was in the middle of reading a web article about the prime-time speech the president of the United States was delivering tonight. Everyone in the country was on edge with the terrorist attack and resulting financial crisis. The nation's citizens were looking to their leader for assurance.

"Check this out. We just got it off QC," Tanner said with renewed energy. He handed the paper to his boss. Helen took a moment to read the brief email, and then she instantly stood up and started walking out of her office.

"When was this email sent?" she asked. She was practically running to the closest available conference room.

Tanner followed quickly behind, filling his boss in on the details. "It was sent last night. The email mentions something in Boise, but I didn't hear anything in the news about that."

Helen opened a door to a secure conference room. "Get that phone number for Derek Cannon. The FBI needs to know about this," she said.

APRIL 25, FBI FIELD OFFICE, UTAH

Derek Cannon was in his office, reviewing the details of Executive Order 13224, when Tanner called. Ironically, the FBI's new Salt Lake City field office was located in the aviation business park, just a stone's throw from Salt Lake International Airport and the site of the terrorist attack. "Wait, you found what?" Derek asked, after Tanner had filled him in.

"We found a suspicious email that mentions Flight 2512. If you can get on a secure line, we'll give you all the details," Tanner said. He gave the FBI agent the number to the secure phone in the NSA conference room.

"Okay, I'll call you back in one minute," Derek said.

A few moments later, Derek dialed the number to a private conference room at the Utah Data Center. Helen answered after the first ring. "Hello," she said.

"Thanks for waiting," Derek said without any other greeting. "I'm on a secure line now with Agent Heywood. First of all, it looks like your executive order checks out. I spoke about it with the Attorney General back in Washington. You haven't violated any personal rights, but the AG says it's not a lifetime exemption on domestic spying. That's the job of the FBI."

"We'll follow the rules," Helen said. "But if we lose our presidential authorization, we won't find information like this." She read the email aloud over the speakerphone to the FBI agents. The information was astonishing.

"How's it even possible that you found this email? I mean, billions of emails are sent across the Internet every day, and that one was encrypted," Sara said.

"We have some unique toys over here at the NSA," Tanner said.

"You said the email was sent last night," Derek said, going back to the topic at hand.

"Actually, it was sent yesterday afternoon," Helen corrected. "The email mentioned something in Boise. What's going on in Boise?"

"Beats me," Derek said. "Boise falls under our Salt Lake City division, but we haven't heard anything up there. I'll contact some of our guys and see what they know."

"Can you fax us a copy of the email?" Sara asked, her Southern drawl pronounced even over the phone.

"You bet. I'll do it right now," Tanner said. "But first, can you get the web hosting company to tell us who owns the email addresses for Rey and Reina?"

"Yes, but I'll bet you a hundred dollars that will just be a dead end. Anyone can register for an email account using a bogus name or phone number. That's why so many criminals use the Internet for communication and coordination. It's a tapestry of pseudonyms," Derek said. "But we'll get a search warrant and officially request the email logs from the hosting company."

Tanner asked an interesting question. "Have you guys considered that you might be dealing with a female terrorist?"

Derek was caught completely off guard by Tanner's keen observation. "Why do you think that?"

"Because one of the people mentioned in the email is named Reina, which is Spanish for *queen*. The way the email is worded makes, it sound like she was the one who actually attacked Flight 2512," Tanner said.

"Maybe it's just a guy using a female alias," Derek said, trying not to reveal more details about the investigation.

"That's always a possibility, but I've had lots of interaction with all sorts of characters on the Internet. It's common for someone to use fake names or address, but most aliases in cyberspace don't change gender. It's too unnatural," Tanner said. "You might want to take a look at it."

"You also might want to focus your investigation on people who speak Spanish," Helen added.

"We will. Call us back if you find anything else," Derek said.

"Definitely," Tanner replied.

"One more thing before we hang up," Derek said. "Good work. This is valuable stuff you found."

NSA DATA CENTER, UTAH

Tanner and Helen stayed in the conference room for a moment after the FBI agents hung up. "Derek didn't like the fact that we were spying on domestic Internet traffic, but once he realized what we had found, he didn't seem to mind," Tanner said.

"That's how it always is. The FBI is the Federal Bureau of *Investigation*," Helen said, with emphasis on investigation. "They want to be the ones to crack a case, but in this situation, they just don't have the power that we do with QC."

"A lot of the credit for finding that email goes back to Rachel and Sidney. They tweaked the algorithms we ran to filter the results by time," Tanner said.

"Too bad we can't go back in time and see if any other emails were sent by this Reina person," Helen said wishfully.

Helen's comment caused Tanner's mind to spin off in another direction. "Maybe we can," he said as he collected his thoughts.

"Once something is put out on the Internet, it never really goes away. That's because the Internet is full of all sorts of appliances to speed up communication. There's a remote possibility that previous emails from Reina are still stored in a caching device out there." Tanner's excitement about the idea grew as his voice sped up. "We'd have to move fast because the longer we wait, the more likely that those caching devices will be overwritten."

Helen was intrigue by Tanner's idea. "How much work would it take to get a program like that going?"

"I'd have to write some new code and tweak Rachel's algorithms again, but I might have a rough script finished in a couple of hours. It will take longer for QC to run the routine and return any results. Scouring the Internet isn't an easy task, even for the fastest computer in the world."

"Let's do it, but also keep our other search going for any new emails from Reina. Maybe we might find another message for the FBI," Helen said.

———•———

It was just after 7:00 p.m. when Tanner finally left the NSA facility. Programming QC to search Internet caching devices was easier than he had anticipated, but it was harder to get the code to run independently without repeated intervention. In the end, Tanner addressed this dilemma by cannibalizing a bit of logic from a well-known computer worm. Unlike a computer virus, which infects individual computer systems, a worm self-replicates and attacks networks, causing denial of service attacks. Tanner's program implemented the worm's inundation technique to encompass the Internet, searching millions of caching devices for any remnants of an email from Reina.

Confident that his program was now dispersing out across the globe, Tanner got in his car and left for home. He turned on his radio, catching the first part of the president's speech about the tragic events of the past couple of days. It was the typical presidential address, filled with phrases like "remaining vigilant," "moving forward," and "prevailing over evil." Tanner wondered if political speechwriters cannibalized phrases from other speeches like good programmers did with computer code. He was positive he had heard some of the exact same rhetoric used just after September 11.

As Tanner drove home on the chilly April evening, he let his thoughts drift away from the stresses at work. It had been a difficult couple of days, and he just wanted to turn off his analytical brain for a while. Tanner felt like he hadn't even taken adequate time to mourn the death of his close friend. Hopefully, the funeral would give Tanner some time to find the closure he desired.

As Tanner turned east on Bangerter Highway, he failed to notice a black Dodge Charger closing in from behind. Reina patiently followed her target in the Honda Civic as he drove home. It would be child's play for Reina to kill Tanner Stone right now, but she was under strict orders not to do that. The murder of another NSA analyst would instantly put the local cops and FBI on alert. Instead, she would have to eliminate Tanner in a way that could only be described as an unfortunate accident.

APRIL 26, ZHEJIANG PROVINCE, CHINA

Although it was just after nine o'clock in the morning, Major General Yang Dao had been at work for hours. Almost sixty−five years old, the major general oozed discipline in everything he did, from his immac−ulately pressed uniform, to his fifteen−hour work days. Yang Dao hadn't achieved the rank of general by slothfulness, and on the eve of his unsanctioned operation against the United States, he couldn't afford any mistakes.

In reality, though, every military operation needed adjustments along the way. Nobody could predict the myriad of unforeseen cir−cumstances that always threatened even the best military strategies. Such was the case with a lone NSA analyst named Tanner Stone. From his source deep inside the United States government, Yang Dao had learned that Tanner Stone was systemically unraveling the major general's coup de grâce. It was a given fact that Tanner would have to die, but Yang Dao was waiting to hear back from his source to determine how much Tanner had already learned about the computer virus. Yang Dao specifically wanted to determine if the Americans knew that the majority of their financial systems were already compromised by the stealthy malware developed by Tang Ju-Long.

The genesis for Tang Ju-Long's computer virus, began several years ago in the industrial city of Shenzhen. Located just north of Hong Kong, Shenzhen was the economic jewel of the People's Republic of China. Thousands of corporations in the United States had moved significant components of their operations to Shenzhen, taking advantage of the skilled labor and cheap manufacturing costs. High-tech factories in the special economic zone assembled millions of computers and laptops to be exported back to the United States. Because of the favorable trade laws mandated by the Chinese government, 70 percent of the components for each of these computers had to be made in China. It was a brilliant move that took control of the manufacturing process out of the hands of the Americans.

For the past three years, every computer system manufactured in Shenzhen contained a specialized microchip with a hidden piece of computer code. Completely obscured from the operating system or any antivirus technology, these microchips were all configured to be activated at the same time, unleashing the full impact of the stealthy computer virus. Nothing could be done to remove the malware because Tang-Ju Long had implanted the code inside a stand-alone microchip. Even if the infected computer system was formatted and reinstalled from scratch, the virus would immediately reinfect its host system upon startup, waiting for its zero day attack.

The true payload of the virus was a closely guarded secret. Only a few people in the world understood how the malware would destroy the financial integrity of the United States. Upon execution, the virus would erase every bit of financial data in every infected computer system across America. The impact would be unfathomable. Bank accounts with millions of dollars would suddenly be zero. Retirement funds would vanish into thin air. Corporate balance sheets would be lost. An unparalleled economic catastrophe would sweep across the United States as every individual, business, and organization became completely and utterly bankrupt. Then, amid the financial chaos in the United States, Yang Dao would rise up and help China reclaim her rightful role as the premier superpower in the world.

•———•

DRAPER, UTAH

Tanner was grateful for the chance to sleep in Wednesday morning, but he still felt guilty not being at work. However, he was soon to be a father, and that was a calling he would carry his entire life, long after he retired from the NSA. He tried to keep that in perspective, even at chaotic times like the past few days.

"What do you think the doctor will say today?" Tanner asked his wife during breakfast.

"He'll probably say that I'm moving along just fine, but to take it easy," Megan replied, eating her omelet. She had experienced some powerful food cravings during her pregnancy, and eggs were at the top of her list. Tanner wondered how much his cholesterol had spiked over the past several months, eating eggs almost every day with his wife.

"We're getting close. It's just a month until the due date," Tanner said. He picked up the dishes and loaded them into the dishwasher.

Megan changed the subject to a more somber topic. "How is Courtney going to survive?" She was referring to Bryan Morrison's spouse.

"I imagine Bryan had some kind of life insurance policy. I know it's a standard benefit for everyone who works with the federal government."

"They just moved into that huge house. I wonder if she'll be able to afford it now," Megan said.

"I don't know. Maybe I should see if we can start some kind of a fund for her at work," Tanner said. He would ask Helen if there was anything else the QC team could do to help out Bryan's family.

Megan seemed satisfied with her husband's response. "I've got to do a quick five-minute conference call before we leave."

"You better hurry up. We might hit rush hour."

Tanner finished doing the dishes while Megan logged on the computer for a web chat with her coworker back in Albuquerque. Ten minutes later, she wrapped up the call as Tanner grabbed their coats out of the closet. Before stepping out into the garage, Tanner helped his wife put on her jacket, giving her a big bear hug from behind.

"I can hardly get my arms around you." He laughed.

Megan gracefully turned her head backward for a kiss, her soft blonde hair brushing against Tanner's face in the process. Tanner kissed his wife passionately, enjoying the brief and carefree moment they had together. He knew the pressure would be back on once he returned to work.

The garage door opened, and the Honda Civic pulled out first, followed by a white Toyota Camry. They each took separate cars to the doctor's appointment so Tanner could go straight to work afterward. The cars drove down the street, passing a black Dodge Charger that nonchalantly blended into the fashionable neighborhood. Inside the parked car, Reina watched as her targets headed off toward Interstate-15.

Reina waited a few additional minutes, and then she grabbed her backpack from the passenger seat. Confident that the couple would be gone for a while, she got out of her car and casually walked toward the vacant house. With her youthful age and modern clothes, Reina appeared to be a college student. Instead of heading off to class, however, she walked up the steps to the Stones' home and rang the doorbell. After the second ring went unanswered, she moved off the porch and around to the side of the house, acting like she had every business being there.

Reina would never have been so flippant about her actions back in China, where the government was always watching, but it was different here in America. Not only were Americans inherently naïve, but political correctness in the US had gone so far that nobody dare offend anyone else by questioning his or her actions. Reina knew that the average American feared being labeled a sexist or a racist more than reporting a crime in progress.

Reina opened the fence gate and walked into the Stones' backyard. She closed the entrance and quickly put on a pair of latex gloves. She began to work on the exterior door leading into the garage. She opened her backpack and took out a black pouch about the size of a book. Unzipping the leather kit, she selected a tension wrench and a small diamond lock pick. Using the white vinyl fence to camouflage her actions, she turned the cylinder on the dead bolt with the tension wrench, while lifting up the internal pins with the diamond lock pick. In a few seconds, the dead bolt was defeated. Next came the tricky part of her operation—she didn't know if the external door to the garage was alarmed. Usually this type of door wasn't monitored, but if there was a sensor, opening the door would start a thirty-second countdown to alerting the monitoring company.

Carefully turning the doorknob and opening the door, Reina listened for the high pitch wail of a siren—it never happened. Confident that the external door wasn't alarmed, she quietly moved across the interior of the garage. Before repeating the same lock picking sequence on the door leading into the house, Reina took out her smartphone and started up an application. The kitchen door would definitely be alarmed, and once opened, she would only have a few seconds to find the console and deactivate the system. Reina again expertly picked the lock and opened the door. She was greeted by the warning beeps from the master console. She found the white control pad mounted on the wall in the kitchen. Analyzing the device, she rapidly queried the app on her smartphone and found the master programmer's code for that specific alarm manufacturer. After punching in the four-digit combination, the beeping suddenly stopped and a polite woman's voice said, "System deactivated. Ready to arm."

Reina carefully rummaged through every part of the four-bedroom house, but she wasn't looking for something to steal. With her smartphone camera in hand, she took a dozen pictures of the home, carefully building a visual profile of Tanner Stone. She quickly learned several things. Tanner was extremely organized. Of course, it might have been his wife who displayed that orderly characteristic, but Reina dismissed the thought after seeing how Tanner had efficiently organized the yard tools in his garage. Everything had its place, but there was something else that communicated more than just someone who was a neat freak. It took a moment for Reina to figure it out, but then she finally realized what she was seeing. Everything in the house was optimized for use and arranged for maximum efficacy. Tanner was a deliberate person. He was someone who didn't waste time or energy. Reina acknowledged that was an admirable characteristic to have in a foe. With his attentiveness to detail, Tanner would surely recognize if someone had turned-down his house. Reina mentally reminded herself again to take extra precautions to make sure she didn't leave any trace of her presence.

Finished with her surveillance work, she went downstairs to the unfinished basement. The area below the main level of the house was vacant, except for a gas furnace and water heater tucked off into a corner. Grabbing a wrench, pliers, and screwdriver from her backpack, Reina opened the cover on the furnace and modified the controller for the exhaust system. The changes she made were small and hardly noticeable, but the result would be deadly.

Because the April sun warmed the house sufficiently during the day, the furnace wouldn't start up again until that evening. The modifications Reina made to the heating unit would cause carbon monoxide to leak out of the furnace and into the house. The colorless and odorless gas would go undetected for hours, building up to dangerous levels until Tanner and his wife died in their sleep from carbon monoxide poisoning. Of course, Tanner's absence from work would be noticed the following day, and eventually the police would respond and investigate the untimely deaths of two people in the quiet neighborhood. In the end, the autopsy report would determine the cause of death to be carbon monoxide from a malfunctioning heating unit in the basement.

Confident that Tanner's death would kill the NSA's investigation into the secret computer virus, Reina threw all her equipment into her backpack and got ready to leave. Walking back through the house, she double-checked to make sure everything was in its proper place. She activated the alarm system and then quietly exited out the rear door of the house. She innocently walked back to her black car, undetected by anyone in the peaceful neighborhood.

APRIL 26, BOISE, IDAHO

The agents at the FBI branch in Boise, Idaho, were surprised to be contacted by Derek Cannon early Wednesday morning. Derek asked his peers up north to dig around and see if they could find any murders that had recently happened in town. A quick call to the local police department confirmed that a John Doe was indeed discovered the previous night at a city park. The local cops didn't think anything of the unremarkable case until the FBI showed up at Boise police headquarters, asking to speak to the detective who ran the investigation.

"I need to see the report for that John Doe you discovered last night," the FBI agent said, removing his dark sunglasses. With his muscular and powerful frame, the special agent looked like he could bench press an elephant.

"There's nothing there. It's just a homeless guy we found in a park," the Boise police detective said. Still chewing on his bagel, he grabbed a folder off his desk and handed it to the FBI agent.

"Who found the body?" asked the agent.

"Some jogger out for a run with her dog," the police detective said. "The dog started barking at the dumpster, and the owner looked inside after she noticed a bad smell. We got the call about 8:00 p.m."

The intimidating FBI agent quickly scanned the paperwork. The John Doe was a white male in his late thirties, about six feet tall and grossly overweight. The report noted there were no signs of trauma or foul play.

"Where's the toxicology report?" the FBI agent asked.

"We didn't run one. It's a waste of time," the detective said. "Like I said, it's just another homeless guy we fished out of a dumpster. They're always scrounging around in the trash, looking for food. This guy probably died of a heart attack or liver failure."

"Just run the lab work and call me when you get the results, okay? I've got a guy down in Salt Lake who says this might be something," the special agent replied. He turned and walked out the door.

NSA DATA CENTER, UTAH

Tanner arrived at his job a little after 10:00 a.m. He went straight to the team's main conference room and quickly realized it was a busy place. Helen, Chad, and Mel sat on one side of the table, with the agents from the Secret Service on the other side. The room smelled of conflict, and the frenzied conversation between the two sides only added to the chaos. Tanner wasn't fazed by the unexplained commotion. He had developed a tolerance for it.

"What do you mean you can't show us how you got the information on the computer virus?" Agent Payne demanded in a loud voice. He suspected the NSA had a new, remarkable way to gather intelligence, and he wanted to see it firsthand.

"You aren't code-word authorized to know about it. That's the rules," Mel said.

"We have a top-secret clearance," Agent Crawford said. He didn't like being put-off either.

"That doesn't matter. You have to get code-word authorized, and that has to come from the admiral," Mel said, referring to the director who oversaw the entire NSA.

Tanner sympathized with the plight of the Secret Service agents, but rejection was a fact of life in the intelligence community. The federal government had truckloads of rules that regulated which agency had access to which classified information. Even though Tanner also had a top-secret clearance, he couldn't just walk over to the FBI or CIA and demand to see their classified documents. The policies managing restricted information were so complex that most federal organizations employed full-time people just to make sense of the rules.

Agent Payne shot back angrily, "Get the admiral on the phone. I'm tired of wasting my time."

The stress and long working hours were taking its toll on everyone. Recognizing that a fight might soon erupt, Helen intervened to diffuse the situation. "Agent Payne and Agent Crawford, I will submit a request to get you access this morning. Unfortunately, the process can take a while, so you'll need to work on something else in the meantime." Then, changing the subject, she acknowledged Tanner's presence at the door. "I need to speak with you for a moment. "

Tanner and his boss walked down the hall a few yards before Helen spoke. "I already told the others, but the funeral for Bryan will be Friday morning at 11:00, with a viewing tomorrow night. I want everyone to attend."

"I'll be there," Tanner said, thinking about his good friend for a moment. "Where are Rachel and Sydney?" He noticed they weren't in the conference room with the others.

"They're waiting for you in the Chamber. Go in there and give them a hand."

Tanner didn't need to be told twice. Anything he could do to avoid Agent Payne and his explosive personality was a relief.

After going through the authorization process to get into the tightly guarded data room, Tanner joined Rachel and Sydney at the main computer terminal for QC.

"We were wondering when you might come in. We didn't find any new emails from Reina last night, but Helen said that you had another program running. We've been trying to figure out what it does, but we can't find any output," Sydney said. She was still a novice on operating QC, and she often got confused navigating the proprietary and obscure operating system.

"Here, let me drive for a second," Tanner said. Sydney stood and he sat down at the console. His fingers flew across the keyboard as he entered in different commands to search the massive computer system.

"Looks like the guru is here now," Rachel said with a mock-laugh, much to the disappointment of Sydney. Tanner sensed Sydney's frown without looking up from the computer screen.

"Don't get frustrated, Sydney. It took me a whole year to figure out how to work this system. Here, I'll show you a few shortcuts." Tanner wanted to mentor Sydney the same way Helen had done for him back when he started at the NSA. He pointed to the screen and spoke. "This is the folder for all the programs that I write. You have to go in here to find my output."

Tanner navigated his way through the complex folder system to the directory where he had collected the results from the unique computer script he created. Taking a couple more minutes to finish the last of his commands, Tanner was thrilled to see several hits from his program.

"I wrote a program before I left last night to scour caching devices on the Internet. I wanted to look for any email residue that might be from Reina," he said. Opening up the first file, Tanner saw that it contained part of a message. The other two NSA analysts looked over his shoulder as he scrutinized the partial text.

"Look at that!" Sydney said. The email contained a list of numbers. Even though the message wasn't complete, Tanner and his teammates quickly noticed that the numbers correlated to airline departure times, and that Flight 2512 was on the list.

"That is very interesting," Tanner said. He was excited at first, but then he turned a little pessimistic. "But without the full text of the email, we can't be sure the exact nature of the message."

Rachel jumped into the conversation. "Yeah, for all we know, this Reina person might be a travel agent."

"Why don't we have the complete message, like the one we found yesterday?" Sydney asked.

"It's because this program isn't running an active search like the other one. This routine is looking for any bits or pieces of emails that were sent from Reina before the attack. We can only find the parts of the message that were cached and hadn't been overwritten yet."

Tanner printed off a copy of the partial email on a specialized laser printer next to the computer terminal. Traditional laser printers used a process called xerography where a laser beam projected the text to be printed on an electrically charged rotating drum. To prevent any eavesdropping, however, all the secure laser printers used by the NSA had a special type of drum that didn't allow anyone to duplicate the printed message.

After the printout finished, Tanner closed the email and opened the other results. The NSA analysts quickly saw that the output in these two messages were false positives. The first email wasn't from a terrorist named Reina, but from a musician who shared the same pseudonym.

"I doubt our suspect is actually a pop singer," Rachel said disappointedly after reading the message fragment.

"The second email is even worse. It looks like it's referring to a private girls' school in California," Sydney said.

Tanner closed the two false positive messages and opened the final email. After quickly scanning the text, a terrified silence gripped him. Like the other messages, this email wasn't complete, but there were more than enough words in the letter to confirm that Reina was intentionally going after Flight 2512:

. . . sure the package . . . tonight . . . Flight 2512 . . .

authorized . . . attack when . . . two NSA analysts . . .
successful . . .

Nobody spoke for what seemed like a full minute. Tanner read the partial transcript over and over again, focusing on the words "two NSA analysts." The revelation that Tanner was indeed a target of the original attack was bloodcurdling.

"Uh, we've got a major problem," Rachel said, but Tanner didn't respond to her comment. He had already printed off the message and was now walking toward the exit.

APRIL 26, FORT MEADE, MARYLAND

Approximately halfway between the cities of Baltimore, Maryland, and Washington, DC, is an army installation called Fort George G. Meade. Arguably one of the most secretive military complexes in the world, Fort Meade is home to surreptitious organizations like the Defensive Information Systems Agency and the United States Cyber Command. The most clandestine group, however, on the military base just off Maryland Route 295 is the National Security Agency.

Billions of radio signals, Internet messages, phone calls, and other electronic communications are captured every day by the NSA. The most pertinent messages are recorded in hundreds of databases for further analysis. In addition to electronic eavesdropping, the NSA also protects critical government communications and information systems. One specific security task the NSA provides is analyzing and categorizing threats from new computer viruses. This work is handled primarily by the Malware Analysis and Response Team, or MART, in the basement of a nondescript building on the NSA campus.

Arthur Dawson and his younger brother, Marcus, were senior analysts on the MART. Working most of the night to unravel the mystery behind the new Chinese computer virus, they had survived on a diet of Mountain Dew Code Red and cold pizza. For the brothers in their late twenties, this was as good as it could get.

Growing up in New Jersey, Slammer and Viper weren't different from other rebellious youth who aspired to be script kiddies. They spent most of their teen years trying to hack into US government installations around the country. They weren't anti-American; they were just curious to push the limits of their abilities. Their initial hacking attempts never amounted to much so, in their late teens, they decided to take an entrepreneurial approach and try their hand at corporate espionage. They pulled off several brilliant jobs, like stealing new drug recipes from pharmaceutical companies and hijacking schematics from electronics firms. Despite their criminal success, it wasn't until the NSA courted them that Slammer and Viper found their true calling.

Slammer and Viper were part of a new breed of spies, where the charismatic looks and physical prowess of a "James Bond" didn't matter one digital bit. Valued for their brains over their brawn, they worked on some of the coolest computer systems in the world. Nothing compared to the rush of full-blown espionage against a foreign government, and the top-secret environment at the NSA only added to the mysterious aura of their job. Of course, the $15,000 paycheck they each received from Uncle Sam each month didn't hurt either. The two brothers were geniuses when it came to computer malware, and their employer didn't balk at their salary requirements or their request for an elaborate, private operations center in the basement of the NSA complex.

Sitting in their darkened operations room, the brothers couldn't tell what time of day it was. The only light not originating from a computer monitor was coming from a neon-green exit sign above the door. They had repeatedly tried to get the annoying light turned off, but apparently the fire marshal had tremendous clout at the NSA.

"It just doesn't make sense," Viper, a.k.a. Marcus Dawson, said before drinking straight out of a two-liter soda pop bottle. "I ran the routine a thousand times, and I keep getting the same thing—nothing."

"The network traffic is still coming from that same server in China, right?" asked Slammer, a.k.a. Arthur Dawson, from his workstation.

"Yeah, but it's just a simple polling routine. The Chinese initiate a ping request from their server, and it goes out across the Internet. I keep expecting the virus execution sequence to follow the ping, but it never does."

"We've been watching this for what, thirteen hours now?" Slammer asked.

"Yep. There's nothing out there that resembles the malware code that the Utah folks sent us. If something was going to happen with this virus, it should have happened by now," Viper said.

"Let's keep monitoring that server until Tanner gets back to us. Maybe he'll have some additional insight," Slammer said before heading off to the restroom. He wasn't sure how much Code Red he had recently, but he figured it was enough to keep an entire classroom awake during a lecture on the OSI Model.

———•———

Tanner came out of the Chamber and went straight to the team's conference room. "Where's Helen?" he urgently asked Mel.

Mel looked up at the doorway with a bored expression on his face. Mel didn't enjoy babysitting the Secret Service agents, who had moved far beyond being just a nuisance to the NSA. All the members of the QC team secretly longed for Friday when the Secret Service guys would finally go back to Washington, DC.

"She had to take a call in her office," Mel said. Tanner quickly turned around and started walking away.

"Hey, wait!" yelled Agent Payne. "We need to ask you some

more questions." It was too late. Tanner was already several steps down the hall, and he wasn't about to go back.

He soon arrived at his manager's office. The door was closed, but he saw through the glass around the door's frame that Helen was on the phone. She acknowledged Tanner's presence and waved him in. Tanner closed the door before Helen put the call on speakerphone.

"I've got Derek Cannon on the line," Helen said. "He has some information about a dead body they found up in Boise."

"And I got something interesting from Reina," Tanner replied anxiously, taking a seat. "But I'll let the FBI go first."

Derek brought Tanner up to date on the investigation on the dead body the Boise police had found in a dumpster. The facts were coming in quickly, with the surprising revelation that the John Doe was the victim of foul play. Derek highlighted the findings from the toxicology report, explaining how the enormous amounts of oxytocin in the victim's body caused death by water intoxication. The county coroner in Boise verified all the police department's findings, adding that the victim suffered a painful and ingenious death.

Tanner shuddered at the details of the murder before asking a follow-up question into the speakerphone. "You said that you haven't identified the victim, but it sounds like he wasn't a high-profile individual that Reina would go after."

"That's right. It's definitely a bizarre murder, but I agree it's a big leap to call it an assassination. We'll know more once we figure out who the victim is," Derek said. "Okay, Tanner, what did you find on Reina?"

Tanner was feeling on edge, and he took a moment to deliberately relax. "We have two emails from Reina that we gleaned off the Internet," he said, showing the printouts to his boss. Tanner then clarified his statement for Derek. "Actually, they're just fragments of emails sent before the terrorist attack."

"How is that even possible?" Derek asked. "Are you saying that you can re-create past email communication?" The FBI agent knew enough about computers to understand that getting access to email server logs required going to the Internet service provider, and that required a search warrant.

Tanner spoke up, justifying his actions. "Whenever an email is sent, it leaves digital fingerprints on network routers and caching devices as it travels across the Internet. Using some very advanced computer equipment that we have, I was able to search cyberspace and look for any digital residue from Reina's emails. I found two messages, both dated the week before the attack on Flight 2512."

Derek asked Tanner to read the emails. His response was urgent. "Okay, that's huge. We've got to move fast on this," he said. "This proves that someone is leaking information to the bad guys."

"It's not us," Helen quickly replied. "We've already been down this road with the Secret Service. There are only five people here that know about this new computer virus."

"Could it be someone else at the NSA, someone who's not in your group?" Derek asked.

"I don't think so. It has to be someone outside the NSA," Helen said.

"I've got to get some more people on this. We'll take a look at both organizations and see if we can find the *mole*," Derek said. The way he emphasized "mole" confirmed Derek's disdain for people who betrayed their own government. Few things energized the FBI more than finding a traitor.

Derek changed the topic. "I'm sure you noticed the fact that the second email from Reina mentions two NSA analysts, not one."

"Yes, I was keenly aware of that," Tanner admitted.

"Hopefully the terrorists think you're dead. It's been three days and the terrorists haven't gone after you again, but I won't take any risks. I'll get the local cops to escort you home and watch your house tonight," Derek said with authority.

Helen voiced her concern. "It looks like Reina was definitely targeting that flight to take out my two analysts."

"I agree, but this is all circumstantial evidence. None of it will hold up in court," Derek said. "Remember, these are just emails. They could be from anyone using *Reina* as an alias. We have to prove, without any doubt, that the emails came from the same person who actually shot down Flight 2512. To do that, we need the actual computer that sent these messages."

"You could track it down by IP," Tanner said. He was referring to the Internet Protocol address. "Both these emails came from the IP address 172.31.20.205. I looked that up in DNS and it's registered to Mountain States Wireless. I'll bet you it came from a wireless modem."

Every computer on the Internet had a unique thirty-two bit number assigned to it called an IP address. The IP address identified a specific computer the same way a phone number correlated to a particular phone. Tanner continued his idea, "You'll have to get the Internet service provider to give you the information, but I'm sure you guys do search warrants for that type of thing all the time."

"We do, but it doesn't move very fast," Derek said. "I'll get to work on it right away. In the meantime, I want you guys to keep a lookout for anything you find from Reina. She's our primary suspect right now," Derek said.

Helen ended the call and leaned forward on her desk. "Are you okay?" she asked. She was worried about the safety of her top analyst.

"I'm not sure what to think right now. At least the FBI is going to provide some security for me," Tanner said. "I don't feel like anyone is after me, but the email is very clear that two NSA analysts were targets."

"Who's leaking this information?" Helen asked with a concerned voice. "Someone is selling us out."

"Could it really have been someone on our team?" Tanner asked.

"I guess anything is possible, but we're a tight group, and I trust everyone. I still think it's someone over at the Secret Service. There's a ton of people that work on the ECTF, and most of them knew we were coming to brief them," Helen said.

"I agree, but without any hard evidence, we have nothing," Tanner said.

"Speaking of the Secret Service, you better get in there and help them out. It's almost noon, and they've been waiting all day to talk with you," Helen said.

Tanner let out a big sigh. He knew he couldn't put off Agent Payne and Agent Crawford forever.

APRIL 26, SALT LAKE CITY, UTAH

Reina enjoyed her lunch of dim sum, a traditional Cantonese food that she had learned to love as a youth. Seated at the kitchen table in her quiet apart—ment, she was proud of both her Chinese and Mexican heritage. Reina considered herself a citizen of both countries, and she was at ease in either culture.

When Reina had first come to Utah, she wasn't sure if she would have access to the traditional foods of both China and Mexico. However, she was pleasantly surprised by the vast array of inter-national cuisine in the Salt Lake area. She had read that Utah was home to thousands of missionaries who had traveled the globe, proselytizing for the Mormon faith. Apparently these missionaries had returned home with refined palates for international food.

Reina had also traveled the world since she went active as a spy for the Chinese government. Her previous attacks focused on minor players who had caused problems for the People's Republic of China. In addition to taking out Jeff Kessler, Reina had eliminated a mob boss in Macau, a military defector in Paris, and a counterfeiter in Thailand. Taking down Flight 2512, however, was by far her biggest job, and it was a positive sign that she was gaining the respect and trust of her uncle.

Looking at her laptop, Reina read over her email draft. Like the other messages she had sent, this one was also addressed to Rey. She would encrypt her email differently this time, using an untested and brand-new encryption program given to her by a specialist on her uncle's staff. Reina's informant in the US government said that the Americans might have compromised some of her emails, and she was now instructed to use a completely different encoding method for all of her future communications. While Reina didn't believe the Americans had the ability to eavesdrop on her message, she followed her orders and began the encryption routine. When the message was finally ready to go, she connected her wireless modem to the Internet and sent the email off into cyberspace without a second thought.

— • —

NSA DATA CENTER, UTAH

It was after 3:00 p.m. when Helen finally came to rescue Tanner from the Secret Service. He had spent the past three hours with Agents Todd Payne and Adam Crawford, trying to convince them of the critical nature of the new computer virus. While the two agents from the Secret Service were interested, they just couldn't accept the fact that something really sinister was about to happen to the critical financial infrastructure of the nation.

Helen took a seat next to Tanner, sensing his dissatisfaction. "How's it going," she asked.

Tanner looked worn out. "I've basically showed them everything we have," he said.

Helen turned toward the Secret Service agents. "What's your opinion?"

"There just aren't enough facts," Agent Crawford said. "Your analysis is great, and I can see how you made your assumptions.

But we need something concrete before we pull the alarm back at headquarters."

"We need to know exactly what this virus does and that it indeed has the ability to compromise our computer systems," Agent Payne added. His sincere comment seemed out of place for a guy who had been so antagonistic the past three days. "Until we have that information, all we can do is watch for any unusual activity."

"That's it?" Helen asked. She couldn't believe her ears. "Can't you warn the banks and financial institutions? You could tell them something bad is coming down the pipes."

"We're not going to do that," Agent Payne said, returning to his defiant personality. "First of all, the financial guys get spooked easily. We're not going to cry wolf for no reason. And second, we don't have anything rock-solid to show them besides a theory from the NSA."

Agent Crawford jumped into the conversation. "Todd's right. You guys have some good stuff here, but you're just analysts, not trained detectives. We'll take all this information back to DC with us and have our team at the ECTF make a recommendation."

Helen looked stunned, but Tanner had known this conclusion was coming. From the beginning he had felt it was going to be a difficult task to convince the Secret Service to believe in the stealthy computer virus.

"So, that's it? You're done here?" Helen asked.

"We'll spend one more day here, finalizing our notes and reviewing a couple of last items. Then we'll head back home Friday morning," Agent Payne said.

"We'll keep you in the loop," Tanner said, offering an olive branch to the two agents. In reality, he didn't know if it would make a difference. Until Tanner had conclusive evidence that a computer virus was attacking America, the Secret Service wouldn't budge.

"Why don't you guys head out for the day? Tanner and I will stay and clean up this mess," Helen said. She gestured to the papers and notes all over the table. Even though the Secret Service had seen all the NSA's information, the documents were still considered classified and needed to be locked up when not in use.

"We'll see you tomorrow morning," Todd said. Helen escorted the two Secret Service agents to the lobby while Tanner waited in the conference room. He was glad to have a few moments to himself.

"Can you believe that?" Helen said. Usually composed and controlled, her frustration was out of place.

"I gave up trying to convince those guys two hours ago," Tanner said. "They just don't think the virus threat is real. Unfortunately, once you see what a virus can do, the damage is already done."

"I've wasted everybody's time. I should have kept you working on QC," Helen said.

"At least we've followed process and notified the Secret Service," Tanner said. "If they don't want to listen, maybe we can get Derek and the FBI to check it out."

Helen wasn't so hopeful. "That's probably a dead end. They'll probably just redirect us back to the Secret Service. This computer virus falls in the Secret Service's jurisdiction. Until there's an actual crime committed, the FBI won't get involved."

Tanner knew his boss was right. The federal government was a spaghetti bowl of confusing rules and regulations regarding which agency had authorization over an investigation. It was clear, however, that the Secret Service was the primary organization to investigate any computer related financial crimes.

Helen decided it was time to end the pity party. "Instead of trying to convince the Secret Service, let's focus our efforts on what we do best. Let's find the full code for that virus and identify exactly what it does."

Tanner took a moment to shift mental gears. Helen was right. They had important work to do. "Let's give those guys at MART a call," he said.

———•———

The unexpected ring startled the two senior members of the MART team. They were busily working in their darkened basement office at NSA headquarters. Slammer picked up the receiver on the secure phone without taking his eyes off his monitor. "Slammer at your service," he said.

"Hey, guys, this is Helen Ripplinger and Tanner Stone at the Utah Data Center. Have you found anything for us on that Chinese computer virus?"

"Yes and no," Slammer said. He put his phone on speaker for the benefit of his brother. "I'll let Viper bring you up to date."

Viper turned on the lights in the darkened room, causing his older brother to shield his eyes from the annoyance. Even though the lights were on their lowest setting, Slammer cowered like a vampire in daylight.

"Sorry about that, bro, but I can't read my notes," Viper said, adjusting his glasses. With his short haircut and glasses, Viper appeared more professional than his older brother, who had a full beard and a ponytail.

"Okay, this virus is seriously weird," Viper began. "There's definitely something out there, but we just can't wrap our heads around it."

Slammer jumped in, beating his brother to the punch in delivering the news. "We found a computer in China that sends out a ping request every hour on the Internet. We know the signal comes from that elite Chinese hacking group in Shaoxing because we traced the time-to-life on the ping relay."

Viper took back control of the conversation. "But the Chinese server doesn't do anything. It just sends out a ping request and nothing else."

"There's no follow up routine," Tanner spoke up, "like code to execute?"

"Nope," the brothers said in unison.

"What about a hidden payload in the ping request? Maybe there's a virus routine embedded in there," Tanner said.

"Already checked it," Slammer said. "It's just a simple packet that's sent out. It's almost like how NTP does its polling," he said, referring to the network time protocol.

Tanner was lost in his thoughts, and nobody else said anything for a moment. Even though she couldn't see it, Helen sensed a connection between Tanner and the two brothers back at Fort Meade.

Viper eventually broke the silence on the call. "What are you thinking out there?"

"When you said NTP, it got me going on something," Tanner said. "You know how NTP synchronizes computer clocks across a network?" he asked.

"Yeah, a master server sends out a data packet over a network to set all the computers to the same time. It's a great protocol for networks with big latency," Viper said.

"Correct, and the master server doesn't care if the target systems respond back. NTP is a one-way communication routine to sync up millions of computers all over the world," Tanner said.

Like a bolt of lightning, a revelation flashed for Tanner and the two brothers. Slammer immediately spoke with awe. "That's it. It's a zero day!"

Helen had to get involved in the exchange now. The conversation was becoming too confusing. "What are you guys talking about?" she asked.

Tanner explained the technical concept, using common language and metaphors that he was so good at. "There's a master computer in China that's using the Internet to communicate with millions of infected computers across the world. Every hour the main system sends out a brief message, saying, 'I'm still here. I'm alive.' The master computer is like a general, making sure all his troops are lined up and ready to attack."

"Okay . . . so the computers are all synced up, waiting to do what?" Helen asked.

"Launch the virus. The target computers here in the states must already be infected with the virus, and they're just waiting for a coordinated time from the master server to begin their destruction," Tanner said.

"It's brilliant," Viper said. "As long as the ping routine keeps coming from the master server, the infected computers just wait. Nothing happens until the ping stops. This setup prevents us from attacking the master server and trying to shut it down. If we do, all the infected computers around the country will assume that the loss of communication is the signal to kick off the virus."

Tanner continued the explanation. "That's why it's called a zero-day attack. Nobody has any time to find an antidote before the virus starts. We'll be caught completely off guard."

Helen probed for more clarification. "We've already determined parts of the code for the Dragon Virus. Can't we just use that to determine which of our computer systems are already infected?"

Tanner shook his head. "The code we found was just the program to stage the virus. We don't know what the actual virus payload is," he said, referring to the destructive routine programmed into every computer virus.

"Unfortunately, we can't find it either," Slammer said. "We've searched all our databases and ran even heuristic scanning on some of the servers in our test lab. There's no virus code out there that matches it."

"Wait!" Tanner shot up. "We're looking in the wrong place," he said. "The virus isn't in the operating system. It's embedded in the hardware, just like Stuxnet!"

Tanner heard Viper swear out loud over the phone. "Rock on!" he shouted. "All our computer parts are made in China. It would be super easy for them to prepackage a virus on any computer system sold back in the US. We'd never know the difference."

Slammer added to his brother's statement. "If the virus is stored on a hardware component, all our antivirus routines will be worthless."

Helen now understood the viciousness of the virus. "Attacking the master server or just blocking its communication will automatically kick off the virus, right?"

"Yep, we're screwed," Viper said dejectedly. "With so many microchips and components on modern computers, it would be impossible to isolate which one stores the computer virus."

"Not necessarily," Tanner said as he stood up. Walking over to a whiteboard, he jotted down his thoughts as fast as his hand could write. "We just might be able to stop this thing from launching."

APRIL 26, NSA DATA CENTER, UTAH

It was nearly 6:00 p.m. when Tanner and Helen ended the conference call with the MART team. After several hours brainstorming different options, Tanner and the others felt they had a good plan in place to thwart the computer virus. Slammer and Viper volunteered to pull another all–nighter, alternating between work and sleep while they cre–ated the code for the virus's antidote. Using a hacking technique called IP spoofing, the antidote would send out a duplicate ping request from QC that would impersonate the master computer system in China. Even if the main server in China suddenly stopped communicating, the infected computer systems in the United States wouldn't launch their virus because they would be tricked by the masquerading signal coming from QC. The plan should work theoretically, but the difficult part was making the switch transparent between the real server in China and QC. Thousands of network packets had to be modified very quickly to appear to be coming from the legitimate Chinese server.

That required massive amounts of computing power, and it was something that was only possible to do with quantum computer like QC.

The group decided that Tanner would go home and get some much needed rest, while the two brothers perfected their program. When Tanner came back to work Thursday morning, he would configure QC to execute the antidote created by the two brothers. With QC masquerading as the master computer in China, the NSA could delay the Dragon Virus from launching for weeks or even months, giving them additional time to find a way to permanently disable the malware.

Helen waited for Tanner in the lobby of the NSA data center while he finished his phone call to his wife. The building was practically vacant this evening. The guard monitoring the front desk was the only other person with Helen in the quiet foyer.

The door to the office area opened a few moments later, and Tanner walked out. He looked haggard and worn. Even from the other side of the lobby, Helen could see dark circles under his eyes.

"What did you tell her?" Helen asked. She was referring to Tanner's phone call with his wife.

"I told her that during the investigation into Flight 2512, the FBI discovered credible threats against NSA employees. I told her that a policeman would bring me home tonight just as a precaution," Tanner said.

"How did she take it?"

"She was worried, of course, but I didn't mention anything about the email from Reina or the seriousness of the threat. I figured that I had already frightened her enough," Tanner said. He opened the front door for his boss. A police cruiser from the Salt Lake County Sheriff's office waited out by the curb.

"It looks like your ride is here," Helen said.

"I hope he's not upset about watching our house all night. That's got to be a boring job," Tanner said.

"Derek said this guy will only be on duty until 2:00 a.m. Another deputy will come to relieve him after that."

Tanner pointed to his car. "I guess I'll just leave my car here in the parking lot for the next couple of days."

"Well, at least it won't get stolen here," Helen replied with a failed attempt at humor. The two NSA employees stopped at the waiting vehicle. The sheriff's deputy got out of the driver's door and walked around the front of the car.

"Hi, I'm Allen Teuloi. I'll be escorting you home tonight." The massive police officer with broad, powerful shoulders and jet-black hair reached out to shake Tanner's hand. As Tanner returned the gesture, he quickly glanced at the officer's name badge to see how he spelled his last name.

"That's an interesting last name. Where are you from?" Tanner asked casually.

"I'm from Utah, but my great-grandparents came to the United States from Tonga," Deputy Teuloi said.

"I'm sorry that you have to babysit me tonight," Tanner said.

"It's no problem. I've done this before. Besides, I like the overtime pay," Allen said. He opened the passenger door for Tanner.

Tanner turned to Helen before getting in the police cruiser. "I guess I'll see you tomorrow morning."

"Six o'clock, bright and early," Helen said.

She watched the police car drive away. Helen worried about her employee, but at least the FBI had found someone to escort Tanner home. Helen hoped that Tanner would be safe with someone like Deputy Teuloi keeping an eye on the place.

The drive to Tanner's house was uneventful. Deputy Teuloi seemed kind enough, and Tanner made small talk to appear relaxed, but his stomach was knotted up with anxiety. He kept thinking about the email from Reina, which specifically mentioned two NSA employees. Someone had sold out the NSA, and it infuriated Tanner that he couldn't identify the traitor. To make matters worse, the direct police involvement in Tanner's life brought back unpleasant memories of his kidnapping in New Mexico.

"Here you are," Al said. He pulled the police cruiser into

Tanner's driveway. "Do you want me to come in and have a look around?"

"No, I think we're okay. My wife works from home, and she's been here all day. She hasn't seen anything out of the ordinary," Tanner said.

"I'm going to stay parked in your driveway and keep watch for stuff out here," Al said. "Don't worry about tonight. I'll keep you guys safe."

"Thanks," Tanner said. He shook the policeman's hand before getting out of the car. Tanner opened the front door to his home and was immediately greeted by his wife.

"I'm so glad you're here," Megan said, giving her husband a tight hug in the entryway. "When you called and told me the police were bringing you home, I got really worried," she said. She didn't give her husband a chance to respond. "How serious is it? Are you really in that much danger?"

"I guess it's serious enough that the FBI feels that I need a police escort home," Tanner said. He immediately walked to the kitchen and activated the alarm system. Then after hanging up his jacket, he turned up the thermostat on the heater to chase off the evening chill.

Megan parted the front shades in the living room to see the police car in the driveway. "Is he going to stay there all night?"

"Yeah, the FBI feels that would be best," Tanner said. He spoke in a casual tone, trying to keep his wife at ease. But Megan, sharp as always, immediately called his bluff. She faced her husband and skeptically crossed her arms.

"Okay, what's really going on? I got a call from Nicole this afternoon," Megan said. She was referring to the Special Agent in Charge of the FBI office in Albuquerque. Apparently, Megan also kept in contact with their mutual acquaintance.

Tanner feigned ignorance. "Really? What did she tell you?"

"Don't patronize me, Tanner Stone," Megan said in her stern voice. "Nicole said that some serious stuff is going on at work. She wouldn't go into the details, but said that you and I both need to be on the lookout for trouble."

Tanner sighed heavily. He had never told his wife anything about his top-secret work, but tonight it had to be different. "I'm starving. Let's make something to eat, and I'll tell you what I can."

Inside the Chamber at the Utah Spy Center, QC continued running her programmed routines flawlessly. Monitoring billions of packets of data as they flowed across the Internet, the quantum computer discovered a new message sent from IP address 172.31.20.205. It was the same IP that was associated with Reina's previous emails, but QC was unable to determine the contents of this message because it was encrypted with an unknown cipher. Nevertheless, the supercomputer made a copy of the encoded letter and stored it on her massive disk array subsystem for further analysis by the NSA employees.

Dinner lasted more than an hour. Taking his time to explain everything, Tanner flirted with the line of demarcation between what he legally could and couldn't tell his wife about the recent events at work. Even though he tried hard to avoid it, Tanner eventually disclosed some classified information regarding Flight 2512 and the new computer virus. He felt guilty for what he had revealed, but in the end, he was glad that he did it. Nicole was absolutely right about keeping an eye out for trouble. If the terrorists knew that Tanner was still alive, they would likely come after him again.

"You're probably safe as long as the terrorists think you're dead," Megan said as she started clearing the dishes.

"Yes, but eventually the passenger list for Flight 2512 will come out, and the terrorists will see that only Bryan's name is on it," Tanner said. He took the dirty dishes from his wife and put them in the dishwasher.

"That might not matter anyway. From what you said, it looks like someone on the inside knew that you and Bryan were going on that trip. So that person probably already knows that you're still alive," Megan said. Her comment renewed Tanner's fear.

"Exactly. That's why the FBI wanted to give me a police escort."

"So, do we just wait for the bad guys to come after us?" Megan asked. Tanner sensed that his wife also felt threatened.

"I'm not sure. I think the police guard tonight might just be a temporary thing until the FBI decides on the best way to handle this. Either way, we need to be flexible," Tanner said.

"That's easier said than done," Megan said, patting her pregnant stomach. "I'm on a time schedule here."

Tanner decided there wasn't any point in speculating on what the terrorists might do. Further discussion would only frighten the both of them. "I'm going to turn on the TV," he said.

It was time for Tanner and Megan's nightly ritual of watching the news together. The lead story focused on the investigation into the attack on Flight 2512. It was followed by another news segment regarding China's decision to stop buying more of the US debt. Fortunately, the stock markets were closed for the rest of the week, preventing further panic in the financial sector. It seemed that the entire nation was in a holding pattern, waiting to see if further bad news loomed on the horizon.

It was almost 10:00 p.m. when the couple decided to call it a day. Tanner was exhausted from the chaos at work, and Megan was extra tired, with the pregnancy taking its toll in the final trimester. Finished brushing their teeth and saying their nightly prayers, Tanner and Megan crawled into bed.

Down below in the basement, the furnace continued filling the house with deadly carbon monoxide.

APRIL 27, DRAPER, UTAH

Tanner woke up in a cold sweat just after midnight. Something was wrong. He tried to get out of bed, but his sluggish body resisted. He felt like a powerful magnet was holding him in place. He struggled to sit up, straining all the muscles in his body to perform the simple movement. The entire bedroom was spinning, and despite several attempts to focus, he couldn't concentrate. Disorientated and nauseated, he collapsed back into his warm and soft bed.

He drifted off into unconsciousness, but from somewhere deep inside him, he felt an innate urge to survive. It was like someone had whispered, "Get up now or you'll die." With renewed vigor, Tanner willed his body to move as he rolled out of bed. He fell to the ground, smacking his head against the nightstand in the process. The stabbing pain on forehead was fortunate, however, because it immediately helped clear his mind.

Instinctively, Tanner knew that his wife was in danger. He kneeled up against the bed and vigorously shook Megan. The easy movement seemed extraordinarily difficult because his body had no strength. He collapsed on the side of the bed for a moment, feeling like he had a severe case of the flu. Again, a thought came to him, "Get to the window."

Like a drunken man, Tanner staggered across the bedroom and parted the curtains before opening the window. The sudden rush of fresh air invigorated his lethargic body. Down below in the driveway, he could see the black-and-silver police car, guarding his home. Tanner tried yelling out for help, but he couldn't get enough oxygen into his lungs. Unsure of what else to do, he lurched for the dresser and grabbed a vase filled with glass beads. Using all his strength, Tanner shoved the container through the window screen and out into the darkness. The vase tumbled to the ground, shattering into a thousand pieces on the concrete porch below.

Deputy Teuloi was reading the sports section of the newspaper when the glass vase crashed against the concrete. The loud noise instantly jarred the policeman into action. Rushing out of his car, Al drew his Smith & Wesson handgun. He immediately saw the broken vase on the front porch. Looking up at the second story, he managed to catch a glimpse of Tanner, collapsed over the window ledge.

Al didn't think. He didn't analyze. His reflexes took over as he sprinted up the porch with his weapon in hand. He tried to open the front door but quickly realized that it was locked. Aiming his pistol at the dead bolt, he rapidly fired three rounds. The loud shots rang out in the quiet neighborhood, waking several of the neighbors. Al didn't hesitate. He kicked the door open with his powerful leg, triggering the alarm system's high-pitched wail. Ignoring the sound, he quickly sprinted up the stairs to the master bedroom, expecting to find an intruder in the home. No stranger was there. Instead, he found Mrs. Stone peacefully asleep in bed with her husband semi-conscious and lying halfway out the second story window.

Al grabbed his radio and immediately called police dispatch as he ran over to render first aid. "I need backup and an ambulance now!" he yelled. He then grabbed Tanner by the shoulders. "What's going on? Are you hurt?"

"Can't breathe . . . wife . . . help her," Tanner mumbled. In a flash of inspiration, Al immediately realized what was wrong—carbon monoxide poisoning. He had seen it last winter during a power outage when a local family tried heating their home with a camping stove. Rushing over to the bed, Al checked on Megan. She was unresponsive with shallow breathing. Grabbing Megan under her armpits, Al carefully dragged Megan next to the open window. Not wasting a second, he then flew down the stairs to his car and yanked an oxygen tank and mask out of the truck. Taking the stairs two-at-a-time, he burst back into the master bedroom and frantically put the oxygen mask on the pregnant female. He didn't know it at the time, but Al had just saved her life.

A few minutes later, the quiet neighborhood was bustling with commotion. Fire trucks, police cars, and an ambulance clogged the road as neighbors stood out on their porches for a better look. Deputy Teuloi helped the paramedics escort two stretchers to a life-flight helicopter, waiting in a church parking lot across the street. The stretchers were quickly loaded onboard, and the helicopter took off in a deafening roar. Watching the medevac disappear into the dark night, Al turned to the remaining paramedic.

"How serious is it?" he asked.

"The husband is in better shape than his wife. She's pregnant, and that makes it extra hard on both her and the baby," the young woman said.

"Will she lose the baby?" Al asked empathetically.

"I'm not sure," she said. "A fetus is very susceptible to carbon monoxide poisoning."

The paramedic's diagnosis was unsettling to Al. In a way, he felt he should have done more to prevent the tragedy. Then Al quickly reminded himself that had he been guarding the family from inside the home, there would have been three deaths that night. Shaking his head in frustration, he looked up in time to see several firemen coming out of the Stones' home. He quickly ran across the street for an update.

The leader of the fire crew removed his mask and wiped his forehead before speaking. "It was definitely carbon monoxide. Our meters indicated six hundred parts per million."

"How high is that?" asked Al.

"High enough to cause death before sunrise," the fireman said somberly. "It looks like you got to them just in time."

"Just in time" didn't sound right to Al, seeing that the victims were in serious condition and on their way to the level-one trauma unit at Intermountain Medical Center. "What caused it?" he asked.

"It looks like it was a faulty furnace. We have an investigator from the county on his way over right now, and he can tell us for sure," the crew chief said.

Al again shook his head in disbelief. When the FBI called him up this afternoon, he had thought the night guard duty was going to be a standard gig. He never felt the NSA analyst was in any serious danger.

⎯⎯●⎯⎯

Phone calls in the middle of the night are never a good thing. When Helen recognized the number for Derek Cannon on the caller ID, her heart immediately sank. She grabbed the phone and answered with trepidation.

"This is Helen," she said in a polite voice. The irony that it was three days ago to the hour that she had received a similar call regarding Bryan Morrison's death didn't go unnoticed.

"This is Derek. Tanner and his wife are in the ICU at Intermountain Medical Center. I'm on my way over right now."

Helen took a calming breath. "What happened?"

"It looks like carbon monoxide poisoning, but I've got one of my folks heading over to Tanner's house to investigate right now," Derek said.

"I'll meet you at the hospital in thirty minutes," Helen said. She arrived at Intermountain Medical Center just before 2:00 a.m. As with most emergency rooms in large cities, this one bustled with people at the early morning hour. She saw both Derek Cannon and Sara Heywood waiting by the front desk. Even though she had never met them face-to-face, Helen knew the look of a FBI agent when she saw it.

"I'm Helen Ripplinger," she said, extending her hand out to the two FBI employees.

Derek took her hand. "It's nice to meet you. This is Sara Heywood," he said, gesturing to his partner. Both agents were dressed in casual clothes and looked like they had been awakened in the middle of the night. On the other hand, Helen somehow managed to appear fresh and alert, dressed like she hadn't even gone to bed.

"Let's go," Derek said. He led the two women up the stairs. The group came out on the fourth floor, which was quieter and calmer than the emergency room down below. At the far end of the hall, Helen saw a police officer, standing guard in front of a door.

"Tanner is on this floor," Derek said. He was walking at a fast pace that required Helen to practically run in her heels. "He's doing better, but his wife is still in serious condition down on the lower level."

"Do you know that she's pregnant?" Helen asked.

"Yeah, the docs told me. Carbon monoxide is more harmful to a fetus than the mother, so even if Megan makes it, the baby might not survive."

The group remained quiet as they quickly covered the length of the hallway, passing the security guard before going into the private room. Inside, Tanner rested on a typical hospital bed. A middle-aged nurse stood close by, watching over him like a momma bear protecting her cub. Several monitors were hooked up to Tanner's chest and arm, providing constant feedback on his condition, and an oxygen mask covered his mouth and nose. After hearing the door open, Tanner opened his eyes and turned to see his guests.

"How's it going?" Derek asked the patient in his light blue hospital gown.

"I'm doing okay, now that they gave me something for the headache and nausea," Tanner mumbled through his oxygen mask.

"Will you give us a few moments of privacy?" Derek asked the nurse. He waited for her to leave the room before talking to Tanner. "I know you feel horrible, but can we chat for a bit?"

"First, tell me where my wife is," Tanner demanded in a feeble yet resolute manner.

"She's not doing so well. They have her in a hyperbaric chamber downstairs to maximize the oxygen in her blood," Derek said.

"What do the doctors say about her?"

"They think she'll be okay, but they're really concerned about the baby. It's too soon to know if the baby will survive or not," Derek said. Tanner digested the bad news solemnly.

Derek pulled up a chair and sat down next to Tanner's bed. "Tell me everything that happened."

Tanner's mind was still foggy from the effects of the carbon monoxide, yet he forced himself to cooperate with the FBI. "It was just a normal night," he said through his mask. He coughed as his body fought against the toxic gas still in its system. "Nothing seemed out of place. We ate dinner and watched TV before going to bed. Then, for some reason, I woke up in a panic. I felt horrible, like I had the flu. The room was spinning, and I couldn't concentrate. Somehow I got the policeman's attention, but I don't remember anything after that."

"The fire department found over a hundred times the normal level of carbon monoxide in your home. They said it came from a faulty furnace, but I'm waiting to hear back from my guy for confirmation."

"No way," Tanner mumbled. "I had the furnace serviced last fall."

"And I don't believe in coincidences," Helen said, entering the conversation. "One of my analysts dies in a plane crash, and now another one in the hospital with carbon monoxide poisoning. Something bad is going on."

Derek nodded his head in agreement. It was going to be a long day.

Anthony Hanks hated his job. He detested everything about it, from the terrible pay to the horrible hours. He tried for months to get off the night shift at the hospital, but it was impossible. Without a high school diploma or college education, the nineteen-year-old knew he was doomed to be a lowly janitor forever.

Tonight was another dreadful shift. After cleaning up vomit on the couch in the emergency room lobby, he had spent the following hour unplugging a toilet on the second floor. By its nature, a hospital was a place of disease, and Anthony came in contact with all sorts of foul messes every day. He particularly loathed his current task—taking out the waste from the emergency room to the locked biohazard dumpster. Pushing his cart out onto the loading dock in back of the building, Anthony tried not to visualize the bloody bandages and used syringes inside the trash bags. He quickly went about his task, disposing of the medical waste before walking around the side of the dumpster and lighting up a cigarette. Smoking in this area was strictly off limits, and in a way, Anthony hoped that someone would fire him for his disobedience.

Lost in his thoughts and misery, Anthony failed to notice a woman as she approached from the far side of the building. It wasn't until she asked for directions that he finally saw her.

"This is a secure area. You shouldn't be here," Anthony told the young Hispanic woman.

"It looks like we're both breaking the rules," the mysterious woman said. She pointed to the obvious "no smoking" sign on the wall.

"What's a lovely lady like you doing out here in the middle of the night?" he asked.

"I'm a private investigator. I'm following up on a case that I've been working on," Reina said. She leaned up against the wall next to the man.

Anthony saw the flirtatious smile on the woman's face. "Oh, yeah? What case is that?"

"I'm tracking down a husband and wife who were ripping off their employer. They were brought in a little while ago. Do you know anything about it?"

"Yeah. I saw them taken into the ER about an hour ago," Anthony said. He wasn't sure where this conversation was going, but if he was going to tell this lady anything, he was definitely going to get something in return for his efforts.

"Maybe you can do me a favor," Reina said. She reached into her purse and pulled out small roll of twenty-dollar bills. She handed the money to the young man. "Why don't you go back in there and see if they're going to make it. I'm sure my client would be happy to know that his cheating business partner is dead."

Anthony stubbed out his cigarette before thumbing through the wad of money. He figured there was about two hundred dollars in his hand. "Give me a moment," he said. He turned and went back inside the hospital.

Distracted by the beautiful woman and the roll of cash, he found the wrong paperwork. The file he was looking at was for a man who was brought into the ER about the same time as Tanner Stone. He saw the words "deceased" written across the bottom of the page and decided that was all he needed. He quickly went back outside to deliver the news.

"He's dead," Anthony callously said as he walked up to the woman.

"Thanks. My client will be glad to know it." Reina flipped her hair back in a playful movement. "Hey, what time does your shift end?" she asked.

"Seven o' clock," Anthony replied.

"I'll see you at the coffee shop across the street when you clock out," Reina said, turning and walking away. She had no intention of seeing the strange man again.

APRIL 27, FBI FIELD OFFICE, UTAH

It was 6:00 a.m., and a lot had happened in the investigation since Tanner and his wife had been taken the hospital. The crowning piece of information was the revelation that someone had tampered with the Stones' furnace. The modification was so slight, however, that even the county investigator and the technician from the FBI had failed to notice the adjustment. It wasn't until a grumpy sixty–four–year–old repairman from a local HVAC company was summoned to dissect the furnace that the alteration was finally discovered. A small wire in the exhaust fan unit had been short–circuited, preventing the furnace from properly expel–ling the carbon monoxide. The investigators on scene quickly relayed the information back to Agent Cannon, highlighting the obvious sign of foul play.

With conclusive evidence that someone had intentionally tried to kill Tanner, Derek pulled out all the stops, kicking his investigation into high gear. His first priority was to secure Helen and the remaining NSA analysts. Someone was trying to systematically eliminate the specialized QC team, and neither Derek nor the FBI would allow that to happen. Under the cover of early-morning darkness, numerous FBI agents secretly escorted Mel, Rachel, Sydney, and Chad back to the Utah Spy Center. While the analysts didn't like the idea of spending their foreseeable future locked up at work, they all agreed that the tightly guarded, top-secret facility was the perfect safe house.

With the remaining NSA analysts now at work, the FBI agents changed their focus to the attempted murder of Tanner Stone. Huddled in a conference room on the first floor of the FBI field office, Helen patiently waited while Derek and Sara anxiously studied a sealed case file. Derek and Sara digested every detail about Tanner Stone, a.k.a. Tanner Zane, and what had happened to him two years ago in New Mexico. It wasn't often that something captivated the attention of an FBI agent, but the mystery behind Tanner's kidnapping and relocation to Utah was almost unbelievable. Except for the occasional comment between the two agents, the conference room was as quiet as a library before finals. Finally, after what seemed like an eternity, Derek and Sara concluded their reading and sat back in their seats.

"You've known about this for how long?" Derek asked.

"Just under two years. I learned about it when the folks in Albuquerque relocated Tanner to Utah and put him on my team. Of course, I couldn't tell you anything about it before now," Helen said apologetically.

On their way back to the field office, Helen had mentioned to the FBI agents that someone at FBI headquarters might have more information about Tanner that would be helpful in the investigation. Derek immediately called the Deputy Directory in Washington, DC, requesting full access to any information the Bureau had on Tanner Stone. When Derek learned that Tanner had a sealed case file, he fully understood the reasoning behind Helen's sly comment.

"Now that we've read his file, is there anything else about Tanner that you should tell us?" Sara asked.

"Not really. I just know what's in the file, but Agent Green in Albuquerque is the expert on Tanner. I suggest we call her and sync up," Helen said.

"It's just after 6:30 a.m. in Albuquerque," Derek said, checking his watch. "I'll text her and see if she can be ready for a call in the next hour. In the meantime, I want to create a timeline of Tanner's history. I think we've overlooked something," Derek said. He stood up and walked over to the large whiteboard on the conference room wall.

———•———

NSA DATA CENTER, UTAH

Everyone on the QC team felt like they were under house arrest. In reality, their situation was more like "work arrest" since they were confined to their work for the next several days. None of the analysts vocalized their frustration, however, because they knew about the serious condition of their coworker and his wife at the hospital. They just hoped there wouldn't be another funeral this week.

After being dropped off by the FBI almost two hours ago, the NSA analysts pondered on what to do next. Without Helen or Tanner charting a course, they felt like a ship without a rudder.

"I'm scared," Sydney said. "When I joined the NSA, I thought that being an analyst was a low-risk job."

"I'd be lying if I didn't say I'm worried also," Chad softly replied. He struggled to keep his mind from racing off into fear.

"It's times like this that I wished I hadn't given up smoking," Mel said. His finger tapped on the conference room table, highlighting his anxiousness.

"Do you think the terrorists were only after Bryan and Tanner?" Sydney naïvely asked.

"Nope," Mel said callously. "Bryan's death could, under extraordinary circumstances, be ruled an accident. Now, three days later, Tanner goes to the hospital with carbon monoxide poisoning. That's no fluke. Someone is definitely coming after us."

"That means we must be doing something right. We must be getting close to finding something about the Dragon Virus that the terrorists don't want us to discover," Rachel said with new optimism. "I say we pick up where Tanner left off." Someone needed to step up and provide direction, and Rachel decided she might as well take the initiative.

"I guess we should go check and see if there's another email from Reina," Sydney said.

"Right," Mel concluded. "I still have to finish up that stock market analysis Tanner asked me to do. I forgot about it with the Secret Service here all week."

"Yeah, what do we do about them?" Rachel asked. "They'll be here in an hour."

"I say we send them up north to the FBI office and let them deal with the Secret Service. We don't have any more time for babysitting," Chad said.

"Good idea," Mel said. "I'll have Helen give the Secret Service a call and explain why we can't work with them today. In the meantime, why don't you two go check on QC, and Chad and I'll get to work on the economic research," Mel said, realizing that being proactive was a great antidote for fear.

———— • • ————

The QC team at the data center didn't know it, but their boss was one step ahead of them. Helen had just called Todd and Adam, asking the two Secret Service agents if they would join her at the FBI office instead of the NSA data center. She didn't expound on the reason for the location change, but she indicated that the FBI had some information that was valuable to both the NSA and Secret Service.

Confident that the Secret Service wouldn't distract her frazzled employees, Helen rejoined Derek and Sara in the secure conference room for an important phone call. Derek punched in the number for the FBI field office in Albuquerque. The phone rang twice before being answered in an unconventional way. "I was wondering when you were going to call," Nicole Green said matter-of-factly.

"What are you talking about?" Derek asked his former mentor. Years ago, Derek and Nicole worked financial crimes in Houston.

"The John Doe you guys found in Boise. I've been looking for that guy for over a year," Nicole said.

"Wait, I'm confused. We're not calling about Boise. We're calling about Tanner Stone," Derek said.

"What about Tanner?" Nicole asked, her tone changing as she sensed that something was wrong.

"Tanner is in the hospital with carbon monoxide poisoning. Our investigation shows that someone tampered with his furnace. We believe it might be related to the terrorist attack on Flight 2512," Derek said.

Nicole was shocked. "When did this happen?" she asked.

Derek summarized the situation. "Last night. Tanner is doing okay, but his wife got more exposure to the carbon monoxide. She's still in intensive care."

"What about their baby?" Nicole asked.

"Megan seems to be stabilizing, but the doctors say it's too early to tell if the baby will make it."

"Okay, my John Doe can wait. Fill me in on what's going on up there," Nicole ordered.

Derek took ten minutes to update Nicole on the investigation. He quickly covered all the details, beginning with Tanner and Bryan's work on the stealthy computer virus. Derek highlighted how Tanner and Bryan were supposed to brief the Secret Service in Washington, DC. He also described the mysterious suspect named Reina, and her possible involvement in the terrorist attack on Flight 2512. He concluded his summary with the obvious fact that someone had tried to kill Tanner.

Nicole listened intently, digesting every detail. "It sounds like you know about Tanner's encounter with the cyber-terrorists down here in New Mexico."

Derek validated Nicole's comment. "The folks back in DC gave us authorization to read his bio. It didn't take much to realize that Tanner is working on the same supercomputer that the cyber-terrorists tried to steal two years ago."

The fact that Helen didn't say anything to confirm or deny Derek's observation made the answer obvious to everyone.

"That's the reason for our call. The bio on Tanner said all the cyber-terrorists died in a fire. Is there anyone else who might want to kill Tanner?" Derek asked. He glanced up at the timeline he sketched out on the whiteboard.

"Wait. You're missing the bigger picture," Nicole said. "This goes back to my John Doe in Boise."

Sara entered the conversation. "What do you mean?"

"I found out about the John Doe this morning. That's why I originally thought you were calling me. His name is Jeff Kessler, and he was Tanner's roommate back at the University of New Mexico," Nicole said. "We've long suspected that Jeff was involved in Tanner's kidnapping and the plot to steal the plans for the quantum computer. But now that Jeff shows up murdered, we think that he was just the middleman, working for someone else."

"China," Helen almost shouted, feeling the surge of electricity that prefaced a major breakthrough in an investigation.

"Right," Nicole concurred. "I bet you a hundred dollars that Tanner's kidnapping has something to do with a larger Chinese operation."

"That sounds like a big assumption. An attack of this magnitude seems too risky for China," Sara said.

"Maybe it's not an official Chinese operation," Helen said. "We know there are factions in the lower ranks of their government. Maybe someone over there is acting alone."

"Either way, I think there's a direct link back to someone China. That's been a key point in our ongoing investigation down here," Nicole said over the conference call.

Derek spoke clearly, summarizing the group's collective thoughts. "So Tanner is kidnapped by Jeff Kessler and a group of cyber-terrorists. Tanner is forced to hack into Los Alamos and steal the plans for the prototype quantum computer. But he escapes, and all those involved die except for Jeff Kessler. Now, two years later, Jeff ends up dead in Boise and murdered in a way that certainly looks like a revenge killing. That proves there was someone else calling the shots."

Nicole continued on, expounding on the plot. "Let's say some-one in China hired Jeff to steal the plans for the quantum com-puter. Jeff gets in over his head and realizes that he can't do the job. So he kidnaps Tanner, knowing that his former roommate has hacking expertise. But Jeff blows the operation, and the Chinese boss eventually kills him," Nicole said before asking a follow up question. "Are the Chinese still after that quantum computer, or are they content with eliminating Jeff?"

"I can almost guarantee they want to shut down our quantum computer because it keeps unraveling their plot to attack the finan-cial networks in the United States," Helen said.

Derek concluded the group's theory. "But the folks in China can't physically get to the quantum computer because it's under lock and key at NSA. So they do the next best thing and start taking out the computer operators. Without the QC team running the specialized operating system, the supercomputer is worthless."

"But who is Reina? Why would she attack an entire airplane just to kill a couple of analysts?" Sara asked. "That sounds too risky."

Helen answered, remembering Tanner's crazy theory from Monday morning. "Tanner and Mel were talking about that. They were looking into the possibility that Reina also brought down the airliner to spook the financial markets."

"What would that do?" Sara asked.

Derek responded to the question. "It would do two things. First, it would get rid of the NSA analysts who know the most about the computer virus. And second, it would destabilize our economy in preparation for the virus's attack."

The group paused, letting their theory sink in. After a few moments, Sara spoke up. "Who told the Chinese about the quan-tum computer in the first place?

"And who's leaking information about our eavesdropping abili-ties?" Helen added.

Nicole answered out over the speakerphone. "It's the same person, and the trail to that traitor starts with Reina."

APRIL 27, NSA DATA CENTER, UTAH

Sydney and Rachel weren't completely surprised when they discovered that QC had found a new message from Reina. However, after a quick examination, the two NSA analysts knew this email was different. The entire message was encoded in a way they had never seen, making it impossible to determine the contents.

"What encryption method was used?" Sydney asked. The NSA analysts were sitting at the computer console for QC inside the Chamber. On the other side of the glass partition, the humming sound of the supercomputer and massive disk arrays continued nonstop.

"It's not AES, but it doesn't look like Blowfish or Triple-DES either," Rachel said, naming off some of the more common ciphers used throughout the world.

"Can we crack it?" asked Sydney.

"That's what QC was built to do," Rachel said. "But first, we need to call Helen and let her know that we might have another email from Reina."

———•———

FBI FIELD OFFICE, UTAH

The secure speakerphone in the conference room at the FBI field office rang, startling Helen and the other FBI agents.

"It's the NSA team," Sara said after checking the caller ID. She quickly punched the button to put the call on speaker.

"How's it going, guys?" Helen asked.

"We've all had better days," Rachel said. "We might have found another email from Reina."

The news immediately caught the attention of the FBI agents in the room. "What does it say?" Derek asked.

"We can't tell because it's encrypted with a bizarre algorithm," Rachel said.

"Then how do you know it's from Reina?" asked Sara.

"Tanner modified his program to search for anything that came from IP address 172.31.20.205. That's the same IP used in Reina's previous emails," Rachel said.

"That's the one that's registered with Mountain States Wireless, right?" Helen asked before turning to Derek. "Did you guys get a search warrant to track down that IP?"

"We served it yesterday. Mountain States Wireless is cooperating, but all of their customers use wireless modems to connect to the Internet," Derek said. "Even if we can positively identify which IP address belongs to Reina, if she's using a laptop, she can roam all over the Salt Lake Valley. That makes it really difficult to track her down."

Sara continued the conversation. "Basically, we have to wait for Mountain States to tell us when Reina is online. Then we can triangulate her location the same way we track normal cell phones."

"How come they didn't call us about this message?" Helen asked.

"We didn't get the notification process ironed out with Mountain States until yesterday afternoon. The email must have been sent before then," Derek speculated.

"That's right," Rachel said over the phone. "We discovered the email yesterday, just after noon."

"But we still don't know for sure if the email is from Reina because it's encrypted, remember?" Sara told the group.

"Don't worry about that. We can crack it," Helen stated confidently. She turned to the phone to ask her team a question. "How long will it take to decrypt the message?"

"We're not sure. The email is using a weird cipher that we haven't seen before. We'll get started on it right away and get back to you when we crack it," Rachel said.

Derek waited for the phone to disconnect before asking Helen a question. "How long does something like that realistically take?"

"It's never an easy process, but with our quantum computer, we can break codes like that in hours instead of centuries," Helen said.

"Really?" Sara asked.

"That's where a quantum computer really excels," Helen said. "We can do things that other nations think are just theoretical. And once we determine the cipher, cracking other encrypted emails from Reina will almost be instantaneous."

"No wonder the Chinese want a quantum computer so badly," Sara said.

Helen let Sara's comment sink in for a moment before asking a question. "Did you notice how Rachel said the email used an encryption method that we haven't seen before?"

"Yeah, is that bad?" Derek asked.

"*Yes*," Helen emphasized. "The NSA knows encryption better than anyone else. We basically invented modern cryptography. It takes a lot of time and resources to create a fully functioning encryption method. If someone out there is using a new algorithm that we've never seen, it means there's a powerful nation at work."

"Is that something China could do?" Derek asked.

"Absolutely. But more troublesome is the fact that Reina's emails are now encrypted using this new technology," Helen said. "The fact that she's changed how she encodes her emails is further proof that someone knows we're listening in on her secrets."

NSA DATA CENTER, UTAH

Mel had never worked with the zeal he felt today. Something bad was about to happen to America, and it was potentially worse than the terrorist attack on Flight 2512. Mel sensed forbidding doom on the horizon, just like he did as a youth back on the family farm in Nebraska when a tornado spawned out of the dark clouds.

Being the economist that he was, Mel always felt this day of financial reckoning was unavoidable. He knew the Chinese wouldn't be satisfied with endless IOUs. The bill collector always came, and the Chinese just might have decided it was time for payback with huge interest. But Mel was astute, and he knew that the national debt wasn't just a Republican or Democrat problem. It was everybody's problem. Government subsidies ranged from small corn farmers to large oil conglomerates as businesses everywhere fought for "free" government money. Americans continued to demand "free" stuff from their government, and the politicians spent it like they had a credit card with an unlimited balance.

With Chad watching over his shoulder, Mel focused all his energy into the task at hand. He was downloading page after page of stock transactions that had occurred the day before and after Flight 2512 was attacked. Somewhere in this pile of digital data Mel hoped to find a clue that would explain the unprecedented drop in the stock markets. He knew the Chinese were up to something, but he lacked the hard evidence to prove anything. He just hoped he could find something to keep the impending tornado from touching down.

———•———

FBI FIELD OFFICE, UTAH

It was almost 9:00 a.m. when the Secret Service agents finally arrived at the FBI office building. Todd Payne and Adam Crawford didn't mind the longer drive through rush hour to a different location. They were almost done with their work in Utah, and the two agents were willing to accommodate the change of venue. Besides, Helen had promised to let them in on something the FBI had recently discovered, and the two Secret Service agents didn't want to be left out of the loop.

"Welcome to command central," Derek said as he escorted Todd and Adam into the conference room. With over a dozen people now on the case, the area bustled with activity.

"Hi, I'm Agent Heywood," Sara said, extending her hand to greet the two visitors dressed in dark suits.

"You already know Helen," Derek said. He pointed toward the leader of the NSA's quantum computing group at the end of the table.

"Thanks for coming up here today," Helen said in her gracious way.

The Secret Service agents joined Helen and the others at the conference room table. Derek spent the next twenty minutes bringing Todd and Adam up to speed. He deliberately took his time, making sure the two Secret Service agents understood how the computer virus related to the terrorist attack on Flight 2512 and the attempted murder of Tanner. Derek told the Secret Service agents everything about the case, except for the specific details regarding Tanner's past life and the ultra-secret quantum computer. Todd and Adam asked questions along the way, but, in the end, they still seemed skeptical that all the events were related.

"That's a powerful accusation about China bringing down the airplane," Adam said. "If it's true, they're playing hardball."

"We already knew about the Dragon Virus, and the NSA told us about their theory that Flight 2512 was intentionally targeted because of that. So the only new piece of information is this Reina character," Todd said.

"There's also the fact that someone tried to kill Tanner again," Helen said, defending her analyst.

"Yes, it appears that someone is after Tanner, but how do you know it's Reina? Maybe Tanner is involved in some other shady business," Todd countered.

Derek saw the discussion was getting off track. "You're right. This is just a theory for now," he said. "We're not even sure if all of China is involved, or just some faction of the government. But we're still going after Reina because she seems to be the focal point for all the events."

"Okay, so how do you track down someone in cyberspace? From what you said, Reina is most likely using a wireless modem and a laptop. She could be anywhere," Adam said.

"We start with the mole. Somebody is leaking information to the terrorists. If we can track down this traitor, he'll lead us right to Reina," Sara said.

"We think the infiltrator is most likely from the NSA or Secret Service. Helen has already agreed to submit her entire team to a polygraph test," Derek said. "Who on the Secret Service side needs to be considered?"

"We've already been down this road with the NSA," Todd said. His face showed his frustration. "I can promise you the leak isn't coming from our organization."

"Agent Payne," Sara said, trying to diffuse the situation, "we understand your high regard for your peers, but we still need to get a list of anyone who knew about Bryan and Tanner's trip back to DC," she said. "That includes administrative people like secretaries or travel agents."

"Let's not waste any time with the NSA," Todd said, sneering. He stood up and removed his jacket. "Since you're so sure the leak is from the Secret Service, let's just start the poly tests right now!" He rolled up his sleeve for effect.

Derek and Sara tensed up at the sudden outburst, but Helen wasn't surprised. She had witnessed Todd's caustic personality before. Silence quickly fell over the entire conference room as the other FBI agents stopped in their tracks to determine the commotion.

"You'll have to excuse my partner," Adam said as he put a hand on Todd's forearm. The simple action helped ease the tension. "We don't like being accused any more than you do, but we understand the reason for the request."

Adam's coolheadedness prevailed as Todd sat down and took a deep breath. The other FBI agents in the room slowly went back to work, and Derek and Sara slightly eased back in their chairs. They had a lot of work to do.

APRIL 27, FORT MEADE, MARYLAND

It was almost lunchtime back at NSA headquarters in Fort Meade, Maryland, but for the two brothers on the MART team, they wouldn't have known. Slammer and Viper had lost track of time as they scrambled throughout the night to finish their unique antidote routine. Even though they didn't know about the supercomputer at the Utah Data Center, they understood the folks out West had the ability to bring the antidote to life. Once the NSA's counterfeit system was in place, it would mimic the ping request, prevent—ing the authentic Chinese system from coordinating the launch sequence for the computer virus.

Confident that their routine was finally ready for prime time, Slammer and Viper called the secure phone in Helen's office. The call went unanswered, and they immediately tried the phone number for Tanner. It also went unanswered. Fortunately, the brothers had the pager number for Helen, and they tried that as a last resort. They were completely unaware of the situation developing in Utah.

FBI FIELD OFFICE, UTAH

"Oh, dear," Helen said in her polite voice studying the number on her pager.

"What is it?" Derek asked. He was sitting across from Helen on the other side of the conference room table.

"I forgot about the people who are doing some work for us back at Fort Meade," Helen said. She quickly brought everyone up to speed on Slammer and Viper, and how they were creating an antidote for the computer virus. However, Helen didn't mention the antidote would run on QC because the Secret Service agents still didn't know about the supercomputer's existence.

Finished with her quick update, Helen dialed the number for the MART team. Slammer answered the phone, announcing himself in his usual manner. "You've got Slammer on the line."

"Hi, this is Helen calling from Utah," she said. "I'm on a conference call with a couple of agents from the FBI and the ECTF."

The long pause on the other end of the call reflected the brothers' hesitancy. In their previous life as computer hackers, Slammer and Viper had done a lot of unethical things, and some other stuff that was downright criminal. Because of their questionable history, they had learned to fear anyone working for the FBI.

"Uh, hi, Helen," Slammer answered coolly. "We have that thing for Tanner."

"I'm sorry I forgot to call you back this morning. There's been an incident with Tanner. That's why I'm with the FBI and Secret Service," Helen said. "Tanner is in the hospital with carbon monoxide poisoning."

Slammer waited for a moment before asking the obvious question that any astute person would ask. "Was it an accident?"

The FBI jumped in to respond. "This is Agent Derek Cannon of the Salt Lake City FBI office. We believe that someone intentionally went after Tanner because of his knowledge of the new computer virus."

Helen and the others could almost hear Slammer gulping down

his fear on the phone. Like most computer hackers, Slammer worked stealthily in the background, never expecting direct harm for his actions.

"Is there anything else we should know about it?" Viper asked, joining his brother on the conference call.

"I don't think you need to be worried for your own safety right now," Helen said. "I'm positive there is no connection back to you."

"What about our code? Can anyone there can run it besides Tanner?" Slammer asked.

"I'm not sure. I'll have to check with the rest of my team. In the meantime, please keep monitoring the network traffic coming out of China, and let me know if anything changes," Helen said.

"Will do," the two brothers answered in unison.

⎯⎯⎯•⎯⎯⎯•⎯⎯⎯

She knew it was a little bit premature, but Reina felt the need to celebrate. Since she arrived in Utah, she had brought down an airliner with SAM, eliminated a former spy in a mysterious manner, and clandestinely killed an NSA analyst with carbon monoxide. Her three hits in one week surpassed all her other assignments. Reina knew her uncle was proud, and even though she hadn't spoken to him directly since the beginning of her mission, she could sense his approval.

Reina was supposed to communicate only when absolutely necessary, but today she couldn't resist the urge to send her beloved uncle a message. She knew there was little risk in doing it, especially since she used encrypted email. The folks back at the First Technical Reconnaissance Bureau in China had assured her there was no computer system on earth that could crack their newest encryption algorithm.

Taking out her laptop, Reina logged onto the Internet. She composed a brief message to her uncle, saying how much she missed him. She acknowledged that she had been away for a long time, but it was her privilege to serve her country on such an important assignment. She ended her message by mentioning that she would be home soon, and how she hoped to take a much-deserved vacation with her uncle to their villa on the Chongwu Peninsula. Finished with her email, Reina started up the encryption program to scramble her message before sending it off into cyberspace.

* * *

Across the Salt Lake Valley, Samantha Bradfield received a text message on her phone, alerting her to an active Internet connection established by IP address 172.31.20.205. The thirty-two-year-old ran back to her office and logged into her UNIX workstation. As the lead system administrator at Mountain States Wireless, Samantha was deceptively proficient with computers. She was the go-to person at Mountain States Wireless when the cops wanted to track down a criminal on her company's network.

Typing with one hand while dialing a phone number with the other, Samantha watched a log file as it listed connection requests on her computer screen. After a few seconds, a voice answered her phone call. "This is Special Agent Cannon," he said.

"This is Samantha Bradfield at Mountain States Wireless. I'm calling about a current connection from IP address 172.31.20.205." As with all the other warrants from law enforcement agencies, Samantha was kept in the dark about the user she was tracking down. She had only been given an IP address to monitor.

"How long has she been on?" Derek asked, hoping to get a good trace on the call.

"Less than a minute," Samantha said. She noticed how the FBI referred to the suspect as a female. Maybe this wasn't just another pedophile she was tracking down. "I'm logging all her traffic and trying to get a trace on her right now." A few more seconds passed, and Samantha spoke again. "Okay, it's coming from an 801 area code."

"Does she have a username?" Derek asked.

"No, we don't require people to have usernames to access our wireless network. The unique identifier for her account is the phone number," Samantha said. Suddenly, she shouted out, "Got it! It's 801-555-6034!"

"Great!" Derek said. He quickly wrote down the number in his notebook.

"The user isn't really doing anything right now," Samantha reported. "She's just logged into a generic email service."

"She's not browsing any other websites?" Derek asked.

"Nope, she's idle right now," Samantha said. "Wait, something's happening. She just signed off. It looks like she uploaded an email and then killed her connection."

"Who got the message?" Derek asked.

"I'm not sure," Samantha said. "Once it's sent to the email hosting site, it's off our network. I can't track it after that."

"Good work," Derek said. "Keep logging any connection information from this user, and call us back if you see anything." Derek ended the call.

Even though Mountain States Wireless couldn't track down the recipient of the email address, Derek did get a valuable piece of information. He now knew the cell phone number assigned to the wireless modem card that Reina used. The next time she logged on to the Internet, it would be simple to triangulate her exact position.

NSA DATA CENTER, UTAH

Sydney and Rachel waited impatiently as QC worked on cracking the email from Reina. Besides making the occasional adjustment to their software routine, there wasn't much else the two NSA employees could do to expedite the cryptanalysis.

"It looks like QC is about 15 percent of the way done," Sydney said, looking at the output. "I thought she'd be farther along by now." When QC cracked SSL, the protocol used in secure web transactions, it took less than four hours. Apparently this new encryption method was significantly more complex.

"It all depends on how similar this new algorithm is to existing ones. If it's a variation of something common like AES, it will likely crack faster," Rachel said. She was referring to the only tried-and-true method to successfully crack a code. Starting with the number one and trying every possible combination of numbers and characters to guess the secret key, brute-force cracking was extraordinarily time consuming but always effective.

"Too bad it's not based off DES," Sydney said. DES was one of the first ciphers used back in the 1970s.

"Yeah, but nobody uses a 64-bit key anyway," Rachel said.

In cryptology, the strength of the encryption algorithm was based on the size of the secret key. The smaller the key size was in bits, the easier it was to crack. As a result, few people used the old-fashioned 64-bit keys anymore because they could be cracked in just a few days with run-of-the-mill computers. On the other hand, if the key length was doubled to 128-bits, the time required to crack the key using a brute-force method skyrocketed to 149 trillion years. To guarantee that a secret key would never, ever be cracked, most serious organizations doubled the key length again to 256-bits, which would theoretically make it impossible for a normal computer to try every possible sequence in a brute-force attack.

But QC wasn't just a normal computer. Using the principles of quantum physics, QC operated with the effective computing power of billions of computers. The one-of-a-kind computer system could simultaneously scan through trillions of permutations every second. It was a closely guarded secret—known only to Helen's team and a select few other people at the NSA—that QC had cracked AES, the Cadillac of computer ciphers.

"Look at that," Rachel said. She changed her focus to another computer monitor on the wall. "I think we just got another email from Reina." She quickly manipulated the keyboard and ran the command to open the message.

Sydney watched over Rachel's shoulder. "It's encrypted also," she said.

"This email was just sent, like in the past ten minutes," Rachel said. "We better call Helen and let her know we've got another one."

—•——•—

FBI FIELD OFFICE, UTAH

Helen's pager chirped, alerting the QC team leader to an incoming message. "It's my team calling," she said. She grabbed the secure conference phone in the middle of the table and dialed the number for the data center. "This is Helen. I've got the FBI and Secret Service with me," she announced, letting her team know that this wasn't a private phone call. "What's going on?"

"We just got another email from Reina," Rachel said. "It looks like she just sent it."

"That verifies what the folks at Mountain States Wireless said," Derek whispered to the other agents in the conference room.

Helen replied into the phone, speaking for the group. "Is it also encrypted?"

"Yes. It looks like it's using the same obscure encryption algorithm as the other message," Rachel said.

"How's it going on the cryptanalysis for the first message?" Helen asked.

"We're over 15 percent done. It looks like the cipher is moderately difficult, but not as complex as something like AES," Rachel said. Her comment let Helen known that it would take less time to crack this Chinese cipher than it took the NSA to originally crack the AES algorithm.

"Good work, you two," Helen said. "Where are Mel and Chad?"

"They're working on the stock market analysis. We haven't seen them in a couple of hours."

"I'll give them a call and let them know what you found," Helen said. "If you see anything else coming from Reina, call me immediately."

"You got it," Rachel said before disconnecting the phone.

Sara spoke to the others gathered around the table as the call ended. "It looks like we're discovering the emails from Reina faster now."

"That's part of our computer's inherent functionality," Helen said. "It's based on artificial intelligence. In a way, our computer can learn to recognize key events. It will keep learning how to find information from Reina, becoming more and more efficient."

"That's impressive," Adam said. "You keep talking about this special computer you have, like it's your ace-in-the-hole. How long are you going to keep us in the dark?"

Todd spoke up. "Yeah, you have something special out there, and it's a major part of this investigation. I want to hear all about it," he said.

Helen knew that she couldn't put off the two Secret Service agents forever. They were fully involved in the investigation now, and it was becoming counterproductive to keep them out of the loop. She decided it was time to let them in on the secret. "Let's call the folks back at headquarters right now and see what they say."

APRIL 27, SALT LAKE CITY, UTAH

It was just past noon at Intermountain Medical Center. In a quiet room on the first level, Tanner gazed solemnly at his unconscious wife through the clear glass of the hyperbaric oxygen chamber. Megan didn't seem ill. In fact, she appeared to be in a peaceful sleep, deceiving Tanner into thinking that she might wake up at any moment. While the doctors continued to be optimistic about Megan's recovery, Tanner grew more concerned about his unborn child's condition.

Tanner turned and walked back to the corner of the hospital room, easing himself into the vinyl recliner with a sigh. The monotonous beeping from Megan's heart monitor echoed in the empty and sterile room. Outside the door, a police officer ensured that only authorized people disturbed Tanner and his wife. Down the hall in the lobby, another plainclothes police detective guarded the hospital entrance as an added precaution.

Tanner looked at the lunch tray next to him. He felt no desire for food, but he forced himself to eat, knowing that it would give him strength. Besides a massive headache and an overall feeling of fatigue, Tanner had mostly recovered from the carbon monoxide poisoning. Unfortunately, that wasn't the case for his wife and child. The doctors wanted to perform an emergency C-section to deliver the baby, but it was too risky to take Megan into surgery until her oxygen level improved.

The isolation and quiet of the hospital room gave Tanner time to ponder over the events of the past few days. He had been so focused on the new Dragon Virus and tracking down Reina that he neglected to examine the broader picture. It wasn't until he was forced to sit still in the quiet hospital that he realized what he had been overlooking—the mole.

Tanner recalled the sequences of events in his mind before coming to his dreadful conclusion. He had tried everything he could do to dismiss the speculation, but he couldn't dismiss the facts. He kept returning to the same result over and over again, and it made his stomach turn. If it wasn't for the antinausea medications the doctors had given him, Tanner might have been sick at the growing realization of who had betrayed him.

Taking a relaxing breath, Tanner looked at the IV in his arm and the oxygen monitor on his finger. He decided that it was time to discharge himself and go back to work. He didn't care if he was fully recovered or not. Tanner felt the stirrings of revenge like he had in New Mexico, but these emotions were more powerful than what he felt when he had been kidnapped. This time somebody had gone after his wife and unborn child.

Tanner looked again at Megan in the hyperbaric chamber. He realized there wasn't anything else he could do for his wife. If she were conscious, Tanner knew she would tell him to get busy tracking down Reina. Determined to find the mole and stop the Dragon Virus, Tanner grabbed the phone by his chair and punched in the number for Helen's pager. It was time to get back to work.

———•———

FBI FIELD OFFICE, UTAH

Helen was surprised to see an unknown number come up on her pager. She excused herself from the FBI and Secret Service agents to make a call in another room. "Hi, I just got a page from this number," she said.

"Helen, this is Tanner. I need you to come get me," he said in a tired voice.

"Tanner, what are you talking about?"

"I'm ready to get back to work."

"Have the doctors okayed this?" Helen asked.

"No, but I'm checking myself out. There's too much work to do," Tanner said with resolve.

"No way," Helen said. "You're staying there until the doctors say you're okay, and you're not going back to work. You're going to stay home with your wife."

"There's nothing more I can do for Megan. If she were conscious, she would tell me to go back to work. I'm the only person who can program the antidote to run on QC. You know that. Besides, we've still got Reina running around out there, and I know more about tracking her down in cyberspace than anyone else," Tanner said.

Helen took a deep breath. Time was of the essence, and she needed Tanner's wisdom and expertise in this critical situation. He had made a very convincing argument.

"Okay, give me a chance to talk to the doctors and make sure you're well enough to leave. But first, I've got to tell you who that dead body was in Boise. You won't believe it."

"Who?" Tanner asked.

"It's Jeff Kessler."

"Wow," Tanner said in shock. If he wasn't so lethargic from the antinausea drugs, he would have been more animated about the revelation of Jeff's death. After all, Tanner and Jeff had been close friends once.

Helen continued her update. "The FBI believes that Jeff was working for the Chinese when he kidnapped you. Apparently, someone in China had a score to settle with him."

The idea that Jeff was involved in Tanner's kidnapping was one of the theories the FBI had been investigating over the years. While Tanner had a long-nagging suspicion that Jeff had turned on him, the FBI hadn't been able to find Jeff to question him. Now it appeared someone had silenced Jeff before he could shed any light on his involvement in Tanner's mysterious kidnapping.

"I bet that somehow Reina was involved in this also," Tanner said.

"That's definitely a possibility because it seems like she's been busy lately," Helen said. "The FBI is still checking out all the facts. Hopefully they'll be able to make the connection between Reina and Jeff."

"So when can you come pick me up?" Tanner asked.

"I'll call you back in thirty minutes, and we'll coordinate how to get you out of there," Helen said. She ended the call.

Finished talking with Tanner, Helen called the hospital and spoke to the chief doctor on the floor. Surprisingly, the doctor wasn't overly concerned about discharging Tanner. She was much more concerned for the well-being of Megan and the child. When Helen asked if Tanner could return to work, the doctor thought it would be okay as long as Tanner could handle the weakness and lethargy for the next twenty-four hours as the effects of the carbon monoxide poisoning wore off.

Helen finished coordinating Tanner's release from the hospital before going back into the conference room to explain the situation to the FBI.

"I'm not authorizing that," Derek said. "Tanner's a sick guy, and he needs to be in the hospital."

"I'm not asking for your permission. I'm telling you that Tanner wants to go back to work. He's as stubborn as he is brilliant, and he'll leave that hospital one way or another," Helen said. "I just spoke to the doctor at the hospital, and she said Tanner would be okay to check out."

"So what do you want from us?" Derek asked.

"We need to send some agents to pick up Tanner and escort him back to the data center to guarantee his safety."

Derek thought about Tanner's return to work and how it might energize the ongoing investigation. "Let's split up," he said. "Sara will go with Helen and Adam to pick up Tanner. You can stop by his house and get him some clothes before heading back to the data center. Meanwhile, Todd and I will stay here and open up a secure conference bridge. We'll have two teams, working simultaneously at each location."

"I like it," Sara said. She was excited about the opportunity to take the lead with the group at the data center.

"I do too," Helen added. "But before I go, I need to brief Todd and Adam here on our unique computer system."

———•———

SALT LAKE CITY, UTAH

When a black Chevy Suburban with tinted windows pulled up to the rear loading dock of Intermountain Medical Center, Tanner immediately knew it was the FBI. His discreet and rapid discharge from the hospital added urgency of the situation, and Tanner didn't wait for the orderly to push him down the ramp to the waiting SUV. Instead, he stood up out of his wheelchair, briskly thanked the orderly, and walked off with resolve to meet his boss.

Helen greeted Tanner with a quick hug. "It's good to see you," she said, smiling at Tanner's unusual wardrobe.

Tanner looked goofy in his loose-fitting hospital scrubs and slippers, but he was preoccupied with other thoughts. As he stooped to get into the vehicle, he noticed another Suburban waiting passively by the entrance to the alley. He assumed that vehicle was also filled with FBI agents, escorting him back to work.

Sliding along the rear seat of the SUV, Tanner recognized Sara behind the wheel and Adam riding shotgun. "Thanks for coming to get me," he said to everyone.

"Here, I'm sure you'll want this," Helen said. She reached into a plastic grocery bag on the floor and removed two items. She handed Tanner a cold Mountain Dew and a bottle of Tylenol. "We're going to stop by your house and pick up some clothes," she added.

"Thanks," Tanner said. He opened the cold soda. "Okay, bring me up to speed."

As the two-vehicle convoy pulled out onto the street, Helen quickly covered everything that had happened since Tanner and his wife were taken to the hospital. "First of all, we know that someone deliberately tampered with your furnace. The FBI is following up on that, but so far they don't have any leads."

"Which means someone broke into my house and was able to disable the alarm system," Tanner said. He head was pounding like a jackhammer, but his mind connected the dots.

"That's what our guy said," Sara replied from the driver's seat. "Fortunately, your alarm system records all the input for that past thirty days. Whoever disabled your alarm did it with the manufacturer's master code." Sara didn't reveal that the FBI also maintained a list of master override codes for every alarm manufacturer in the United States.

"That doesn't give me a warm fuzzy," Tanner said. "I imagine there aren't any fingerprints or other evidence."

The SUV accelerated up the on-ramp to Interstate-15. "Nothing so far, but we've got folks turning your house upside-down for clues," Sara said.

Helen continued with her briefing. "We also have two more emails from Reina, but they're both encrypted with some obscure cipher that we haven't seen before."

"She's using a new cipher?" Tanner asked. "That means someone has told her that we can snoop on her messages."

Helen marveled at Tanner's snappy observation. The carbon monoxide hadn't seemed to affect his ability to reason. "The team is running the algorithms through QC to see if we can crack it. Since it's an unknown key, it's taking longer, but we're about 20 percent done," she said.

Tanner looked at his boss with surprise, obviously wondering why Helen mentioned the ultra-secret computing system in the car of mixed company. "It's okay," she said. "The Top Brass at headquarters gave us permission to brief Sara and Derek, along with Adam and Todd. They all know the basics of our computer system."

"How much of a *briefing* did they get?" Tanner asked.

"Just the high-level stuff, but the specifics are still classified," Helen assured her analyst.

Adam spoke from the front passenger seat. "Now I understand how you've been getting your information on this computer virus and Reina. I'm impressed."

Tanner paused at the mention of Reina. Apparently the FBI had also briefed the two Secret Service agents on the primary suspect in the terrorist investigation. "So, I guess we're all on the same page now?" he asked.

"Yes, and I think it's better this way," Helen said. "The FBI and I are operating on the theory that the Dragon Virus, the attack on Flight 2512, the death of Jeff Kessler, and your attempted murder are all related."

"Do the Secret Service guys buy into this?" Tanner asked.

Adam spoke up, answering the question. "I agree with the FBI. There are too many coincidences going on here, but Todd is still doubtful."

That didn't surprise Tanner at all. He knew that Todd was skeptical of any theory that didn't originate inside the Secret Service. "Have you heard from our guys back East?" Tanner asked.

"They have the script ready to run," Helen said. "By the way, the FBI and Secret Service also know about the MART team."

"Everything goes back to Reina," Sara said as she turned the SUV onto Bangerter Highway. "Tracking her down is our number one priority."

Tanner felt exposed with all the new information Helen had revealed to the FBI and Secret Service, but he realized now wasn't the time to argue. He remained intently focused on finding who had tried to kill his wife and unborn child.

Helen spoke up again, bringing Tanner out of his thoughts. "There's one more thing. You're dead."

"What?" Tanner asked in shock.

"According to the hospital staff, you died last night from carbon monoxide poisoning," Helen explained.

"We felt that was a good way to buy us some time. Hopefully, the terrorists will think you're dead and back off now," Sara said.

"What about my family and friends, or the people at my church? They'll be horrified when they find out!" Tanner exclaimed.

Helen tried to calm Tanner's anxiety. "Your name hasn't been released to the public yet. Nobody in your neighborhood or church group knows exactly what happened," she said. "We've instructed your church leader to spread the word that you were rushed off to the hospital because of complications from your wife's pregnancy."

Adam added more details. "Only the local cops and few medical personnel know what's actually going on."

"And Reina," Sara said. "She's the only one who will pick up on the news report that an unnamed man died at the hospital last night from carbon monoxide poisoning."

"But eventually the press will want the name of the deceased person, and it will cause a lot of panic," Tanner said.

"It usually takes a couple of days for the cops to notify the victim's family. When that time comes, we'll blame the whole thing on a mix-up at the hospital. Another man did, in fact, die at the hospital last night. We'll tell the press that the names got switched," Helen said.

Sara closed the discussion from the driver's seat. "Don't worry. We'll smooth this all out in the end, but the main thing right now is that you're dead, and that gives us a huge advantage in trying to track down Reina."

Tanner didn't like the charade about his death, but he decided to let it go. He had more important things to worry about than his fictitious and premature demise.

ZHEJIANG PROVINCE, CHINA

Halfway across the world in Shaoxing, China, Major General Yang Dao looked out across the darkened valley from his large office window. The city below appeared extra peaceful early in the morning. Taking his time to finish his herbal tea, the general allowed the quiet stillness of the empty office to soothe his mind. The general had arrived two hours before his normal starting time of 6:00 a.m. He wanted to be alone with his thoughts before the office staff barged in, ruining the peace he currently felt.

Yang Dao pondered on the email he recently received from his niece. He should have been more upset with her for breaking protocol and contacting him directly, but Yang Dao couldn't really be angry with his precious niece. The major general had never married or had kids of his own, so he had raised her as his own daughter.

When he first brought her back to China, Yang Dao gave his niece the name of Yang Qiao. The name meant "skillful," and his niece had proven that she rightly deserved the name. Yang Qiao had done everything precisely as directed. She had accomplished all her tasks in a proficient manner, eventually earning her an elite status among the hundreds of special assassins employed by the People's Liberation Army.

Yang Qiao's recent success was only the beginning. Tomorrow, the First Technical Reconnaissance Bureau would achieve history, unleashing their potent computer virus against the Americans. Nobody knew it, but the virus had already worked its stealthy magic in the stock market crash just a few days ago. The virus's commencement might have gone unnoticed, but its finale would be seen by everyone. The virus would erase the electronic balance on bank and retirement accounts all across America. It would destroy the records of every financial transaction, making it impossible for anyone to re-create their missing information. It would be months before the Americans understood what hit them, but the catastrophe would never be linked back to China. The Americans would only be able to trace the cyber-attack to a virus that mysteriously originated from inside their own computer systems.

Among the financial ruin in America, Yang Dao would lead out, helping China rise up and become the premiere economy in the world. Nobody would be able to stop the outcome. Of course, the major general knew the Chinese had no ambition to rule a political empire. That wasn't the goal. Yang Dao and the others in his secret group knew real power came from economic dominance, not political leadership.

• • •

APRIL 27, NSA DATA CENTER, UTAH

In a secure conference room at the Utah Data Center, the QC team welcomed Tanner back from the hospital with handshakes and hugs. For the first time in almost two days, Helen had her team together in one room. Despite the haggard and worn expressions on everyone's face, Helen felt the renewed vigor of the group. The pizza that she had picked up on the way back to the data center helped soothe the stress of the day, but Helen knew it wouldn't last for long. Unfortunately, she was about to throw everyone back into the fire.

"We've got serious problems to solve," she said, standing at the front of the conference room. Her analysts listened intently as they ate. "The events of the past four days have been a disaster. And now, with the attempted murder of Tanner and his wife, it appears another disaster is now imminent." She placed both hands on the table and leaned in for effect. "I know you are tired and scared. I am too," she said. "I know this seems like a bad dream that won't end, but what we do here as a team, in the next twenty-four to forty-eight hours, may be the most important work you will ever do. I need you all to dig deep and hunker down because you are probably the best option we have for dealing with the tidal wave that is coming for America."

Helen turned to their guest. "This is Agent Sara Heywood of the FBI. It seems our discovery about an obscure computer virus has morphed into a full-blown FBI investigation. Sara will bring you up to speed on everything that is going on and how we can help out."

Helen sat down and let Sara start her briefing. Over the next twenty minutes, Sara touched on all the points of the FBI investigation. She wove the disparate facts into a single tapestry, showing how the virus, the attack on Flight 2512, and the attempted murder of Tanner were all related. She talked about the imminent damage from the computer virus, and the need for the NSA to find a way to stop it from launching. Most important, she highlighted how everything pointed back to Reina. When Sara finished her briefing, there was no doubt about the two main objectives for the NSA—stop the Dragon Virus from executing and crack Reina's emails.

⸻

Reina couldn't have been happier. With the confirmation on the morning news that a man had died last night from carbon monoxide poisoning, she knew that her work was done. Later tonight, she would take a red-eye flight to Tokyo before switching planes for the last part of her trip to Beijing. When the computer virus initiated its final deathblow at noon on tomorrow, she would be safe back home, watching the financial tsunami as it crashed on America.

Reina decided it was time to take the last run of her brief stay in America. She laced up her running shoes, pulled her silky black hair into a ponytail, and put on a light jacket before leaving her apartment. The afternoon sun deceptively tricked Reina into thinking that it might be warmer outside, but her body told her summer was still several months away.

Reina ran east for half a mile before veering off course and running across Veterans Memorial Park. Located in the middle of the Salt Lake Valley, the one hundred-acre park was a popular destination for outdoor enthusiasts. The city park was often crowded, highlighting a mix of different people doing different activities. Reina liked running through the park because the terrain was flat and simple to navigate. More important, the park provided the perfect location for dead drops with other members of her espionage cell.

Long considered a fundamental element of the spy tradecraft, a dead drop allowed two individuals to exchange information or money without having to meet face-to-face. A dead drop was usually defined by a signal that appeared as a common, everyday mark to everyone but the spies. In the case of Reina's spy unit, the signal for a dead drop was a red chalk line on the restroom wall at this exact park.

Running across the outfield of the baseball diamond and past the playground area, Reina approached the bathroom in the park. She had run this route more than forty times over the past two months, but she had never seen the mark. With her duties over and her flight home in just eight hours, Reina assumed today wouldn't be any different. She was wrong. A few moments later, she was shocked to see the obvious yet plain red chalk line on the top right hand corner of the bathroom wall. The location of the mark high up on the wall signified the urgency of the message. Reina was to stop all her activities and immediately respond to the communication at once.

Reina's team preferred using digital methods of communication like email, but the presence of the red mark on the bathroom wall indicated that she would receive her information the old-fashioned way—on paper. Obviously, the other member of her spy unit felt that digital communication was too risky for this specific message. Reina rehearsed in her mind the exact instructions she was supposed to follow if she ever saw the red mark.

She quickly turned south and ran toward the new city library complex at the far end of the park. Walking into the lobby, she casually strolled past the reference desk, being careful not to raise any suspicions. She went into the nonfiction area of the main floor and looked for a book whose title she knew well. Finding the classic work *The Art of War* on the second shelf, she quickly flipped to the beginning of chapter thirteen. There she found the dead drop from her teammate.

Reina read the note three times just to be sure that she completely understood the message. Rey was in Utah, and he wanted to meet face-to-face. The note instructed Reina to skip her flight home and meet Rey tonight at the predetermined rendezvous point. She didn't know what the meeting would be about, but the urgency was obvious. Putting the note in her pocket, Reina folded the top right corner of the page in the book, signaling back to Rey that she had received his message. She quietly walked out of the library and headed back to her apartment.

APRIL 27, DRAPER, UTAH

At the Stones' house in Draper, Utah, a technical computer consultant named Ricky Hawes arrived on scene. Dressed in a shirt and tie, he was determined not to blow his first job with the FBI. Consulting with the Feds was a lucrative business, and Ricky hoped to use his professionalism to encourage future contracting opportunities with the government. After a quick round of introductions with the other law enforcement people on scene, Ricky was shown several of the Stones' personal computers. There was a laptop on the counter in the kitchen, and a tablet on the nightstand in the master bedroom. However, it was the main computer workstation in the office that demanded Ricky's attention first.

"Let's start here," Ricky said to Josh Butler, the FBI agent who was overseeing the investigation at the Stones' home. "I always like to begin with the primary computer system and work out from there," Ricky said. He casually grabbed the webcam off the monitor and turned it over in his hand.

"What are you going to do first?" asked Josh. The FBI agent wasn't completely ignorant when it came to computers, but his knowledge paled in comparison to people like Ricky, who the FBI contracted with to do technical forensic work.

"I usually crack open the case and copy the entire contents of the hard drive for analysis," Ricky said. "The hard drive is basically the brains of the entire computer system. Everything is stored on it." Ricky put down the webcam and opened up his leather bag, taking out his personal laptop. He then removed an electronic gadget and connected it to the laptop with a USB cable.

"What's that?" asked Josh.

"It's a disk reader. I can take the hard drive out of any computer and connect it to my laptop. That way, I can read the entire contents of the disk and bypass any security locks or anti-tampering software. It also maintains the data integrity of the hard drive in case you want to prosecute the owner."

"I don't think you need to be worried about that. The owner isn't a suspect. He's the victim," Josh said.

"Really?" Ricky asked with a puzzled look. He removed the last screw on the back of the computer case and looked at Josh. "Then why do you want to run forensics on his system?"

"We think someone broke in to the house and was looking for information. We want to make sure the suspect didn't tamper with this computer or try to steal any information from it."

Ricky was surprised by the agent's summary of the investigation, but in the end Ricky didn't care what the crime was. He was here to do a job. "It won't take long to copy the entire contents of the hard drive to my laptop. Then I'll be able to run some programs to check who accessed the computer recently," he said.

Working efficiently, Ricky finished removing the hard drive from the Stones' computer and connected it to his laptop. He then started up a computer program to dump the entire contents of the hard drive to his laptop. But Ricky didn't wait for the copy routine to finish before he kicked off another routine, searching the installed programs and access logs on the hard drive. "Do you know what this computer is primarily used for?" he asked.

"Mostly just home computing stuff, I guess," Josh said.

Ricky's fingers typed all over the keyboard. "Is the computer owner a database administrator?" he asked. It was an out-of-the-blue question.

"No," replied Josh. Then he remembered the briefing from the folks back at the office about Mrs. Stone and her occupation. "But his wife does stuff like that."

"That explains all the database files I see on here," Ricky said. He typed a few more commands. "It looks like she telecommutes to a company back in Albuquerque."

"Yeah, she does," Josh said in amazement. "How did you figure that out?"

"There's a VPN client installed on the computer. People use those to create secure connections to other networks like a business or such. The VPN client has a company logo on it. I just Googled the name and got a hit for a company that does payroll systems in Albuquerque."

Josh looked over Ricky's shoulder at the computer screen. "Yeah, that's the company she works for," he said.

"That probably explains the webcam. She probably uses it for video conferencing with her coworkers," Ricky said.

A few minutes passed as the contents of the hard disk transferred over to Ricky's laptop. He continued searching for any sign that the computer had been tampered with, but he wasn't having any luck. "Everything that I'm seeing legitimately relates to the wife's job. I don't see anything out of the ordinary," he said.

"Well, make a full copy of everything so we have it on file . . . ," Josh said.

Ricky quickly held up his hand, cutting off Josh's response. "Wait, this is weird," he said. "I just copied over a huge file. I mean, it's like gigabytes."

"What kind of file is it?" Josh asked.

"It's a video file, WMV format."

"Is that a movie?" asked Josh.

"No, movies are usually recorded in MPEG format. This file is the format that is used by a webcam," Ricky said. He pointed to the webcam resting on top of the monitor.

"Why is the file so large?"

"I don't know. Maybe someone forgot to turn off the camera after using it," Ricky speculated.

A zap jolted Josh, and he immediately thought of a strange idea. "Can we search through that video file to see if it captured anything unusual when it was left on?"

"It's hard to search for a specific frame on a video. It would be easier to browse it in fast forward," Ricky said. "But this file is huge, and it could be hours long."

"Let's try it. I've got a feeling that we might get lucky," Josh said..

Ricky queued up the file on his laptop and started playing it. The opening image on the screen was a woman with blond hair sitting at the computer.

"That's the wife," Josh said.

The image on the monitor was nothing spectacular. It showed a woman dressed in casual clothes, silently talking to someone via a headset. The picture remained unchanged for almost three minutes before the woman stood up, exposing her pregnant belly.

"Whoa, she's pregnant," Ricky said. An unknown man entered the video frame, giving the woman a hug.

"That's her husband," Josh said. He watched the video clip of the husband helping his wife put on her coat. "It looks like they're leaving," he said. "Can you tell what time of day this was taken?" he asked.

"Not really, but I'd say this part happened sometime in the morning, since they're putting on their coats," Ricky said.

Josh and Ricky watched the two individuals disappear off the screen. The camera stayed on, recording the same picture over and over again. "Let's speed it up," Josh stated.

Ricky entered a command on his laptop, and the video speed

forward even faster. For fifteen minutes the video scrolled by on fast forward, and the only noticeable change was the line of sunlight, moving slowly up the wall. Then suddenly, something happened as a dark shadow quickly moved across the computer screen.

"What was that?" Ricky asked.

"Rewind the video and slow it down," Josh ordered. He instinctually leaned in toward the monitor for a better look.

"That was definitely a person's image, but I can't make him out," Ricky said. He replayed the clip again at a slower speed.

"Okay, let's see if we can see who this is," Josh said.

The video continued forward at normal speed, and for seven minutes, nothing happened. Then the shadow quickly crossed the computer screen again. "Rewind it," Josh said.

Ricky looked down at his keyboard and started typing in a command, but he stopped when Josh shouted out excitedly. Looking up at the monitor, Ricky saw what had surprised the FBI agent. In the middle of the computer screen, clear as day, was the facial image of a Hispanic woman looking directly back at them.

"It's a woman," Josh said in amazement.

The silent video clip was eerie, like the woman could see who was watching her. "She's just staring at the monitor. I bet she didn't realize the webcam was turned on," Ricky said.

"Can we print off her picture?" Josh asked.

"I don't have a printer, but I can crop it and email it to someone if you want," Ricky said.

"Do it. We've got to send this off to the office," Josh emphasized. He pumped his fist with excitement.

———•———

FBI FIELD OFFICE, UTAH

Derek Cannon was ecstatic. He couldn't believe his luck. Josh had just emailed him a picture of the intruder who had likely tampered with the Stones' furnace. Derek carefully studied the image on his computer monitor—it was a photo of a young Hispanic woman. Derek thought back to the security video taken from the golf course clubhouse just after the SAM was launched. The fact that both images revealed a petite, young woman was not coincidental. Derek now had a valid photo of the mysterious Reina, and that piece of critical evidence renewed the tired agent.

Derek printed off the photo of the anonymous woman. He left his office and headed back to the conference room that served as the command center for the investigation. Inside, he showed Todd and the other FBI agents the latest discovery.

"A woman?" Todd asked, surprised at the finding.

"Yeah, and we're almost certain this is the same person who shot down Flight 2512," Derek said.

"Do you know who she is?" Todd asked. For the first time all day, he seemed engaged in the investigation.

"Not yet, but I'm going to send this photo back to FBI headquarters. We have some facial recognition software that can search through the NCIC and look for matches," Derek replied. He was referring to the National Crime Information Center database the FBI maintained.

A female FBI agent studied the photo. "She's awfully young for a criminal," she said.

"With looks that could kill," added a male agent.

Derek was just about to remind the agent that the female was a murder suspect and not a prom date, but the phone in the middle of the conference room table rang loudly. Derek punched a button, putting the call on speaker. "This is Derek," he answered.

"Hi, this is Sara I have Tanner, Helen, and Adam on the line with me. We just finished briefing the down here, and we—"

Derek stopped Sara in mid-sentence. "You won't believe this, but we got a possible ID on Reina," he said excitedly. "We pulled an image off Tanner's home computer. It showed a young woman snooping around the home."

"Wait. How did that happen?" Sara asked.

Tanner spoke up on the conference call, interrupting the exchange between the two FBI agents. "It was the webcam, wasn't it?"

"Yes, it was dumb luck that we even found it," Derek said.

"It's probably not as random as you think," Tanner said. "My wife uses the computer for video chats with her work back in Albuquerque. I've told her to make sure she turns it off when she finishes her calls, but she often forgets and the hard drive fills up with endless video. She probably forgot to turn it off before we went to the doctor's yesterday."

"Why does she record her calls? That seems weird," Derek asked.

"Megan often works at night. She records all her calls so she can go back and review what her boss told her during the day," Tanner said.

"This is a huge break," Derek acknowledged. He spoke to both groups seated at different locations. "This shows that Reina was involved in the gas leak at Tanner's house, or at least that she was at the house the same day the furnace malfunctioned."

"Can you send us a copy of the photo?" Sara asked.

"Yes, I'll fax it over right now," Derek said. It took less than a minute for the fax to get to the NSA data center. Helen was the first to speak. "She definitely looks Hispanic," she said.

"Look how young she is. I bet she's in her early twenties," Sara said over the phone bridge.

Adam spoke out over the phone call. "Do we really know she's Reina? Wouldn't she be more Asian looking if the Chinese were involved with the virus and everything?"

"Unless China is trying to distance itself from all the attacks," Derek said. "If it looks like China hired someone else to take care of the murders, they can deny involvement. It's a perfect setup."

"Look at how young and innocent she seems. I doubt that's the face of a killer," Adam said.

"Don't get suckered in by her looks," Derek replied. "I've seen a lot of strange things in my career, including a seventy-eight-year-old grandmother, who drowned her husband of fifty-five years in a bathtub. This photo is the best lead that we have right now, and I'm pulling out all the stops to identify this woman."

APRIL 27, NSA DATA CENTER, UTAH

While Tanner and Helen reviewed the photograph of Reina, Mel and the other members of the QC team busily worked inside the Chamber. The analysts had just finished loading all the financial stock transactions into QC, and they were ready to look for any clues as to whether someone had tampered with the stock market. Mel eagerly anticipated the results they might find. To be honest, Mel had wanted to do something like this ever since he joined the NSA, except that using the supercomputer for personal gain was strictly prohibited.

Mel's first love had always been economics. After graduating from the University of Michigan, he quickly realized that he wasn't cut out for the suit and tie crowd of Wall Street. Looking for something completely different, Mel signed on at the NSA, hoping to meld his mathematical skills with cutting-edge cryptology.

"How long until we see some results?" Mel asked Sydney.

"I don't know. It could be a few minutes or a few hours," Sydney answered. Rachel sat in a chair next to Sydney at the console, while Mel and Chad stood behind and watched the main monitor.

"So how is this going to work?" Chad asked.

Rachel spoke without looking back at Chad. "My algorithm will search through all the stock market transactions that you and Mel downloaded. It will look for anything that can be tied back to the Chinese."

Chad thought about Rachel's reply for a second. Then speaking up, he asked, "How do we know what we can trace back to China? It's not like they highlighted all their stock transactions for us."

"No, but we have a list of foreign and domestic brokerages that act in behalf of the Chinese government," Sydney said. "We also know about several Chinese multinationals that trade in the financial markets. We've programmed QC to look for transactions made by those groups specifically."

"Let's put the output on the big screen so we can all see," Mel said. He pointed to the 55-inch LCD monitor mounted on the wall.

It took almost ten minutes until the QC team started seeing results from Sydney's computer program. At first the hits were slow and random. Then, as QC continued to "learn," she uncovered more and more data that correlated to numerous Chinese actions in the stock market. A few minutes later, QC began charting the results.

"The X-axis will show the time of day, starting twenty-four hours before the terrorist attack," Sydney said. "The chart will mark off every ten minutes the stock market was open during the week."

Mel offered a play-by-play as he pointed up to the large monitor. "That's our baseline forming. It shows the normal Chinese stock activity before Flight 2512 went down. See how the line is relatively uniform and steady?"

"Yeah, it's appears to be pretty consistent," Rachel said.

"I bet we'll see increased Chinese stock activity as we get closer to the attack on Flight 2512," Mel said.

Looking up at the monitor like they were watching a movie,

the NSA employees waited in anticipation as QC began her stock market analysis on the day of the plane crash. The red line on the graph held steady until just after the opening bell of the market, then a jump in the Chinese stock transactions suddenly occurred.

"Look, it just went up," Rachel said.

Mel acknowledged Rachel's comment. "I would have expected it to be more of a spike, but the sell-off seems to be consistent with what other nations did. It was just fear selling."

The red line representing the Chinese stock transactions stopped rising and then dropped back down. "It seems like the Chinese went back to normal trading after the initial sell-off," Sydney said. She highlighted the graph's timeline with her mouse cursor.

The timeline on the bottom of the screen continued scrolling, signaling that it was approaching the first pause in trading activity. "We're getting to the point where the market stopped trading for an hour because of the 10-percent drop," Mel said. At 10:28 a.m., the program reached the time where the first circuit breaker kicked in, and the line representing the Chinese transactions dropped down to zero.

"That's what we'd expect, right?" Rachel asked. "Nobody should be trading for the next hour."

"Correct," Mel answered. "Let's have QC skip forward to just before the stock market reopened at 11:28."

Sydney entered in a few commands, instructing the supercomputer to jump forward forty-five minutes in the time sequence. The analysts watched the line representing the Chinese stock transactions remain at zero. "We're approaching the time when the market reopened," Rachel said.

"Remember, after it reopened the first time, the stock market held steady for a while before dropping rapidly. We might not see much trading from the Chinese at first," Mel said.

At 11:28 a.m., the line showing the Chinese stock market activity slowly climbed up to normal levels. "That doesn't look too bad," Sydney said.

"Let's skip forward until right before the stock market shutdown the second time," Mel suggested. Again, Sydney changed QC's parameters to jump forward in time.

"This is about twenty minutes before the second pause in trading activity," Sydney announced. The line showing all the Chinese stock transactions had actually decreased slightly from before.

"It looks like they're down a little bit right now," Chad said. He pointed to the decreasing slope on the graph.

"Wait for it," Mel said, predicting the second major sell-off was about to occur. For almost ten minutes nothing happened. Then, at 1:14 p.m. on the time chart, the line representing Chinese actions in the stock market rocketed upward. The analysts had a difficult time understanding what had happened because the line shot up so fast that it disappeared off the top of the monitor.

"Adjust the scale of the chart," Rachel ordered. Typing feverishly, Sydney made the necessary changes. A few seconds passed, and QC redrew the chart, showing the Y-axis now increased ten thousandfold. Something was wrong.

"Stop the analysis!" Mel shouted.

Sydney quickly typed a command to pause the program's output. "That can't be correct," she said. "According to the chart, the Chinese activity in the stock market went up in orders of magnitude."

"We screwed up on a calculation somewhere, like multiplying by a hundred instead of ten," Mel said. "That can be the only explanation for the unbelievable increase."

"It's not my math. I doubled-checked it," Rachel said, defending her work. "The calculations are right."

Mel chuckled. "Your math is wrong. That has to be the answer," he said before speaking to Sydney. "How hard would it be to put up another line on the graph showing the volume of the stock market? I've already loaded in the values, so it should be pretty simple."

"What's the volume?" Chad asked.

"It shows the overall number of stock transactions for the entire day. If we can get Sydney to chart that number next to the Chinese stock activity, you'll see the problem," Mel said.

It took just five minutes for Sydney to change her program to chart the number of Chinese stock transactions compared to the overall transactions for the entire market. QC quickly redrew the red line representing the Chinese stock trades and then added a blue line, showing the volume of every trade on the stock market. The two lines overlapped when the massive spike occurred.

"See that," Mel said. He pointed up at the monitor. "The two lines overlap. That shows we screwed up somewhere because there's no possible way that every stock transaction at that time of day was done by the Chinese."

"But we're focusing on just the time period right before the second shutdown. Let's zoom back out to the beginning of the day," Rachel said.

Sydney quickly made the necessary changes to the graph. A few seconds later, the chart reformed on the monitor with the same red and blue lines. However, at the start of the trading day, the red line representing the Chinese trading was significantly below the blue line showing the overall stock activity. The two lines remained far apart for the entire morning time until they quickly merged together and spiked up just before the second shutdown in the stock market.

Rachel highlighted the difference. "See this. At the beginning of the day, the Chinese line and the overall trading line are separated. That shows that my algorithm is correct. Otherwise the two lines would be overlapping from the very beginning."

"That's impossible," Mel said. "According to the chart, there were over one billion shares of stock changing hands. Are you saying that every single transaction was tied back to the Chinese?" he asked. "No way. There are millions of mom-and-pop traders out there. The Chinese couldn't have dominated a trading session like that. It's impossible. Let's go back to the beginning and check the numbers again."

The team started over and reloaded all the stock market data into QC from scratch. Rachel reviewed her algorithm for the third time, walking the team through her logic process. Sydney dissected her computer routine again, making sure she didn't forget to close out a statement or improperly escape a loop. After forty minutes, the analysts were ready to try it again.

"Start at the market open, but let's compress the time scale on the X-axis to see it play back faster," Rachel said.

Sydney tweaked her routine, and then she executed the program. Starting at 9:30 a.m. EDT, the chart showed the blue line representing the total stock activity much higher than the Chinese red line. "It looks the same so far," Sydney said.

"Let's wait and see what happens. I bet it will be different," Mel countered. The team watched both lines drop down to zero during the first circuit breaker. An hour after the pause, both lines increased again, but the red line representing the Chinese trading in the stock market remained far below the blue line.

"We're coming up on the spot where the two lines merged last time," Sydney said eagerly. All four analysts were focusing on the red line, unaware that someone was coming into the Chamber. At precisely 1:14 p.m., the red line representing the Chinese stock activity shot up and overlapped the blue line. Rachel shouted out in celebration, vindicating her algorithm, while Mel threw out a few choice swear words.

"That's impossible!" Mel shouted. "There has to be a glitch or something that is giving us inconsistent data. There's no way the Chinese controlled every transaction on the stock market at that time of day."

"Yes, there is," a male voice said from behind the group. The four analysts quickly turned around and were surprised to see Tanner and Helen standing behind them. "Print off those charts and come back to the conference room with us. We've got a lot to talk about."

APRIL 27, FBI FIELD OFFICE, UTAH

With a fresh cup of coffee, Derek pressed forward like a basketball superstar, trying to score the winning shot in the final seconds of the NBA play-offs. The photograph of Reina had lit up the radar of the folks back in Washington, DC, and Derek was grateful for the added resources they provided in the investigation. Right now, two dozen agents at FBI headquarters were running the picture of Reina through the Bureau's databases, looking for additional information.

The speakerphone on the middle of the table blared out, startling Derek and the others in the conference room. He checked the caller ID and recognized that it was Sara calling from the NSA facility. He answered the phone. "What's up?"

"The NSA just found some interesting evidence regarding the collapse of the stock market," Sara said over the phone bridge. "It looks like the Chinese had a hand in the crash."

Todd suddenly became very interested in the conference call. "What do you mean?" he asked.

"It looks like the Chinese sold off a bunch of stock, maximizing the effect of the crash," Sara said. "I'll let Mel explain since he did the analysis."

There was a brief pause before a scratchy voice came on the line. "Hi, this is Mel. I'm a member of the team here at the NSA," he said. "Just after the stock market crash on Monday, we tossed around the idea of something more to the crazy drop in the financial system. Even after 9/11 we didn't see a drop like this," he pointed out before continuing. "Tanner asked me to run some numbers and see what I could find. I didn't believe it at first, but we quadrupled-checked all our info, and it's solid. We think the Chinese manipulated the stock market by selling off billions of dollars at the same time."

"How could they do that?" Derek asked.

"We're still trying to figure it out, but from our data, it appears they somehow simultaneously controlled all the electronic trading sessions of the stock market.

"Aren't there safeguards in place for something like this?" Derek asked. "I don't know much about the computer systems that run the stock market, but it seems like there would be some kind of fail-safe for this." Derek glanced across the conference room table at Todd. He knew the Secret Service had responsibility in this area.

Todd felt a chill run down his spine. His normal, combative appearance suddenly vanished. "Actually," he began. He cleared his throat, trying to save face. "I was on a team at the ECTF that investigated this scenario back in 2010." He paused and then continued with a word of caution. "What I'm about to tell you isn't top secret, but it's very sensitive data. In the wrong hands, this information would definitely cause economic chaos." He spoke slowly, taking his time to craft a response that deflected away some the pressure he felt. "The New York Stock Exchange is highly automated. It's been that way for years. All the trading is done by computers, and we only use humans to trade as a backup process. The computer systems that run the stock exchange used to be located in different warehouses all over the East Coast. But over the years, as the trading became more and more computerized, the distributed systems became too slow. About two years ago, the folks that run the stock exchange built a 400,000 square-foot data center on an old rock quarry in northern New Jersey. It's similar to what you folks at the NSA have here in Utah," Todd said. "The data center for the stock exchange is massive, with long avenues of computer servers that control all the transactions on Wall Street. There's a failover site located just outside of London, connected together by a high-speed data link in case of another *event*." Todd emphasized the word "event," reminding everyone of the tragedy on September 11, 2001.

"What about access controls and security?" Mel asked over the phone bridge.

"It's all state of the art. It's a hardened facility with biometric scanners and the works. The entire network is isolated, firewalled from the outside world. Our investigation two years ago concluded that nobody on the outside could get access to the systems and manipulate stock trading," Todd said.

"Then it had to be an inside job," Helen countered.

"We looked at that also. Everyone who has access to that facility goes through a massive background check. It's very similar to the same process we use for a security clearance. The entire trading system is segregated into components to make sure that there isn't a single point of failure. It would be impossible for one person to simultaneously control all the systems to affect trading the way Mel described," Todd said. "It just couldn't happen."

Tanner spoke up on the call, offering an unlikely, but scary clue. "Unless it's already in the wild," he said.

"What was that?" Derek asked.

"Unless the Dragon Virus is already in the wild," Tanner repeated before explaining. "It means the Dragon Virus is already up and running and we don't know it. Or at least components of the virus are already running inside the data center for the stock exchange."

"You think this virus somehow got past the network security and firewalls for the stock exchange system?" Derek asked.

"I can't be certain since we haven't really isolated the source code for the virus. But I'd bet the virus was already installed on those computer systems before they went into the new facility," Tanner said.

"Okay, how do we determine if that happened?" Todd asked sincerely. He felt a personal connection to the virus now, seeing that it might have compromised the exact financial systems that he had vetted two years ago.

"We need to know the model and serial number that all those systems were manufactured under. If we can trace them back to a single manufacturing company in China, that might be the conclusive evidence that we need to show the systems came to America preloaded with the virus," Tanner said.

"I'll do it," Todd said. Everyone noticed that his combatant personality was gone. "I still have a couple of contacts at the stock exchange. I can get that information within the hour."

"We'll get our people at FBI headquarters to personally interview the entire staff that works at the stock exchange data center. Someone there might be involved," Derek said.

"We also need the logs for those systems during the day the stock market crashed. That will show us for sure how someone might have coordinated the massive stock sell off," Mel said.

"What about the Dragon Virus?" Adam asked on the conference bridge. "If it's already running out in the wild, how can we stop it from doing any more damage?"

"Leave that to me," Tanner said. He knew that Slammer and Viper had been waiting all day to execute their code on QC. It was time to get it done.

APRIL 27, SALT LAKE CITY, UTAH

Back at her apartment, Reina knew something was terribly wrong. While she was thrilled to see another member of her team, Reina was also apprehensive about the details of the late–night meeting. The operation had somehow deviated off course. That was the only justification for the sudden and unexpected visit from Rey.

After she had found the note hidden in the library book, Reina rehearsed every step of the operation. *Have I messed up somewhere?* She was absolutely positive that she had accomplished all of her assignments, yet something in her gut told her she was in trouble. The computer virus was scheduled to launch in less than twenty-four hours, but the unexpected change in her travel plans made Reina doubt the outcome of operation's final goal. Anxious for answers, she let her youthful impulsiveness get the best of her. She decided to violate the strict communication blackout and send a direct message to her uncle.

Reina glanced at the oversized clock hanging on the wall in her apartment. It was almost 5:00 p.m. local time, which meant that it was 7:00 a.m. Friday morning in China. She knew her uncle was an early riser, and that he would already be at work. Reina grabbed her laptop off the table and began crafting an email. She asked her uncle to elaborate on the unexpected meeting with Rey, and if it had anything to do with her performance. Always eager to please her uncle, Reina quickly summarized her accomplishments in America. She had done everything her uncle had asked of her. Reina ended the email by emphasizing her love and respect for her uncle before encrypting the message and sending it off.

Less than ten miles south of Reina's location, the fastest computer system in the world encountered a message from the IP address associated with Reina's computer. QC made a copy of the email and flagged it for further analysis by the NSA team before adding it into the decryption queue. The quantum computer now had three encrypted messages from the same user, and three was a magic number for cryptanalysis.

With three points of reference, QC could now positively identify repeating strings of characters that might otherwise be considered coincidental in just two messages. Rapidly crunching on all three emails at the same time, QC soon made the first connection. The string "43$jMPgtQ#6ts7" in all the messages equaled the letter "R."

—————•—————

NSA DATA CENTER, UTAH

Tanner and his boss ducked into an isolated conference room for a private conversation. Tanner didn't have much time to chat because Rachel and Sydney were waiting for him to go into the Chamber. But something had been on Tanner's mind, and he needed a moment alone with his boss to express his feelings.

Helen closed the door to the conference room. "What's up?" she asked. She sensed something was bothering her primary analyst.

"I wanted to tell you this when you picked me up, but I needed to wait until we were alone," Tanner began. "While I was in the hospital, I had time to look at the larger picture of everything that has happened. I started with the attack on Flight 2512 and analyzed all the major steps that got us to this point. Despite my reluctance, I keep coming back to the same awful conclusion."

"What's that?" Helen asked.

"I think I know who the mole is," Tanner said. "And if I'm right, this situation is a lot worse than any of us could imagine."

Tanner took the next three minutes to explain his reasons for discerning the traitor. Helen listened intently, her face becoming whiter and whiter with each point Tanner articulated. When Tanner wrapped up his summery, Helen had to sit down to keep from fainting.

"I can't believe that Bryan is the mole," she said.

"I know," Tanner said. "What do we do now?"

Helen took a moment to compose herself before speaking. "We've got to let the FBI know, but we need to keep it quiet."

Tanner took a deep breath. "I'll call Derek and tell him," he said. His stomach knotted up at the thought of openly accusing his deceased friend.

———•———

FBI FIELD OFFICE, UTAH

While Tanner and Helen were finishing their private conversation, Derek was speaking with Samantha, the systems administrator at Mountain States Wireless. Samantha had called Derek when she received the notification that IP 172.31.20.205 had logged in to the wireless network. Even though the connection time was brief, Samantha was able to get a lock on the call and triangulate the position.

"Are you sure that's the location of the call?" asked Derek. He scribbled the address down on a piece of paper.

"Positive. I verified it with the cell towers in the area, but it's only good down to an area of about five hundred meters," Samantha said, highlighting the main limitation of the process called multilateration. "But that should give you a good idea of where to start looking."

"Great work. Thank you very much," Derek said.

"You're welcome. I'm just glad I got the notification when I did because I was just about to head out to pick up my kids from day care," Samantha said.

"Well, don't keep them waiting," Derek said.

"I'll let you know if I see any further connections from this computer, but I'm sure this is your suspect," Samantha said, ending the call.

Back at the FBI field office, Derek logged onto his laptop that was connected to the projector in the conference room. He brought up the location Samantha had given him on Google Maps. The phone call came from the vicinity of 7800 South and Redwood Road. It was time to get everyone's attention.

"We have a potential location on Reina!" Derek shouted. Ten different agents and staffers in the conference room suddenly came to attention. Derek stood up and pointed to the crossroads on the map. "She's right here," he said.

"What's the chance that Reina was mobile when she made the call?" asked a junior agent from the other side of the room.

"That's a good possibility since she's using a wireless modem, but this is the best lead we have so far," Derek said. "I want a sur-veillance team dispatched to that area, immediately."

$$\bullet\!\!-\!\!-\!\!\bullet$$

NSA DATA CENTER, UTAH

It was early Thursday evening when Tanner implemented the antidote from the MART team. His programming routine was a little sloppy, but it would have to do the job. Tanner was having a difficult time concentrating on some of the technical aspects of his work right now. His mind was hazy from the effects of the carbon monoxide poisoning, and he kept agonizing over Bryan's possible involvement with the terrorist group. Tanner wondered if there was anything else he could do to positively identify Bryan as the traitor. Despite the argument he had laid out for his boss, Tanner knew that his theory was still just a theory without solid evidence.

"So, is that it?" Rachel asked over Tanner's shoulder, bringing him out of his thoughts. Tanner was seated at the console to QC with both Rachel and Sydney watching as he executed the program.

"Yeah, we should be good to go now," he said.

"How can we test it?" Sydney asked. "I know the program is supposed to mimic the synchronization signal from the master server in China, but how do we know for sure that it will work?"

"We can't. There's no way to test it except for shutting down the system in China, and we don't have access to do that. We'll just have to keep our fingers crossed and hope for the best," Tanner said.

Rachel gestured for Tanner to move out of the chair in front of the keyboard. "Now that you're done with your program, let me check and see how far we are on cracking those emails from Reina," she said. Typing up a command, she quickly noticed that there were three encrypted emails now instead of two.

"Hey, look at this. We got another email just a little while ago. We now have three messages from Reina!" she said excitedly. The NSA analysts in the Chamber immediately understood the positive impact of having three encrypted emails from the same source.

"How far are we in the decryption now?" Sydney asked.

"We've jumped up to 80 percent on the first email," Rachel said. "But with the third encrypted email, we should be done cracking everything in a couple of hours."

Just then the door to the Chamber opened up, and Chad and Mel stormed in. "Helen wants you all back in the conference room for an update. I guess the FBI just got a clue where Reina is hiding."

APRIL 28, ZHEJIANG PROVINCE, CHINA

Major General Yang Dao was both stunned and infuriated. When he arrived at work an hour ago, he found a very unusual letter on his desk. The message was from Rey, but it wasn't in his typical form of communication. Instead of an anonymous email, this message was a handwritten note delivered overnight via diplomatic pouch. Unfortunately, because of the time required to get the letter from America to China, the message was nearly eighteen hours old.

According to Rey, the Americans understood far more about the sinister computer virus than anyone had previously suspected. To make matters worse, the NSA had the ability to read the encrypted emails circulating among the Chinese spy cell. Rey highlighted that continued use of digital communications would only compromise the mission further. But there was still more in Rey's shocking message, and it was the last part that completely caught the major general off guard.

Rey revealed that the pesky NSA analyst, Tanner Stone, was none other than Tanner Zane, the same computer hacker that Jeff Kessler had kidnapped two years ago. After Tanner had escaped his captors in New Mexico, the FBI relocated him to Utah, gave him a new identity, and put him to work at the NSA. Rey emphasized that Reina had not succeed in killing Tanner, and that he was now unleashing the full power of the quantum supercomputer in an attempt to thwart the computer virus from executing.

The entire message from Rey was nerve-racking, and it caused Yang Dao to have doubts about the overall success of his grand operation. To complicate his precarious situation, the major general had just received another odd email from Yang Qiao. Again, his niece broke communication protocol by sending a message directly to her uncle. Unfortunately, Yang Dao didn't dare reply to his niece because that would tip-off the Americans that there was an active Chinese spy among their ranks. In the end, however, Reina's impulsive and foolish email served a purpose. She mentioned that she was going to have a late night meeting with Rey. Working together, Yang Dao fervently hoped that Rey and Reina would somehow find a way to stabilize the decaying situation.

APRIL 27, NSA DATA CENTER, UTAH

In the conference room, Helen and the members of the QC team listened to Derek's update over the speakerphone. The FBI agent said he had a solid lead on Reina's whereabouts, and that a surveillance team was en route to the vicinity of 7800 South and Redwood Road. He also mentioned that the Attorney General back at FBI headquarters was fully plugged into the investigation now, and that Derek would be delivering hourly briefings on their progress.

When Derek finished his update, Tanner offered some news of his own. "We have a couple of things to report on at this end as well," he said. "First of all, I executed the program that will delay the launch of the Dragon Virus." Tanner paused as he remembered that he hadn't contacted Slammer and Viper yet to let them know that he had started their code. He made a mental note to do that after this briefing. "We also recently got another email from Reina," he said.

"That's probably the same email that allowed us to track down her location," Derek said from over the phone bridge.

"There's more to that," Rachel added. "With three encrypted emails from the same source, we can decrypt the messages faster."

"When do you think you'll have that first message cracked?" asked Sara, who was sitting across the table from Rachel and Tanner.

"I think we'll have something back within the next couple of hours," Rachel said.

Helen entered the conversation. "It should work out perfectly then," she said. "That will give us a chance to go to the viewing."

"What?" asked Mel. His confused expression begged for more information.

"The FBI has agreed to allow us to visit Courtney Morrison and her family before the viewing officially starts at 7:00 p.m." Helen briefly looked at the clock on the wall. It was 5:30 p.m. "We won't have much time with her, but it will allow us to pay our respects in a private way."

"You'll be escorted by several FBI agents, just as a precaution," Sara added.

"What about Tanner?" Sydney asked. "Will he get to go?" While the other members of the QC team were isolated at the data center for their protection, Tanner was also kept there to remain out of sight.

"Unfortunately, no," Helen said. She felt terrible that Tanner wasn't going along with the rest of the team, and her voice reflected her sincere disappointment. "Reina still thinks that Tanner is dead, and we can't have him walking around out in public. He'll remain here and keep an eye on stuff while we're gone."

Derek spoke up over the speakerphone, explaining the decision.

"It wasn't Helen's call, Tanner. I wanted to keep you at the data center."

Mel didn't like the FBI's decision to keep Tanner at the data center. "So what do we tell people at the viewing if they ask where Tanner is?" he asked.

"We'll tell them that Tanner's wife is in labor, and that he's at the hospital. That's a completely reasonable explanation for his absence," Sara said to the NSA analysts seated around the table.

"We don't have much time," Helen said. "I want everyone ready to go in ten minutes." Then turning to Tanner, she spoke, "I'm truly sorry that you can't come. We'll bring you something back to eat."

"I understand," Tanner said. While he was disappointed not to pay his respects, Tanner knew it was best that he remain out of sight. Besides, he already had plans for what he was going to do while the others were gone, and it was something that he had to do alone.

APRIL 27, FORT MEADE, MARYLAND

At NSA headquarters in Fort Meade, Maryland, two brothers geared up for another night of work. It was long past quitting time for the normal rank—and—file office workers, but Slammer and Viper decided they needed to stick around and help out with the Dragon computer virus. After taking quick naps on the floor on their office, they planned ahead to make their stay tonight a little more comfortable.

The NSA facility had a secret warehouse filled with emergency supplies like bedding, food, and clothing in case of a national crisis. It took a few phone calls to managers in his chain-of-command, but eventually Slammer found someone to bring two cots over to the mini-data center in the basement of building six. Unfortunately, the emergency supply warehouse didn't stock Mountain Dew, but that problem was remedied by the pizza man, who had promised to bring ample amounts of soda pop when he delivered the brothers' pizza.

"I hope that pizza gets here soon. I'm starving," Viper said. He checked the digital clock on the wall. It was already after 7:00 p.m.

"Who's going to pick it up this time?" Slammer asked. Even though they could get pizza delivered to the NSA complex, the delivery man could only take the food as far as the perimeter gate. At that point, one of the brothers had to leave the confines of his secluded workplace and drive across the NSA facility to pick up their dinner.

"I'll play you for it. Loser has to get the pizza," Viper said.

Slammer smiled. "You're on."

The two brothers walked to the far side of the room. Tucked away in the corner of their cluttered office space was an air hockey table. It was a great way to blow off steam, but getting the game table into the top-secret NSA facility proved to be difficult. Fortunately, Viper came up with a solution to their dilemma. He convinced a vendor, who supplied computer hardware for the NSA's data centers, to smuggle in pieces of the table mixed in with miscellaneous items. After two weeks of deliveries, the brothers finally had all the parts necessary to secretly reconstruct the game table in their basement office.

Slammer flipped on a ultra-violet light, mounted with duct tape over the air hockey table. The purple light created an eerie glow in the darkness as the brothers took their positions at opposite ends of the table.

"First one to five?" Viper asked.

"We should just play the first goal wins. The pizza will be here soon," Slammer said. He placed the florescent yellow puck on the table and smacked it with his paddle.

The brothers played in silence, completely focusing on the task at hand. From their youth, Slammer and Viper had a fierce sibling rivalry. Although Viper was three years younger, he was naturally bigger and stronger than his older brother. To neutralize his brother's strength advantage, Slammer often relied on his keen intellect. However, it didn't matter if the brothers were playing air hockey, picking up on women, or writing computer code, they were closely matched in everything they did. Their equality created both a jealousy and a bond that was reminiscent of twins.

A loud ring split the silence of the room, startling the brothers in the middle of their game. Viper momentarily lost focus as he turned toward the phone on his desk. Slammer noticed his younger brother's distracted state, and he quickly smashed the puck into Viper's goal.

"Hey, no fair!" Viper shouted like a nine-year-old kid.

Slammer let out a boisterous laugh. "Looks like you're on pizza duty," he said. He left his paddle on the air hockey table and sprinted across the room to answer the phone. He put the call on speaker for his brother to hear. The caller ID showed it was coming from Utah.

"We've been waiting for your call," Slammer said.

"Hey, guys," Tanner said in a weary voice. "Sorry I didn't get back to you sooner."

"We heard about your trip to the hospital. Is your wife okay?" Viper asked.

"She's getting better, but her recovery seems to be going a little slow," Tanner said.

"Did you get our code loaded okay?" Slammer asked, jumping to the business at hand.

"Yes, and I think it's going to work," Tanner said. "You guys did a great job on that."

Slammer took the compliment in stride. "We're staying here all night, so let us know what we can do to help," he said.

"I will," Tanner said. "Are you guys still monitoring the ping signal coming out of China?"

"Yep, and nothing's changed," Viper said. He glanced again at the monitor, listing the packets on the network. "We'll know as soon as the Chinese kill the signal on their side."

"Okay, our system here will be ready to resume the sync signal when that happens," Tanner said. "There might be a few milliseconds delay between the time when the Chinese kill their signal and we start ours," he said.

"That shouldn't be a problem. I don't think the infected computers in the US will recognize the difference," Slammer said.

Viper jumped into the conversation. "That must be some system you have to fake the Chinese signal. We definitely don't have anything like that here."

"Tell you what, if we get by this Dragon Virus with minimal damage, I'll make sure you guys get a trip out here to see our system," Tanner said.

"Sounds good, but make it sometime during the winter. That way we can hit the ski slopes after our visit," Viper said.

"Will do," Tanner said. "Keep me posted if you see any changes from the Chinese."

"We've got you covered," Slammer said before hanging up. His stomach grumbled loudly, signaling it was dinnertime.

"I guess it's time to go get the pizza," Viper said, conceding his loss.

Slammer laughed loudly. "Better luck next time, bro."

NSA DATA CENTER, UTAH

Tanner paused as he stared blankly at his desk. He was burned out, but talking to Slammer and Viper gave him renewed hope. The brothers' eagerness was contagious, and it compelled Tanner to move forward despite his uncertainty. His upcoming actions required him to do something illegal, but first he had an important phone call to make.

Just before Tanner left the hospital that afternoon, the doctor overseeing Megan's care gave Tanner her personal cell phone number as a means for backdoor communication. Taking a slip of paper from his pocket, Tanner dialed the doctor's direct number.

"This is Cassandra," Dr. Tappen said.

"Dr. Tappen, this is Tanner Stone. I'm calling about my wife."

"Good. Do you have a moment to talk?" asked the doctor.

"Yes," Tanner said. "How's my wife?"

"Her condition has stabilized, and she seems to be recovering. We're hoping to remove her from the hyperbaric chamber soon,"

180

Dr. Tappen said and then paused. Tanner noticed the doctor's hesitation, and he prepared for the upcoming negative news.

"But . . . ," Tanner said.

"Your baby isn't doing as well," Cassandra said. "The baby's oxygen level is still low, and her heart rate continues to be quite high. We're concerned that your wife might lose the baby," the doctor said solemnly.

Fear gripped Tanner. "What can we do?"

"With your wife stabilizing now, the pediatrician and obstetrician both feel that we need to deliver the baby. That's the best chance for survival."

Tanner took the negative news as best he could. "What's your plan?"

"Basically, we take your wife out of the hyperbaric chamber, sedate her to make sure she stays unconscious, and perform an emergency C-section. Once the baby is delivered, we'll rush her over to the NICU," Cassandra said. She was, referring to the neonatal intensive care unit that would ensure the baby's survival after delivery

"Megan isn't due for another month. Will the baby be all right?" Tanner asked.

"The hospital has a great level-two NICU. The baby would be born at thirty-six weeks, but the chance of survival that far along is very good," Cassandra said.

Tanner thought about Megan. He didn't like the idea of his wife unconscious and undergoing a C-section alone. On the other hand, the baby wasn't doing well and might not survive much longer inside the womb. It didn't take long for Tanner to reach a conclusion. "Do it. I won't be there, but do what you need to do to save Megan and the baby," he said. He would miss the birth of his first child.

"Okay, we'll do it right now. You'll be a father shortly," Cassandra confidently announced. "What about you, Tanner? How are you holding up?"

"I'm doing okay, but the headache won't go away," he said.

"What about the blurry vision? Is that getting any better?" asked Cassandra.

Tanner hadn't told the others on his team, but in addition to his massive headache, his vision had been slightly out of focus ever since he left the hospital. "It's still about the same," he said.

"That should have started getting better," Cassandra said. She had a bit of concern in her voice. "Are you still really fatigued?"

"Yeah, but I'm running on adrenaline right now, so it's hard to say," Tanner explained. He held the phone receiver between his head and shoulder, and vigorously rubbed both eyes, trying to get his vision to focus.

"Try some coffee. It will speed up your metabolism, and force your body to hasten the dissociation of carbon monoxide from the carboxyhemoglobin."

Tanner had no idea what the doctor had just said, but his response was the same answer for whenever someone offered him some coffee. "I don't drink coffee."

"Oh, yeah, you're a Mormon," Dr. Tappen remembered. She glanced down at Tanner's chart on her desk and verified the letters "LDS" on form. "It's not the coffee, but the caffeine that helps. I'm not sure where you stand on colas, but drinking a Coke or two would help," the doctor said.

"Okay, I'll give it a shot," Tanner said. "Call me back on my cell when you know about the baby."

"Will do," Cassandra said. "Good luck."

"You too," Tanner said. He ended the call, wondering why the doctor had wished him luck, but he didn't have time to ponder the doctor's strange farewell. Glancing at the clock, Tanner noticed it was already 6:00 p.m. He had to leave.

Tanner opened up his desk drawer and took out a spare key to his car. He was always paranoid about locking his keys in the car, and he determined the best way to alleviate that fear was to keep a spare key at work. Tonight the extra key proved to be invaluable.

Tanner grabbed his jacket and walked out of the administrative area of the NSA data center. With his team gone to the viewing, nobody was around to watch Tanner leave, except for the security guard at the front desk. Fortunately, the guard had no idea that Tanner was supposed to remain inside the safety of the data center.

"Good night," the guard said as Tanner walked out the security exit.

"Have a good one," Tanner replied with feigned casualness.

Tanner noticed the sun was already setting as he walked out into the nearly vacant parking lot. His Honda Civic was conveniently parked in the same spot since the previous night when the sheriff's deputy had escorted him home. Tanner started up his car and drove through the exit of Camp Williams, heading south toward Lehi, Utah. He stopped at the first convenience store he saw and bought an energy drink. Guzzling down the amped-up beverage, he noticed a strong taste similar to sugared candy. He kept drinking the liquid, hoping that the enormous amount of caffeine would help with his fuzzy vision and headache. Getting back into his car, he pulled out onto Redwood Road and continued south.

Even though he couldn't see clearly, Tanner knew exactly where to go. His stomach sank at the thought of what he had to do, because breaking into someone's house was a crime, pure and simple. Although Tanner knew the house would be vacant, it still didn't calm his nerves. The home belonged to someone he had trusted completely.

Tanner quickly navigated toward Bryan Morrison's home. Built within the last year, the new home was enormous and immaculate, but Tanner didn't stop his car in the half-circle driveway. Instead, he turned the corner and parked in the cul-de-sac at the end of the street. He took a couple of deep breaths to calm his nerves and noticed that his vision was already starting to sharpen.

Tanner quietly exited his car, glancing around to see if anyone noticed him. He figured that most of the Morrison's neighbors would be going to the viewing tonight, but Tanner still didn't take any unnecessary risks. Casually walking along the sidewalk, he approached the magnificent home and rang the doorbell. To his relief nobody answered. Looking around for any signs of activity, Tanner concluded that he was alone. He reached out and discreetly tried to open the front door but found that it was locked.

Tanner was unfazed by the closed door. He walked indifferently off the front porch and headed diagonally across the front yard toward the sidewalk. Reaching an area of shadows between the Morrison's and their neighbor's house, he darted back toward a gate in the white vinyl fence and into the Morrison's backyard. He quickly closed the gate and crouched down on one knee. He remained perfectly still for almost a minute, listening for anything out of the ordinary. Besides his heavy breathing, the only thing he could hear was a dog barking off in the distance.

Tanner felt more at ease now that he was obscured by the fence and the shadows in the Morrison's backyard. Taking his hand out of his coat pocket, he turned on a small LED flashlight that he kept in the glove box of his car. He carefully approached the rear door of the home. He wasn't worried about an alarm system because he remembered that Bryan had recently said that he still need to find a monitoring company for his new home. Preparing to smash out a window, Tanner was thrilled to see that the rear sliding door was left unlocked. He let himself into the darkened house and was immediately blanketed in silence. He became keenly aware that even the slightest noise would be amplified throughout the entire home.

Tanner started his search for evidence in the master bedroom, assuming that if Bryan had any secret information, he would have hidden it in there. Tanner spent a minute looking through the drawers in the nightstand and dresser before checking under the king-sized bed. Nothing seemed out of the ordinary.

Tanner then turned and headed toward the walk-in closet on the far side of the bedroom, but he stopped in his tracks, shaking his head in frustration. He suddenly realized how stupid his cloak-and-dagger mission was. He had originally hoped to find proof to implicate his former coworker as the mole, but that theory just vaporized. If Bryan had committed espionage, he certainly wouldn't have left any evidence around his house.

Besides underestimating Bryan's intelligence, Tanner had missed a more obvious and vital clue. But he didn't beat himself up too much, writing off the mental error as a side effect from carbon monoxide poisoning. Bryan had died four days ago, yet someone was still feeding up-to-date information to the terrorists. Someone had told Reina that Tanner survived the plane crash, and that was probably the same traitor who also told Reina to use a different encryption method on her emails. In the stillness of the Morrison's home, Tanner realized his mistake. If Bryan was part of the conspiracy, he wasn't acting alone.

APRIL 27, PROVO, UTAH

The room was quiet. Even though people were talking, every sound was dampened beyond normal, in a mysterious way that only seemed possible in a funeral home. A small but diverse mix of people filled the room. Family members of the deceased were dressed in their Sunday best, but the coworkers of the departed wore casual jeans and T–shirts. Adding to the strange allure of the environment, two FBI agents and a lone Secret Service agent casually strolled about, keeping a low profile as they watched over the guests.

Courtney Morrison stood at the front of the room next to an empty casket. She wore a conservative black dress with white pearls. The official viewing for her husband started soon, yet she didn't know how she could handle it. Fortunately, some of Bryan's coworkers had showed up early to help ease the window into the difficult evening.

"We're so sorry for your loss," Sydney said with tears in her eyes. She leaned in and gave Courtney another embrace.

"We're also sorry that we didn't come dressed appropriately. We've all been working overtime, trying to figure out exactly who is responsible for attacking Bryan's flight," Helen said.

Courtney nodded her head. "It's too bad that Tanner and his wife weren't able to make it. Bryan would have wanted Tanner here," she said.

"I know he would have come if he could, but his wife is in labor right now," Mel said.

"I'm so glad that you were able to stop by for a visit. It means a lot to me," Courtney said. She broke down and started crying again.

"We hope to be at the funeral tomorrow afternoon, but with the way things are at work, it might be difficult to make that happen," Helen said.

"Our prayers and thoughts are with you," Sydney said.

The NSA analysts each took a minute to say their final condolences before getting in the car and making their journey back to work. It would be a difficult night for everyone.

———•———

LEHI, UTAH

Tanner's cell phone rang loudly, startling him out of his thoughts. He had completely forgotten to silence his phone before breaking into the Morrison's home. Although there was little chance that anyone outside the enormous house had heard the ring, Tanner felt like it was loud enough to wake the entire neighborhood.

He quickly grabbed the cell phone out of his coat pocket and silenced the ringer. He then looked at the caller ID and clearly saw that the call had come from Dr. Tappen. His vision was definitely getting better.

"Hello," Tanner answered with a whisper. He stepped into the master bedroom closet and shut the door.

"Tanner, this is Dr. Tappen at the hospital. I have someone who wants to say hi to you." At first, it was difficult for Tanner to hear anything on the receiver. Then, he recognized the faint noise of a baby crying. "Congratulations. You're a father," she said.

Tanner was awestruck. He didn't know what to say. Feeling like he had just woken up from a bad dream, he muttered out a response. "Is everything okay?"

"Yes, everything is fine. Your daughter was born at 6:18 p.m., but I had to wait until the NICU got her cleaned up and in the incubator before they'd let me see her," Dr. Tappen said. "She's going to be okay."

The reality of Tanner's new fatherhood sank in as tears welled up in his eyes. "What about Megan? Is she okay?"

"She's still sedated and unconscious, but that isn't necessarily such a bad thing after a C-section," Cassandra explained. "The good news is that she's is not in the hyperbaric chamber any more. As soon as the baby was born, your wife's vital signs all returned to normal."

Tanner's legs felt weak, and he quickly knelt down on one knee to stabilize himself. He was a father! In the midst of the horrible, messed-up events of the past week, a ray of light broke through the ominous clouds. Tanner's emotions suddenly overcame him, and he wept with joy.

"Tanner, are you okay?" Dr. Tappen asked.

"Yeah, I'm all right. Just feeling a little overwhelmed right now," he said.

Tanner imagined what his new daughter looked like. He longed to hold her in his arms. "Thanks for calling me, doc," he said.

"You're welcome. I'll call you back if we see any changes with your wife," Dr. Tappen said. She disconnected the call.

In a closet at the Morrison's home, Tanner quietly pondered his fatherhood. Even though the birth of his daughter came in a completely unexpected way, Tanner embraced the moment. With one knee already on the ground, he thanked God for the birth of his new daughter and for the improvement in his wife's health. Tears of gratitude rolled off Tanner's checks as he asked God for strength to assume the new the responsibilities in his life. Ending his humble prayer, Tanner remained motionless for several moments before standing up. It was time to get back to the data center.

APRIL 27, SALT LAKE CITY, UTAH

The charcoal-gray van waited for the red street light at the corner of 7800 South and Redwood Road. The vehicle didn't look any different than thousands of other Ford 350s in the Salt Lake Valley. Even a very observant onlooker would fail to give this vehicle a second glance. But the unassuming exterior of van was just a facade, hiding the van's amazing contents.

The driver was a forty-two-year-old FBI agent in plain clothes. Slightly overweight with shaggy hair and a goatee, Agent Cameron Skidmore didn't fit the profile of a typical cop. As an undercover agent, he wasn't supposed to be noteworthy. He was supposed to blend in and be anonymous. Obscured in the back of the van, two other men prepared for their upcoming surveillance work. One was a seasoned FBI agent with twenty-five years of experience. The other was much younger and not a sworn agent, but part of the technical staff that supplemented many of the functions at the FBI field office.

"Okay, let's get online," Agent Lloyd McMahon said. When it came to understanding the law, especially surveillance, there were few people better than Lloyd McMahon. "I'm on it," the technician answered. Just shy of thirty years old, the younger man was a whiz when it came to operating the gadgets in the surveillance van. The light turned green, and Cameron nonchalantly drove the van through the intersection and into a grocery store parking lot. He spoke out loud, but nobody was in the passenger seat. If a passerby happened to be looking at Cameron, it would have appeared that he was talking to himself or maybe to someone else on a hand-free cell phone. In reality, Cameron was speaking into a hidden microphone, updating his teammates riding in the back of the van.

"I just pulled into a grocery store parking lot," he said.

"Roger that," said Lloyd from his position the back of the van. "We're warming up the gear now."

The rear of the surveillance van was amazing. Gray carpet covered the floor and walls, and two leather chairs provided a comfortable workspace for the surveillance crew. Sitting in one of the chairs, Lloyd felt like he was piloting the Starship Enterprise. On a small desk were two laptop computers and a color printer. Four different audio recording devices were obscured on the sides of the van, each one able to eavesdrop on conversations at different ranges. Two DVRs inside the van were connected to hidden video cameras for recording suspects. The coolest feature, by far, was a 360-degree camera that popped up out of the roof of the van. The camera was similar in function to a periscope on a submarine, although much smaller and less obtrusive. To people on the outside of the van, the camera had the appearance of a flat Frisbee.

"I'm heading into the store to grab some food. Be back in a minute," Cameron said. It would be too obvious if he just sat in the driver's seat all the time, so part of his cover was to behave like a normal citizen.

"Bring back some doughnuts," the young technician shouted into his microphone.

Lloyd rolled his eyes. "Are we ready to go yet?" he asked.

"I'm just about online." The technician finished entering a command on one of the laptops. He was starting up a special program called Stingray that they used to track cell phone communication. Although they didn't know when Reina might use her wireless modem again, the surveillance crew wanted to be ready to pinpoint her location when she did.

·————·

NSA DATA CENTER, UTAH

Tanner was relieved to see that the rest of his team hadn't returned from the viewing when he pulled his Honda Civic back into the same parking spot at the data center. As he quickly returned to his desk, he thought about who might be the mole. He hadn't been seated long before his secure, gray phone started ringing. Tanner checked the caller ID and saw that the call was coming from the lobby inside the NSA complex.

"Hello," Tanner answered anonymously.

"Tanner, we're back, and we brought you some food," Helen said. "We're heading over to the conference room right now. Come get something to eat."

Tanner didn't feel like eating. He wasn't sure if his stomach was still upset from the carbon monoxide poisoning, or if he was nauseated from the thought of another mole running around. In the end he decided it didn't matter how his body felt. There was work to do, and he needed to be with his peers. "Okay. I'll meet you there in a second," he said.

APRIL 27, SALT LAKE CITY, UTAH

R eina waited anxiously, wondering what to do next. She hadn't seen Rey in almost a year, and she could hardly contain her excitement. Unfortunately, her anticipated rendezvous wasn't scheduled for another three hours, and the clock seemed to be moving stubbornly slow.

Rey was much more than just Reina's partner in crime. Rey was her older brother, and in many ways, he was more secretive and elusive than his sister. After their parents' tragic death in Ciudad Juarez, Reina and Rey were adopted by their uncle, Yang Dao. Reina moved to China while her brother went to live with Yang Dao's extended family in San Francisco. Rey spent his teenage years in California, returning to China to visit his sister during the holidays.

After Rey graduated from high school, Yang Dao pulled some strings with shady contacts he knew in the United States. Rey was quickly accepted to college. While he was at the university, Yang Dao worked his magic again and got his nephew full-fledged US citizenship. With the forged documents all in order, Rey was now an

American, and able to secure a job within the United States government. For the past several years, Rey had been Yang Dao's number one spy. Rey had access to vast amounts of classified data, and he frequently forwarded the information back to his uncle in China.

Reina stared at the clock on the wall. It was still two and a half hours until her meeting with her brother. She decided she needed to burn off some of her nervous energy. She put on a pair of tennis shoes and a jacket and then left her apartment for a brisk evening walk to the grocery store.

———•———

Agent Skidmore stood in the checkout line with an arm full of food. It wasn't a healthy selection, but the snacks were perfect for reconnaissance duty. A couple of bags of chips, chewy red licorice, beef jerky, doughnuts, and a twelve-pack of soda would hold the surveillance crew over for a while.

Cameron was in line behind a young woman with black hair. He couldn't quite see her face, but he imagined she was very attractive. Although she appeared to be much younger than the FBI agent, Cameron still liked to think he had "game" with the ladies. Not in any hurry, he decided to strike up a conversation.

"The bakery must be really good here," he said to the unknown woman. She held a blueberry muffin in her hand.

Reina turned around and smiled faintly to the chubby man behind her. He was tall and muscular, but the potbelly around his waist said that he needed to take better care of himself. "I like the muffins. I come here a couple of times a week," she said.

"What's the best kind?" asked Cameron. He noticed a faint scar that ran across the younger woman's face. It didn't really detract from her beauty, but he wondered what had happened.

"I usually get the bran muffins, but this one looked better tonight," Reina said. She wasn't really in the mood to talk, much less flirt with the man behind her. She paid cash for her dessert and then spoke in parting to the stranger. "Have a good evening," she said.

"You too," Cameron said. He briefly watched as she walked

toward the exit. He then paid for his snacks and made his way out of the supermarket toward the surveillance van.

Cameron hopped into the driver's seat. "I've got food and drinks," he said into his hidden radio.

The rear compartment of the surveillance van was separated from the driver by a steel wall. At the base of the divider was a small hatch where items could be passed back and forth. Upon hearing that Cameron had brought food, Lloyd opened the two-by-two-foot door to receive the goodies.

"Thanks, Cam," Lloyd said. "We got something for you. Here's a photo of our suspect, just in case you see anything out there." He passed an eight-by-ten picture of Reina back through the hatch.

Cameron reached down and took the color photo from Lloyd's hand. Holding the picture up to the overhead light in the cab, Cameron instantly recognized the young woman's face.

"I just saw her in the store. She was in line right in front of me!" Cameron shouted.

"Who?" Lloyd asked over the microphone. The hatch between the front and rear of the van was now closed.

"Our suspect. She was in the store with me!" Cameron said. He quickly jumped out of the driver's seat and sprinted into the parking lot, but it was too late. The mysterious woman had already vanished into the night.

———•———

NSA DATA CENTER, UTAH

Tanner ate a quick dinner with his teammates in the conference room. Helen ordered takeout from a local Mexican restaurant and picked up the food on the way back from the viewing. The meal was good, but it didn't quite compare to the chili verde Tanner had learned to love while living in New Mexico.

"What happened to the other two?" Tanner asked. He noticed that Sara and Adam hadn't return with the rest of the group.

"Sara wanted to get back to the FBI office," Helen stated. "And Adam has an early morning flight back to DC tomorrow."

Mel expanded on the situation. "The Secret Service folks think they can follow the investigation from DC just as well as here."

Sydney shook her head in frustration. "They come into our building, tell us our data isn't sufficient, and then leave." Her frustration was evident to everyone in the conference room.

"That sounds about right," Rachel said.

Helen quietly listened to her team's banter. They were a tight group, even with the loss of Bryan. She just hoped they could stay focused because they weren't out of this mess yet. "Let's plan our next steps. We need to be ready to assist the FBI folks at a moment's notice. We should probably work in shifts throughout the night so we can get some sleep," she said.

The team decided on strategy to work around the clock to provide accurate and up-to-date information to the FBI. Rachel and Sidney volunteered to work the first shift since they had originally started the decoding process of Reina's emails. They would monitor QC until 2:00 a.m. At that time, Mel and Helen would take over, allowing Tanner to continue sleeping through the rest of the night. Chad volunteered to stay in the team's main conference room and listen for the phones.

As everyone finished up their dinner, Tanner took the opportunity to give a personal update. He didn't like to talk about himself, but he couldn't keep the good news bottled up anymore. Before everyone headed out to their assigned duties, Tanner informed his close friends that he was now a father and that Megan was recovering quickly. The lingering sadness from the viewing seemed to dissipate as Tanner's coworkers smiled and congratulated him. For the first time in days, the NSA analysts felt like they might actually make it through the miserable week.

———•———•———

FBI FIELD OFFICE, UTAH

Thirty miles north of the NSA data center, the conference room at the FBI field office bustled with commotion. With no less than a dozen people working in the command center, Derek tried to maintain order among the chaos. He was extremely grateful to have Sara back, and even more grateful to be rid of the Secret Service. While Derek didn't have anything against the ECTF agents, he didn't want them loitering about the area either. This was clearly an FBI investigation, and Derek didn't see a reason for Todd and Adam to stick around.

Derek prepared for a long night. Even with Sara helping out, he knew he wouldn't get any sleep. Derek found new resolve, however, when the surveillance team announced they had a positive sighting of Reina. Even though the trio didn't see where Reina had gone, they were confident she was close by. Unfortunately, the FBI couldn't go knocking on everybody's door just yet. They needed Reina to use her wireless modem again to pinpoint her exact location.

Despite assistance from the State Department and CIA, nobody could positively identify Reina. She was a ghost, and it was maddening to Derek that someone could still exist completely off the grid. From the day of their birth, everyone began a long and complex identification trail. Birth certificates, vaccination records, driver's licenses, high school diplomas, marriage certificates, and passports always provided a physical record of someone. Living anonymously in a modern society was extremely difficult to do—unless a person was an illegal foreigner. Derek felt that was likely the case with Reina. Unfortunately, the FBI's turf was domestic crime, and Derek didn't have access to foreign documents or records to see what other countries knew about Reina.

Derek pondered his dilemma when he suddenly felt his cell phone vibrating. Looking down at the device, he noticed a quick text message:

Call me, privately—Tanner

Derek noticed the text message included a different call back number than he was used to. He excused himself from the others in the conference room. "I'll be back in a second," he said.

APRIL 27, NSA DATA CENTER, UTAH

Rachel and Sydney stared at the glowing monitor as if they were telepathically absorbing the digital bits of information on the screen. It was past 8:00 p.m., and the two analysts were settled into their six–hour shift. Neither of the women stirred as they eagerly waited for QC's output from the first encrypted email. The decryption process would be done any minute now.

"Come on," Rachel said, willing the supercomputer to move faster. "You're almost there." All three emails from Reina were being simultaneously decrypted, but the oldest message was the furthest along.

The decrypted email flashed up on the main monitor. "It's done!" Sydney yelled. Both analysts quietly read the message, looking for signs of clues:

Rey,
I received your message about Tanner Stone. I have already

driven by his home, and I don't think this job will be very dif-
ficult. I'll do it tonight, and in a way that can only be thought
of as an accident. Don't worry. I'll be very discreet.
    Love,
    Reina

"Well, there's no doubt now they were going after Tanner," Rachel said dryly.

Even though the attack had already happened, the message still sent chills up Rachel's spine. She looked over at Sydney for her input, but she wasn't paying attention. Her eyes were focused on the large monitor mounted on the wall in front of them.

With the first email decrypted, something magical happened. QC now understood the complete cipher that Reina had used to encrypt her messages. With the decryption key stored in memory, QC instantly unlocked the contents of the other two emails. The other two messages quickly displayed side-by-side on the monitor.

Rachel and Sydney read the contents of the last two emails, digesting the information. The tones of these messages were very different from the first. Instead of the sterile and straight-forward communication in her first email, Reina seemed to be communicating with someone she highly respected. These last letters were also addressed to someone named Bobo instead of Rey.

"We need to show these to Helen," Sydney said. The contents of the emails were both fascinating and condemning.

"Yeah, that's an excellent idea," Rachel said, starting up the classified printer

$$\bullet\!\!-\!\!-\!\!\bullet$$

FBI FIELD OFFICE, UTAH

At the same time that Rachel and Sydney were reading the secret contents of Reina's emails, Derek was having a private telephone conversation with Tanner.

"I know it seems farfetched, but I think Bryan might be involved in this mess," Tanner said over the phone.

"You think Bryan is the mole?" Derek asked. He wasn't completely shocked at Tanner's allegation. As a trained investigator, Derek knew elaborate crimes often required help from someone on the inside to be successful.

"I doubt he's *the* mole, but my gut tells me that Bryan was involved somehow," Tanner said. "Nobody knew more about the Dragon Virus than Bryan, but I can't believe that he intentionally sold out his country. Maybe he was blackmailed into leaking information or something like that," Tanner said.

Derek could tell that it bothered Tanner to accuse his former coworker. Nevertheless, the allegations had some merit. Blackmail or financial troubles were the two biggest reasons why a person would commit treason.

"I'll have Sara look into it. Maybe someone found a way to manipulate Bryan," Derek said. "In the meantime, let's keep this quiet. If Bryan was working with someone on the inside, we don't want to scare away that person."

"Sounds good. I'll let you know if I think of anything else," Tanner said.

"Okay, I've got to get back to the war room," Derek said. He ended the call.

Derek pondered Tanner's theory on his walk back to the conference room. When he arrived a few moments later, he was greeted by a wild commotion among his peers.

"The NSA cracked Reina's emails. They just faxed us a copy over," Sara said excitedly. She handed Derek a paper. He took the document and read the three separate emails:

Rey,

I received your message about Tanner Stone. I have already driven by his home, and I don't think this job will be very difficult. I'll do it tonight, and in a way that can only be thought of as an accident. Don't worry. I'll be very discreet.

Love,
Reina

Bobo,

I have been away much too long. My heart aches for my homeland. It has been my privilege to serve you and our country on such an important assignment. I will be home soon, and I would very much like to go with you on a vacation to the Chongwu Peninsula. It is one of my favorite places on earth.

With love,
Yang Qiao

Dearest Bobo,

I received an important message that Rey wants to meet with me. My heart leaps with joy to see him again, but I'm confused as to why he insists on meeting this late in our operation. Have I done something wrong? I feel like I have completed all my assignments faithfully and professionally. Did I not cause the crash as you directed? Did I not exact the revenge on Jeff Kessler that you wanted? Have I not killed the two NSA analysts that discovered our secret? I love you dearly, and I would never do anything to disappoint you.

With love,
Yang Qiao

Derek shook his head in disbelief as he finished reading the emails. The details of the messages were inconceivable. "We've hit the jackpot," he said. He couldn't believe his luck.

"I know," Sara said. "The emails are very clear. Reina takes credit for everything from the terrorist attack on Flight 2512 to the attempted murder of Tanner. It's all in there."

An anonymous agent spoke out, asking an interesting question. "Doesn't it seem strange that she was so clear and direct in her emails?"

"Maybe not," Derek said. "She probably didn't use code words or phrases because she assumed her encrypted emails were secure."

Sara turned to the group in the conference room. "Does anyone know where the Chongwu Peninsula is?"

"I'm working on it right now," someone said from the other end of the large table.

Derek walked over to the whiteboard on the wall. He wrote "Reina" in the middle of the whiteboard and drew a circle around it. Then on either side of the name, he wrote "Rey" and "Bobo." He connected all three names together with a line.

"Okay, we've got three people who are somehow tied to each other," Derek said. "From the tone of these emails, it sounds like Rey is a peer or partner to Reina, while this Bobo person is someone completely different."

"Who's Bobo?" Sara asked. The entire group of FBI agents and staff were focused on Derek, brainstorming together to find answers.

A rookie agent on the other side of the room spoke out. "Bobo is Chinese for uncle," he said. The rookie was fresh out of the FBI academy in Quantico, Virginia. Until now, he hadn't said a word during the entire investigation.

"What?" Derek asked. He turned around to see who had spoken.

"Yeah, it's what someone would call his father's brother in Chinese," the rookie said with a little more confidence.

"How do you know that?" Sara asked.

"I served a mission for my church in Taiwan. But that was eight years ago, so I'm rusty now," he answered.

"Is Bobo Reina's uncle?" Sara asked.

"I'd think so. The way Reina phrases her letters to Bobo is very endearing. It's just how a young Chinese person would address her elder."

Derek wrote the word "uncle" above the name Bobo on the whiteboard. "What's this word *Yang Qiao*?" he asked, trying to pronounce the name at the bottom of the emails.

"That's just a name. There's probably not any significance to it," the rookie said.

Sara asked a question. "The emails all came from the same computer. Do you think Reina is also Yang Qiao?"

"Reina is Hispanic, not Asian," Derek countered. "But I guess she could have multiple aliases."

Another staffer interrupted the conversation. "Sir, I just found some info on the Chongwu Peninsula," he said. "It's in southeast China. It's a popular vacation area with a famous beach."

"Reina might not be Chinese, but she's obviously spent a lot of time in China," Sara said. "She references going back to the beach with her uncle."

"Is this Bobo character Chinese or Hispanic?" Derek asked out loud.

"It could just be a bunch of aliases meant to throw us off," Sara said.

Derek nodded his head in agreement. The emails from Reina were fascinating, but Derek needed expertise that he didn't have in this office. "Let's make copies of these emails and send them back to headquarters. I want to get one of our linguists and psychologists to analyze them."

"I'll take care of that," the rookie agent said. He stood up to take the paper from the senior FBI agent.

"I also want these scanned in digitally so we can put them on the projector," Derek said. He then turned to Sara and whispered. "I need to talk with you in my office."

APRIL 27, SALT LAKE CITY, UTAH

Despite what Hollywood glamorized in the movies, surveillance duty was repetitive and boring. Few people understood that better than Special Agent McMahon. In his thirty years of service with the FBI, Lloyd had spent weeks of his life in the back of a cramped surveillance van, waiting for the scarce moments of action in a prolonged stakeout.

Even though Cameron had met Reina face-to-face, the two FBI agents hadn't been able to glean any further information on their suspect after interviewing the employees at the supermarket. They had only learned that Reina visited the grocery store several times a week, and that she always paid for her food in cash. She was friendly and quiet, yet nobody seemed to know her real name or where she lived.

With no other leads to follow, Lloyd and his surveillance team casually meandered around the area of 7800 South Redwood Road. Cameron kept a close lookout for their suspect as he drove the charcoal-gray van through different residential areas. In the back of the vehicle, the technician monitored the Stingray cell phone tracking application, patiently waiting for Reina to use her wireless modem again.

"There must be a dozen apartment complexes within a mile's radius of here," Cameron said into his hidden microphone.

"That means we got our work cut out for us," Lloyd said from the rear of the van. "Criminals flock to apartments like vultures to roadkill."

Because of the constant change in occupancy, apartments were an ideal place for illegal activity. Although the situation had improved somewhat after September 11, when the government mandated that landlords have identification for their tenants, it was still possible for a criminal to get a lease with fake credentials.

"We need her to use her laptop again so we can get a trace," Cameron said.

"There's nothing we can do about that. We'll just keep driving around in the meantime. Maybe we might get lucky and spot Reina again," Lloyd said.

———•———

It was time for her rendezvous. Reina anxiously left her apartment, dressed in casual and unassuming clothes. Her dark green jacket and blue jeans blended in with the foot traffic of her anonymous neighbors. She walked across the grassy commons area of her apartment complex and veered toward her car. She quickly got in the black Dodge Charger and drove away, passing a charcoal-gray van as it pulled into the parking lot.

Reina went east toward Interstate-15. Her meeting with Rey would happen in an open area with lots of people. She continued the same direction until she came to a light-rail station. Officially called "Trax" by the Utah Transit Authority, this light-rail system crisscrossed the Salt Lake Valley in all major directions. Reina pulled into the Trax parking lot just as a train arrived and released a dozen commuters. She didn't get out of her car, but only unlocked the passenger door and waited. A few moments passed, and a man approached the Dodge Charger from the rear. Rey quickly got in the passenger's seat without looking at Reina or saying a word.

Reina waited until she was completely out of the parking lot and back on the main street before she looked at Rey. He was dressed in casual clothes, with a dark jacket, a baseball cap, and a fake moustache. Looking into the man's empty brown eyes, Reina quickly recognized her sibling.

"*Hermano*," she endearingly said. She hadn't seen her brother in over a year. He appeared older, with faint areas of gray beginning to show on the side of his short black hair. He also appeared to have gained a little weight from his desk job.

"*Querida, Hermana*," Rey said. He leaned over and gave his sister a half-hug. It was indeed good to see her again. He switched to English, feeling more comfortable speaking the language he used day in and day out. "Keep driving. We've got to move quickly."

"What's going on?" Reina asked. She was surprised by her brother's unexpected visit so late in the operation. She was under the assumption that she wouldn't see him until after the launch of the computer virus.

"The Americans know about the virus, and they've figured out a way to stop it from working," Rey said.

"How is that possible?" asked Reina.

"They have a new computer system that can take secrets right off the Internet. In fact, it's the exact same computer that Uncle tried to steal the plans for two years ago," Rey added. "The computer system is fully operational, and until we can shut it down, our plan will not succeed."

"Does Uncle know about it?" Reina asked.

"Yes, I gave him a brief update. I had to send it in a diplomatic pouch because the Americans can read all our email. That was a couple of days ago," Rey said.

Reina accelerated the car as it headed southbound on I-15. She made sure to obey all the speed limits and traffic laws. Now was not the time to get involved with the local cops. Reina's fake identification was a good cover, but her brother's identification was very real and very legitimate. It had to be for his employment with the US government.

"What do we do now?" Reina asked.

"I already have a plan in place. Tang Ju-Long is on his way out to help us," Rey said, naming the creator of the computer virus.

Reina was surprised that her brother had used Tang Ju-Long's real name and that the architect of the virus was actually coming to America. "Does Uncle know that *he* is coming?" Reina still didn't feel comfortable speaking Tang Ju-Long's real name out loud.

"No," Rey said. "I knew that if I asked our uncle, he would reject my idea. I had Tang Ju-Long leave without anyone's knowledge."

"When does he get here?" Reina asked. She wasn't sure that it was such a good idea to remove Tang Ju-Long from the safety of China's borders and put him into the lion's den. Nevertheless, Reina completely trusted her older brother, and she decided to go along with his plan.

"I need you to pick Tang Ju-Long up at the airport at midnight. Then, both of you will meet me back at this location," Rey said. He handed his sister a piece of paper with a hotel's address and room number on it. Rey paused for a second before continuing. "Do you know that Tanner Stone is still alive?"

"What?" Reina asked in shock. "That's impossible. I had someone double-check at the hospital."

"It was a cover up. The authorities lied about his death," Rey said matter-of-factly.

Reina gripped the steering wheel in frustration. It wasn't her fault that Tanner had escaped his first death when Flight 2512 crashed, but the fact that she had failed to kill Tanner the second time was humiliating. "Where is he now? I'll finish the job immediately," she said.

"That time has passed," Rey countered bluntly. Then, feeling like he was being too hard on his little sister, he changed his tone. "Don't worry. We need Tanner alive now. My plan depends on it."

Rey quickly highlighted the rest of his strategy as his sister drove the Dodge Charger. When Reina stopped at the Trax station further down the road, she felt like her brother's plan would work. The two siblings had to move fast, but there was a good chance they could still get the stealthy virus to launch tomorrow at noon.

"Take care," Reina said. She gave her brother a prolonged hug.

"See you in a couple of hours," Rey said. He got out of the car and headed toward the crowd of people on the train platform. Checking his watch, he noticed the entire trip with his sister took less than fifteen minutes.

———•———

Special Agent Cannon and the others in the conference room listened to the briefing from FBI headquarters in Washington. A linguist, who was fluent in Chinese, verified the meaning of the word *Bobo* and concurred that Reina was most likely writing to her uncle. A psychologist then briefed the FBI agents, highlighting something that was originally missed. Going back-and-forth between the context of the emails and the digitally enhanced picture of Reina, the psychologist stated that Reina was both part Chinese and part Latino.

"How sure are you of this?" Derek asked.

"I'd say 80 percent or higher. Our technicians ran this enhanced photo through our facial recognition software. Reina definitely has physical features from both races."

"Is Rey also part of the family?" another agent asked. It was one of the many theories the FBI agents had tossed around.

"It's impossible to tell. I'd need a photo or an email response from Rey to analyze his writing style," the psychologist said. "Do you have anything like that?"

"Unfortunately, no," Derek said. He rubbed his weary eyes. It was approaching midnight. "Please let us know if you think of anything we might have missed."

"I will," the psychologist said.

Derek ended the call and stood up to stretch his legs. Sara wasn't in the conference room, because she was in her office working on a special assignment from Derek. He decided now would be a good time for a visit.

"What have you found?" Derek asked as he quietly stepped into Sara's office and closed the door.

"It looks like Bryan passed his annual poly test. That was over a year ago, and he was due for another one," Sara said. She was referring to the mandatory, annual polygraph test for all NSA employees.

"What about his financial situation? Have you pulled his bank records?" Derek asked. Fortunately for the FBI, they didn't need a search warrant to get the information on Bryan. As part of the condition for getting a top-secret clearance, all NSA employees agreed to background checks and personal investigations at any time.

"Yes, it looks like he received an inheritance from his grandmother last year, but it wasn't very much," Sara said.

"Does he have any judgments against him?" Derek asked. A court order might show if Bryan was in financial trouble.

Sara checked the computer monitor on her desk. "Nope," she said.

Derek thought about another area to check. "What about his taxes?"

"They're all paid in full," Sara said. "Besides a huge mortgage, his only other debts are a couple of auto loans."

Derek nodded his head in agreement as he looked at the bank statements on the monitor. "Anything else that seems suspicious?" he asked.

Sara shook her head. "Not really."

"Well, keep digging. I think Tanner is on the right track with another mole running around out there. We just need to determine if there's a link between that mole and Bryan Morrison," Derek said.

He left the room and started heading back downstairs. On the way, he stopped by the break room. He needed some Tylenol for his increasing headache.

APRIL 28, SALT LAKE INTERNATIONAL AIRPORT, UTAH

It was just after midnight when a black Dodge Charger pulled into the passenger pickup zone at the Salt Lake International Airport. Reina had arrived early enough to make sure she was on time, but not too early to draw unwanted attention. After all, it was just five days ago that she had brought down Flight 2512, and the airport was still under very tight security.

Although Reina had never met Tang Ju-Long, she quickly identified him as he exited the international terminal of the airport. With a Yankees baseball hat, reading glasses, and tan overcoat, he was dressed just like Rey had said he would be. Tang Ju-Long was older than Reina had envisioned, and she decided that he was probably in his early fifties. He appeared lankly and uncoordinated, punctuated by the difficultly he was having with his luggage, but Reina didn't get out of the car to help him. She knew that the airport had hundreds of surveillance cameras, and she wanted to remain out of sight from the prying eyes of the local authorities.

Reina just popped open the trunk and let Tang Ju-Long manage the bags himself.

After loading his stuff in the trunk, Tang Ju-Long came around the side of the Dodge Charger and opened the passenger door. "Is this the right car?" he asked in Chinese.

"Get in!" Reina ordered in fluent English. She shook her head in disgust. Obviously, this idiot was a computer nerd and not a spy. No secret agent would break cover by asking such a stupid question in his native tongue.

Tang Ju-Long sheepishly got in the car. He hadn't even buckled his seat belt before Reina drove away. "I'm sorry, but I didn't know who was picking me up. I was only told to look for a car that matched the description of this one," he said in English.

"You're not in China anymore," Reina said. Her voice had a sharp edge. "The Americans are lazy but smart. They're very good at figuring stuff out," she warned.

The car drove across an overpass and away from the airport. Checking the rearview mirror, she decided nobody was following them. She allowed herself to relax for the moment.

"Can you please tell me what this is about?" Tang Ju-Long asked. He had never met the mysterious woman before, and while she had Asian eyes, she looked more Hispanic than Chinese.

"The less you know, the better," Reina said. "But it seems your computer program needs some last-second modifications."

Tang Ju-Long nodded his head in silence as he stared out the window into the dark night. While he wasn't athletic or sophisticated, he was bright. He had figured something was wrong with his computer virus routine, but he wondered why he had to fly all the way to America to fix it. He could have easily made the modifications from China.

———•———

NSA DATA CENTER, UTAH

The activity level at the NSA data center had slowed down dramatically. After cracking the code on Reina's encrypted emails almost five hours ago, the members of the QC team hadn't seen much action. Rachel and Sydney passed their time in the Chamber, watching for any new messages from Reina. Their shift would end soon, and they eagerly waited for their peers to take over.

In the team room on the first floor, Helen, Mel, and Chad tried to get some rest. Unfortunately, the conference room chairs reclined awkwardly and didn't provide much comfort. Helen had found a better sleeping arrangement for Tanner, who was in desperate need of more rest than the others. He was sound asleep on the couch in the women's restroom on the second floor. Helen wasn't worried that anyone would disturb Tanner at two o'clock in the morning. But just to be sure, she did put a note on the restroom door as a precaution.

"I can't get comfortable enough to doze off for more than just a few minutes," Mel said as he readjusted his chair.

"You could just lie down on the floor like Chad," Helen said. She was too wired up to sleep, but apparently Chad didn't have that problem. Curled up in the fetal position under the large oak table, he slept like a baby.

"I'm too old to sleep on a bare floor," Mel said. "It would kill my back. Besides, our shift starts soon. I'm going to get something to drink."

"Get me something too," Helen said. Food or drink wasn't permitted in the Chamber, but that rule was completely disregarded tonight. Without something to keep the analysts awake, nobody would be able to monitor the supercomputer for very long.

Mel walked out just as Rachel and Sydney strolled into the conference room. "Your turn," Sydney said with a yawn.

"Any word from the FBI?" Rachel asked. She took a seat in an empty chair and kicked off her shoes. She propped her feet up on the table and leaned back against the wall.

"Nothing in the past hour," Helen said.

"Is Tanner still out, like Chad?" Sydney asked. She pointed to her coworker under the table.

"Yes, and we're going to let him sleep as long as possible," Helen said. She stood up and smoothed out the wrinkles in her skirt.

"What should we do?" Sydney asked.

"There's not much we can do unless the FBI calls for help. In the meantime, try to get some sleep," Helen said. She walked out of the conference room and disappeared into the hallway.

● ——————— ●

SHAOXING, CHINA

It was 4:00 p.m. on Friday. Even though it was the weekend, Yang Dao worked a normal business day. The lack of communication from his operatives in America was disturbing. He knew email wasn't an option because they feared the Americans would eavesdrop on their conversation. However, his spy cell had access to diplomatic couriers. While that was a slower method of communication, it was very secure.

Yang Dao stood in the back of the room, nervously watching the technical staff in the operations center. He looked up at the digital clock mounted on the wall. The clock counted down the time until the launch of the computer virus. The red numbers glowed brightly, showing seven hours and forty-five minutes. His staff had assured the general that everything was ready for launch, yet Yang Dao felt uneasy. *Have I overlooked something?* He decided he needed to reach out to the virus's creator for advice. Yang Dao excused himself from the presence of his subordinates and went upstairs to his office to call Tang Ju-Long.

APRIL 28, FBI FIELD OFFICE, UTAH

Agent Cannon's cell phone rang, interrupting his conversation with Sara. Looking at the caller ID on the phone in his hand, he didn't recognize the number. He answered with a cautious "hello" while Sara watched her partner for signs of who might be calling.

"Good news," Derek said after ending the call. "That was the hospital. Tanner's wife is awake and recovering in a normal room. She wants to see her husband."

"Is it too risky for him to go?" Sara asked.

"I don't think so. We can escort Tanner to the hospital and take him in the back way, so it should be fine," Derek said.

Sara thought of an idea. "I'll pick him up and head over. It will give me a chance to ask Tanner if he has any more information about Bryan Morrison."

"Can you stay awake for the drive down?" Derek asked. It had been a long day and night for both of them.

"I'll be okay. My internal clock is kicking in with the start of a new day," Sara said. "I'll give you a call when I get there."

"Okay, get a Suburban and pick him up. I'll call Helen and let her know you're on the way."

⸻

Tanner didn't want to wake up. He felt someone shaking his arm, but he pushed away the annoyance and turned over on his side.

"Tanner, get up," Sydney said. She vigorously shook Tanner, but he still wouldn't budge. She decided to try another tactic. Going over to the sink in the bathroom, she cupped her hand and filled it with cold water. She then sprinkled the liquid on Tanner's face in an unfriendly manner.

"What the—" Tanner shouted as he flinched with the rude awaking. He brushed the water off his face, looking for the offender.

"Sorry, but I couldn't wake you up," Sydney said. Tanner focused his blurry eyes on his coworker. He was about to say something, but Sydney beat him to the punch.

"The hospital just called. Your wife is awake. She wants to see you!" Sydney announced excitedly.

Tanner shot straight up. "What time is it?"

"It's five-thirty in the morning. The FBI is on their way to take you to the hospital right now."

Tanner followed Sydney downstairs to the main conference room. He was surprised to see all his teammates when he arrived.

"Isn't it wonderful?" Helen asked. Her eyes looked tired and heavy. "First your baby is born, and now your wife is awake." She gave Tanner a quick hug of celebration.

"When did she wake up?" Tanner asked.

"About an hour ago. She's been asking for you," Helen said.

"Am I going over right now?"

"Yes. Agent Heywood is on her way to escort you," Helen said.

"What about you guys?" Tanner asked.

Mel responded before Helen could. "We'll be fine. Besides, the only thing you've been doing for the past six hours is holding down a couch," he said.

"Thanks, everyone. I appreciate it," Tanner said. He raced off to his desk to get his jacket. Helen then walked Tanner out to the lobby.

"Take as long as you need with your wife and baby. We'll hold down the fort while you're gone," she assured him.

"I guess you can call me at the hospital if you need to," Tanner said. Helen gave him one final hug, and Tanner slipped out into the early morning darkness.

The FBI Suburban was already waiting for Tanner in the parking lot. He ran up to the SUV just as the rear passenger door opened from the inside. Tanner jumped in and closed the door before realizing the woman sitting next to him wasn't Agent Heywood. It was Reina dressed in a blonde wig and wearing Sara's clothes.

It took Tanner a moment to realize that he was being kidnapped. He reached for the door handle to escape but found that it was locked from the outside. He hastily turned around to fight back, but recoiled when he saw Reina pointing a large, black gun at his head.

A familiar voice called out from the driver's seat. "Relax, Tanner." Tanner looked at the driver and dropped his jaw in shock. It was Adam Crawford of the Secret Service.

APRIL 28, ZHEJIANG PROVINCE, CHINA

Yang Dao was certain that some-
thing was wrong. After a lifetime of planning operations
for the Chinese military, the major general had developed
the keen ability to sense when trouble was looming on the horizon. Unfortunately, his sixth sense didn't give him the clairvoy-
ance he needed to understand exactly what was troubling him.

The major general had been unaware of Tang Ju-Long's last-
minute trip to America. He wondered what the programmer could
possibly be doing in the United States right now. Surely, Tang Ju-
Long remembered that his virus was about to be unleashed, and
going to America just before that grand event was sheer stupidity.
To make matters worse, Yang Dao had absolutely zero contact with
his spy cell in America. He assumed his team was doing everything
possible to ensure the successful launch of the computer virus, but
with less than six hours to go, there was still too much uncertainty.
And uncertainty, in any conflict, was just as lethal as bullets or
bombs on a battlefield.

SALT LAKE CITY, UTAH

Besides Adam and Reina, there was nobody else in the black Suburban with tinted windows. Tanner hastily played out several possible escape scenarios in his mind, but they all seemed futile. Reina was a full arm's length away from Tanner, and her pistol was aimed at his head with unwavering precision. She would have ample time to pull the trigger before he could get to her. However, there was something else about the young Latino woman that was more frightening then the 40-caliber Smith & Wesson she held in her hand. Reina's dark brown eyes were void of emotion. She was a killer—an assassin with no conscience. Although she hadn't spoken a word, Tanner knew that Reina would kill in a second if needed.

"Tanner, you've caused us all sorts of trouble," Adam said. He calmly drove the Suburban out of Camp Williams. He didn't want to alert the sentry at the gate that someone was hostage in the back seat. "I had foolishly hoped that you would give up, especially after the second attempt on your life, but your persistence was quite impressive."

The traitor indeed came from the Secret Service, but Tanner thought the mole would have been Todd with his caustic personality, not Adam. Tanner had even grown to like Adam over the past week, and the thought that he had seen all the NSA's secrets on the Dragon Virus caused the bile to rise in Tanner's stomach.

Tanner searched for something to say. "Where's Sara?" he asked.

Adam ignored Tanner's question. It was time to get down to business. "You're in way over your head. You've screwed everything up, but in a few minutes, you'll get your chance to fix it all."

Even though Tanner's stomach was turning with anxiety, he tried to remain calm. His kidnapping in New Mexico was a nightmare, but he had learned a couple of valuable things from the horrible ordeal—remain calm and buy time. Tanner knew the longer he could stay alive, the better chance he would have of escaping or being rescued.

"What do you want from me?" Tanner asked. He wanted to keep Adam talking. Tanner had learned that, for some reason, the bad guys always liked to talk—except for Reina. She hadn't said a word since Tanner had gotten in the SUV.

"You'll find out shortly," Adam said. He drove the Suburban up the on-ramp to Interstate-15.

"What if I don't want to cooperate?" Tanner asked. There was a hint of sarcasm in his voice. He had nearly died yesterday, and he didn't need to take any abuse from a slimy traitor.

Unfortunately, Tanner's arrogance came across as too much for his kidnappers. Adam quickly shouted something in Spanish, and Reina moved before Tanner had a chance to react. In a fluid and rapid motion, the sinister woman smashed the butt of the handgun against the back of Tanner's skull, knocking him unconscious.

———

FBI FIELD OFFICE, UTAH

Derek was perplexed. It was past 7:00 a.m., yet Sara hadn't checked in from the hospital. His repeated calls to Sara's cell phone immediately went to voice mail, indicating that her phone was off or out of range.

Derek needed to get feedback from someone at the hospital. He called the number for the police officer stationed outside Megan's room. Derek was surprised to hear Sheriff's Deputy Teuloi answer the call. He was the cop that had miraculously saved Tanner and his wife from the carbon monoxide poisoning the previous night.

"This is Al," the deputy answered.

"Hi, Al. This is Derek Cannon. I didn't know you were on duty over there."

"Yeah, I just switched out with the other guy about ten minutes ago. I figured it was the least that I could do to help out," he said. Al still felt responsible that Tanner and his wife almost died on his watch.

"I've got a problem," Derek said. "Sara was supposed to come

218

over with Tanner to see his wife, but I can't get a hold of either of them. Have you seen them around?"

"I haven't, and the cop that I just replaced said it's been quiet ever since Megan had her C-section," Al said.

Derek's ears perked up. "Wait, what did you say?"

"Megan had an emergency C-section to deliver her baby. She's still unconscious, but the doctor—"

"What's this about a baby and Megan still being unconscious?" Derek asked.

Al started over from the beginning. He wasn't sure why he was repeating everything to the FBI because he had thought they already knew the story. "The doctors performed an emergency C-section last night about 7:00 p.m. They said the baby was having a hard time from the carbon monoxide in Megan's blood. The emergency surgery went well, and as soon as the baby was delivered, Megan's oxygen level started coming up."

"You said that Megan is still unconscious, right?" Derek asked.

"Yes, she's still unconscious," Al replied. "What's going on?"

Derek quickly summed up the call he had received from the hospital earlier that morning. It became instantly clear to both law enforcement officers that Derek had received false information.

"Someone is lying to you, because that's not what I'm seeing here," Al said.

"This smells rotten, Al. I want you to double-down and keep a watch on that place. Let me know immediately if you see Tanner or Sara," Derek commanded before hanging up.

Flipping through the caller ID on his phone, Derek called back the same number that had called him earlier in the morning. The phone rang five times before being transferred to another extension. "Intermountain Medical Center. How many I direct your call?" the operator politely asked.

"Yes, this is Special Agent Derek Cannon of the FBI. I received a call earlier on my phone from extension 1480. I was trying to dial that number back. It's supposed to go to a Dr. Cassandra Tappen."

"One second, please," the operator said. "That's not Dr. Tappen's number. It appears that extension goes to a phone in the cafeteria. That's why it rang back to me when nobody answered."

"Thank you," Derek said. He didn't even give the operator a chance to say good-bye before he ended the conversation.

Something bad was happening, but Derek didn't have time to get all the facts. Instead, he initiated a full-blown manhunt. He ordered his team in the conference room to alert every cop within a hundred mile radius of Salt Lake City to be on the lookout for a missing FBI agent and a NSA analyst. He also put out a high priority bulletin for a black Suburban with special government license plates. If the Suburban was traveling anywhere in the state, Derek hoped a cop would see it.

NSA DATA CENTER, UTAH

Helen was worried by the call she had just received from Derek. It didn't make sense that Tanner wasn't at the hospital, but Helen trusted Derek's intuition. If the FBI thought someone took Tanner, Helen didn't want to argue. She immediately got her team involved.

"I just spoke with Derek at the FBI. Tanner never made it to the hospital," Helen said. "Furthermore, it seems that someone lied about Megan coming out of her coma."

Mel spoke up, immediately asking the question that everyone was thinking. "Was it Reina?"

"We can't be sure, but I personally watched Tanner get into the Suburban with Sara earlier this morning. So if something happened to them, it had to be on their way to the hospital," Helen said.

"Are we sure they didn't just get side tracked or something?" Rachel asked.

"We aren't sure of anything," Helen said. "But the FBI is organizing a manhunt right now. They'll let us know as soon as they find anything."

"So what can we do about it?" Sydney asked. Even though Tanner's teammates were concerned, they recognized they weren't in a position to go out and look for him.

Helen took a breath as she posed an interesting question to her team. "Is there any way that Tanner can disable the virus blocker?" Fortunately, before Tanner had gone to the hospital, he updated his teammates on the function of the program that he had put in place to keep the virus from launching.

"Why would he do that?" Mel asked.

"Maybe that's why he's missing. Maybe someone is forcing him to turn it off," Helen said. "That would explain Tanner's mysterious disappearance at such a critical time."

Rachel spoke up. "Let's say Reina kidnapped Tanner and was holding a gun to his head. He still couldn't turn off the program. He'd have to do it at the console," she said. She was referring to the isolated computer terminal inside the Chamber.

"So then why kidnap Tanner?" Helen asked. "I don't believe for one second that his disappearance is coincidental."

"That's a good question," Mel said. "Maybe Reina or whoever took Tanner doesn't realize that he can't stop the virus blocker from the outside. It's a waste of time."

Helen shook her head back and forth. "I can't put my finger on it, but we're still missing something."

"Let's call those guys at the MART," Rachel said. "They're the ones who helped Tanner create the virus blocker in the first place."

FORT MEADE, MARYLAND

In a basement office at NSA headquarters, Slammer and Viper battled in an intense game of air hockey. Copious amounts of Mountain Dew and pizza kept the two brothers awake, but now they found themselves on edge. In an effort to burn off some nervous energy, they engaged their favorite pastime.

The phone started ringing, but they ignored it for a full thirty seconds until Viper scored the winning goal. Slammer threw down his paddle in defeat and ran over to the phone.

"This is Slammer," he said. He sounded out of breath.

"Hi, this is Helen Ripplinger at the Utah Data Center. I've got my team on the line. How's it going over there?"

"Good. We're not seeing any changes on the virus front," Slammer said. He put the phone on speaker for his younger brother to hear.

Viper entered the conversation. "The ping requests are still coming from that server in China."

"We've got a problem here," Helen said, skipping to the critical point. "Tanner's missing."

"Like, voluntarily or involuntarily missing?" Viper asked.

"Involuntarily," Helen said.

"That's not good," Slammer said. "Are the cops looking for him?"

"Yes, the FBI is working on finding Tanner and one of their missing agents," Helen said. "We've been brainstorming why someone might want to kidnap Tanner. Is there any way that Tanner can disable that antivirus routine that you guys created?"

Slammer thought for a moment before answering. "That depends on what you mean about disabling."

"Explain that, please," Helen said. Even in her tired and worn-out state, she still maintained her social etiquette.

"Tanner can't turn off the program because it's running on a private, isolated network at your data center. He'd have to be on site to do that, right?" Slammer asked.

"Correct," Mel answered for his teammates.

Viper then finished his older brother's line of thinking. "But Tanner could tell the Chinese how to alter their ping program in a way that would completely ignore our countermeasures."

Slammer took back control of the conversation. "Basically, the Chinese would be able to craft a work-around and bypass our blocking routine."

"How difficult would that be?" Rachel asked.

"I don't know how elaborate the computer virus is, but theoretically it might be as simple as changing just a couple lines of code," Slammer said. "But why would Tanner want to help out the Chinese?"

"We're thinking the Chinese might have kidnapped Tanner, and they're forcing him to modify their virus so it will still launch even after the pings stop," Helen said.

Slammer let out a whistle, expressing his deflated mood. "Then we're screwed, because with Tanner's insight, there's no possible way for us to know how the Chinese might alter their virus. We won't be able to stop it."

APRIL 28, SALT LAKE CITY, UTAH

For the second time in just an hour, Tanner was rudely awakened by someone throwing cold water on him. This time, however, it wasn't Sydney splashing just a handful of liquid on his face. It was Reina who jolted Tanner into consciousness by dumping an entire bucket of icy water over his head.

"Wake up, Tanner!" a male voice shouted.

It took Tanner a few moments to get his bearings because of the massive headache at the base of his skull. He was in a large hotel room, sitting in a chair with soaking wet clothes. Reina stood directly in front of him, staring penetratingly into his eyes. She was holding a plastic ice bucket, like the standard kind found in every hotel room in America. She had discarded her blonde wig, and she now had her jet-black hair pulled back in a tight ponytail. Standing next to her was Adam. With his arms folded across his chest, he appeared to be studying his victim for signs of alertness.

"Tanner, can you hear me?" Adam asked impatiently.

Tanner didn't say anything. He just slowly rolled his head around as he gazed about his periphery. He noticed a third person sitting on a couch at the far side of the hotel suite. Older than both Reina and Adam, this man was distinctively Asian in his appearance. He looked like a college professor with the wire-framed glasses on his taut face.

Adam spoke again with more urgency. "Tanner, answer me."

"Yeah, I can hear you," Tanner weakly replied.

"Good," Adam said. "I need you to focus. Do you understand?" He approached Tanner and offered him a towel. Tanner took the white towel and wiped the water from his face and head, realizing that he wasn't tied up or restrained in any manner.

"I knew the mole had to be someone in the Secret Service, but I thought it was Todd, not you," Tanner said.

"Payne?" Adam said with a pompous laugh. "You disappoint me, Tanner. I thought you were smarter than that."

"Why did you do it?" Tanner asked.

"That's a fair question," Adam said. He paced to the other side of the room as he gathered his thoughts. "Why do people commit treason?" he rhetorically asked. "Money, power, glory . . . ," he said. He let his words trail off and then turned toward Tanner and gave his honest answer. "Revenge."

"Revenge? For what?" Tanner asked. The fog was fading from his mind, and he was becoming more alert.

Adam's face showed resentment. "For killing our parents," he said.

"What?" Tanner asked. He was sincerely confused.

"I'm not even an American. Do you know that?" Adam said. "I was born in Mexico, just over the border from El Paso. So was my sister." He pointed to Reina.

The revelation that his captors were siblings shocked Tanner. He quickly made the connection in his mind. *Rey and Reina, king and queen, brother and sister.* Tanner looked over at Reina for confirmation on what her brother had just said, but she didn't flinch. She only stared back, keeping a watchful eye on their captive.

Adam continued his soapbox rhetoric. "We're orphans. Our parents were killed in the crossfire between rival drug gangs. Those are the same gangs that traffic drugs over the border into the United States—to feed *your* country's drug addiction!" He was becoming more agitated and animated, shouting at the top of his lungs. "Drugs have destroyed my country, and now I'm going to destroy yours. It's payback time for our parents' death, twelve years ago to this exact date!"

Something snapped inside Adam. He had become completely unglued, and he started shaking. Tanner wasn't a psychologist, but he decided that Adam might have some sort of a mental illness. It was frightening how quickly the Secret Service agent changed personalities. Then Reina, sensing her brother's out-of-control emotions, quietly said something in Spanish. Adam turned away from Tanner and looked at the closed drapes. A second later, he turned back around. Just as fast as Adam's crazy personality had arrived, it was gone.

"I've got a friend who is going to ask you a few questions about the computer program you wrote to block our virus," Adam said.

The Asian man on the couch stood up and walked over. He grabbed a chair and put it next to Tanner. It was then that Tanner recognized the mysterious man was Tang Ju-Long. The virus's architect sat down and placed his fingers on his laptop keyboard.

"How do I bypass your countermeasures?" he asked in perfect English.

Tanner didn't say anything. He let a few moments pass.

"Don't waste our time," Adam said. "We know you can tell us how to defeat it."

"I am ready to make the change. Please tell me how to do it," Tang Ju-Long said. His voice had a tone of pleading. It seemed that he knew something bad was about to happen.

It did.

Tanner was completely blindsided by a hit from Reina. She punched Tanner with a martial arts move that landed perfectly on his side. Tanner doubled over in pain, sure that the assassin had just broken one of his ribs. Even though he wanted to yell out, Tanner stifled his scream. He didn't want to give Reina the satisfaction of knowing that she had hurt him.

"How do I defeat your program?" Tang Ju-Long again pleaded.

Gasping for breath, Tanner turned back toward the Asian man. His eyes showed fear. Tanner said nothing.

Again, Reina attacked Tanner. This time she kicked Tanner's left shin in a quick and sharp manner. Tanner's tibia and fibula both broke with an audible snap. He fell out of his chair, shrieking in agony.

Adam was surprised that Tanner was still resisting. A person could live with a broken rib, but Adam knew that a fractured shin was an extremely painful injury.

"We can keep breaking bones all day until you give us the answer!" Adam shouted. "Quit wasting our time, and tell us how to defeat your program!"

Tanner knew he was in a no-win situation. Refusal was the only card he had to play. Laying on the floor in agony, Tanner made his patriotic decision. He would never let the Chinese launch their computer virus, even if it meant that he would die in this hotel room. Expressing his refusal, Tanner closed his eyes and bowed his head, bracing himself for another blow.

Adam stood over his victim, looking down in disgust. "So, that's how it's going to be?" he asked. "Very well, then."

Adam looked up and nodded toward Reina, giving her free reign to do with Tanner as she pleased. But instead of striking Tanner again, Reina quietly said something to her brother in Spanish. The siblings retreated to a corner of the room and spoke in private for a moment. Although Tanner couldn't hear their conversation, he could tell the two were debating something. After a minute, Adam came back over to where Tanner was on the floor.

"My sister believes that you won't talk regardless of how much she hurts you, but we've found a solution that will work better for everyone," Adam said.

Tanner glanced up in time to see Reina grab her coat and storm out of the room.

APRIL 28, NSA DATA CENTER, UTAH

It was 7:30 a.m. on Friday morning, and Helen patiently waited for her phone call to be answered. After learning that the Chinese could create a work–around with Tanner's insight, Helen didn't suppose that her analyst had been kidnapped. She *knew* that Tanner had been kidnapped, and she was determined to convince the FBI of the same conclusion.

"This is Agent Cannon," Derek said, answering his phone.

"This is Helen. Where are you?" She could hear the road noise in the background.

"I'm on the way to the hospital with a couple of agents. We're going to interview the staff watching Megan. Something isn't right over there," he said.

"We know what happened to Tanner," Helen said.

"What?"

"We think the Chinese kidnapped him, and they are forcing him to create a work-around so their virus can still attack us," Helen said.

"How do you know that?" Derek asked.

"Yesterday afternoon Tanner executed a program that effectively blocked the Dragon Virus from launching. Somehow the Chinese found out about this, and they grabbed Tanner on his way to the hospital. They're probably making him disable his program right now," Helen said.

"That means someone on the inside is still leaking information to the Chinese," Derek said.

"Where are those Secret Service agents?" Helen asked.

"They're probably at the airport," Derek said. "Their flight leaves this morning."

Helen went for broke. "It has to be either Todd or Adam. We've felt since the beginning that someone in the Secret Service was selling us out."

"What about someone on your team?" Derek asked.

"That could be, but everyone is here with me. Except for going to the viewing last night, nobody has left this building," she said.

Helen spoke with such urgency that she convinced Derek to follow up on the Secret Service agents. "Okay, I'll see if I can track down Todd or Adam. I still have their contact information somewhere. In the meantime, keep your staff together in one place," he said.

———•———

Derek hung up the phone and flipped through the notebook on his lap. He found the mobile number for Agent Payne just as the SUV pulled up to the main door of Intermountain Medical Center. He dialed the number.

"This is Agent Payne," Todd answered in his typical, unfriendly voice.

"Todd, this is Derek. Do you have a second?"

"Make it quick. I'm just about to drop off my rental car," he said.

"I need you and Adam to come back into the office. Something urgent has come up," Derek said. He continued his conversation as he briskly walked through the hospital entrance with two FBI agents in tow.

"I can't miss my flight," Todd said. "But you can probably still catch Adam. His flight isn't until later this afternoon."

"Adam isn't with you?" Derek asked.

"Nope," Todd announced. "He said he was going to push back his flight so he could do some sightseeing before he left."

That sounded odd to Derek. "When was the last time you talked to him?"

"Last night before he went to bed. Why?"

"Tanner and Sara both disappeared this morning on their way to the hospital, and now it seems that Adam might be missing also."

Todd suddenly recognized the gravity of the situation. "Okay, how long has everyone been missing?"

"Tanner and Sara have been gone for over an hour, and Adam might have been gone since last night," Derek said.

"Have you tried his cell?" Todd asked.

"I'm just about to interview some of the staff here at the hospital. I was hoping you'd be able to call him," Derek said.

"Okay, I'm turning around right now. I'll call Adam and tell him to meet us at your office," Todd said.

———•———

Driving back toward the FBI field office, Todd hit the speed dial for his partner's cell phone. The call instantly went to voice mail. Driving with one hand while he worked his phone in the other, Todd brought up the number to the hotel where he and Adam had stayed for the past week. Fortunately, the number was still stored in his call log.

"Room 854, please," Todd told the hotel receptionist who answered the call.

"I'm sorry, but he has checked out," she said.

"This is Agent Todd Payne of the Secret Service. Adam Crawford is my partner. You probably remember us staying there the past week."

"Yes, I remember you," said the hotel clerk.

Todd was sincerely confused. "You said Adam has already checked out?"

"Yes, it looks like he left last night," she said.

"Wait, he checked out last night?" Todd asked. Something wasn't right.

"Yes, he checked out around 11:00 p.m. Is there anything else I can help you with?" she asked.

"No thanks," Todd said. He ended the call.

Todd's thought about the strange ways his partner had behaved the last couple of days. Adam had acted more aloof and secretive as the week went on, and checking out of the hotel early was very unusual. In retrospect, Todd now recognized that something wasn't right with his partner. He stepped on the gas and zoomed past the exit to the FBI field office. He had somewhere else to go.

———•———

It was the most pain that Tanner had ever experienced. His entire leg felt like it was on fire, and no amount of water would stop the burning. Every time he took a breath, his side hurt like it had a knife stuck in it, yet Adam did nothing to ease Tanner's discomfort. He just left his victim on the floor where he had fallen out of his chair.

Adam sat motionless on the foot of the bed. He stared at the blank TV screen, watching nothing in silence. He was lost in a dissociative trance. On the other side of the room, Tang Ju-Long cowered alone on the couch. He wasn't used to the violence, and he had moved as far away from Adam as possible.

Tanner accepted the fact that he was going to die. He found comfort and solace in knowing that his death would bring relief from his physical pain. On the other hand, his heart ached with remorse. His imminent death meant that he would never see Megan again or be able to hold his newborn child. Nevertheless, if this was how God wanted his life to end, Tanner decided to calm his thoughts and prepare for his fate.

After what seemed like an eternity, the phone in the hotel room started ringing. It rang several times and, for a while, it appeared that Adam wouldn't snap out of his trance. After a dozen rings, he quietly stood up and answered the call. He spoke a couple of words in Spanish and then walked over to his victim.

Tanner rested in an awkward position on the floor, trying to support his broken leg and rib. But Adam didn't care about Tanner's well-being, and the Secret Service agent forcefully turned Tanner's head to the side before putting the phone receiver next to his ear. "There's someone who wants to talk to you," he said.

Tanner listened on the phone, expecting a familiar voice, but all he heard was the high-pitched wailing of a newborn baby. His face lit up.

"That's your baby girl," Adam said. His eyes burned with a psychotic vigor. "Since you don't care what happens to you, maybe you'll care what happens to your daughter." He grabbed a fistful of Tanner's hair, lifting his victim's head off the floor. He stared directly at Tanner. "I'm going to ask you one more time to tell us how to defeat your computer program, or your entire family dies, starting with your baby girl."

Tanner wasn't sure how Reina had managed to find his newborn baby, but the situation had changed. While he was fully prepared to die, Tanner wasn't willing to sacrifice his family. His innate, fatherly desire to protect his newborn daughter prevailed.

"Okay," Tanner said with a defeated, short breath. "I'll do it."

"That's a wise decision, but I'll tell my sister to stay at the hospital until I'm sure that you've done your part," Adam said. He took the receiver away from Tanner's ear and spoke a couple of Spanish phrases to his sister. Adam ended the call and then and looked over at Tang Ju-Long in the corner. "Get over here!" he shouted.

Tang Ju-Long stood up and started walking over toward Tanner. Suddenly, the exterior door to the hotel room flew open. A large man lunged through the entrance, and forcefully pushed Tang Ju-Long to the ground.

"Get your hands up!" Todd shouted. He pointed his SIG Sauer P229 firearm directly at his partner.

Time stopped as everyone held their positions. The two Secret Service agents were only twelve feet apart. Adam kept his hands above his shoulders, stalling for time as he planned his next move. An evil smile slowly formed on his face.

"Don't do it!" Todd yelled.

Adam swiftly reached for the gun tucked under his belt, but his actions were futile. Todd had anticipated the move, and he quickly fired off two shots, hitting Adam in the chest and then in the head. He was dead before he hit the floor.

"Stay there!" Todd shouted to the Chinese man on the ground. Tang Ju-Long willingly complied, realizing that this frenzied situation was a lot more than he had bargained for.

Todd lunged forward and kicked the gun out of Adam's hand before assisting Tanner. Although he wasn't exactly sure what had happened, Todd could tell that the Tanner's shin was broken by the awkward angle it rested on the floor.

"It's okay," Todd said. "Help is on the way."

Far off in the background, Tanner heard sirens approaching. He clenched his teeth in pain. "It's not okay. She's at the hospital," Tanner said.

"Who?" Todd asked. He had a puzzled expression on his face.

"Reina," Tanner gasped. "She has my baby."

APRIL 28, SALT LAKE CITY, UTAH

Just as the chaotic situation was calming down at the hotel, a panic was forming at the hospital. Derek and two FBI agents had just checked in on Megan. She appeared to be doing well, but she was obviously still in a coma.

"She's been unconscious ever since she arrived at the hospital," Dr. Cassandra Tappen said. She quickly escorted the FBI agents down the hallway to another location in the hospital. "I've been here the entire time, and I didn't authorize anyone to call you."

"I want to interview the entire staff," Derek said. The group stopped at the nurse's station in the middle of the third floor. "Let's start with everyone on duty now, and then get the names of whoever was on duty for the past twenty-four hours."

A faint buzzing sound began, and it was soon followed by a loud ring. Derek took his cell phone out of the holster on his hip. Checking the caller ID, he saw the call was from Todd. "This is Derek," he said.

"Reina is at the hospital right now. She has Tanner's baby!" Todd shouted.

"What?" Derek asked. He put a finger to his other ear to quiet the noise around him.

"I found Tanner at a hotel. He's hurt, but okay," Todd repeated. "He says Reina kidnapped his baby."

"She's here right now?" Derek asked. The other two FBI agents and medical staff stopped talking. Something important was happening.

"Yes, but you've got to move fast," Todd said.

"You said you found Tanner. What about Sara?"

"She's not here, but there's no time to explain. Go!" Todd shouted.

Derek put his phone away with a confused look. "Where's Megan's baby?" he asked.

"I assume she's still in the NICU on the lower level," Cassandra said. She was referring to the neonatal intensive care unit. "What's wrong?"

"That was someone at the Secret Service. He said that our suspect is here at the hospital, and that Megan's baby is in trouble." Suddenly, the urgency of the situation encompassed Derek. "Show me where the baby is now!"

Bypassing the elevator, the FBI agents followed Cassandra down the stairs of Building 4 to the lower level. When they opened the door to the labor and delivery unit, they were greeted by a hospital security officer and the head nurse on duty, Caroline White.

"The nurse's station up on three said you were coming down. How can we help?" asked Caroline. She was an older woman with gray hair. In every way, she resembled the image of a sweet, little grandmother.

"Where's the Stones' baby?" Derek asked.

"We moved her out of the NICU and into the main nursery about three hours ago," Caroline said.

"Show us the way," Cassandra ordered before Derek got a chance to say anything. In a hospital, a doctor outranked a senior FBI agent.

"Follow me," Caroline said. She quickly led the group down the hall. When they got to the nursery, she scanned her ID badge to unlock the door. "It's for security purposes," she said. She opened the door and ushered the group into the room.

The nursery at Intermountain Medical Center was large and state-of-the art. Derek quickly surmised that every woman in Utah must have delivered her baby at this hospital. There were dozens of bassinets, all filled with newborns wrapped in pink or blue blankets.

"Where's my staff?" Caroline asked. "There should always be a minimum of two nurses in here." Then she heard a faint sound coming from the supply closet in the back. She tried to open the door, but it was stuck shut. Someone had jammed an object in the keyhole.

"Move over," Derek said as he gently pushed the head nurse aside. The former basketball star raised his size sixteen shoe and kicked the storage room door in a powerful movement. The handle snapped off, and two female nurses spilled out of the closet.

"She took the baby! She took the baby!" the youngest woman cried. She pointed to the empty bassinet where the Stones' baby had been. "I tried to stop her, but she pointed a gun at me and took my ID badge."

The other, middle-aged nurse spoke in a calmer fashion. "She left with the baby about ten minutes ago."

"Where did she go?" Derek asked.

"We didn't see. She locked us in the closet," the younger nurse shouted. She was so frantic that she was almost incoherent.

Caroline grabbed Derek by the arm. "She can't leave the floor. All the babies have monitors on their ankle. It would trigger an alarm," she said.

"So she has to be hiding somewhere on this floor?" asked Derek.

Caroline nodded her head with urgency. "Yes."

Derek turned toward his junior companions. "I want some agents up here right away. We're going to search every room!"

Caroline stayed to comfort the two weary nurses, while the rest of the group ran out of the nursery toward the main desk on the floor. "I want this level sealed off," Derek shouted as he sprinted down the hall. "Nobody gets in or out."

The hospital security officer acknowledged Derek's order and radioed for backup from the local police department. Derek then turned to the medical staffers at the main desk and gave them further instructions. "I want two of you to take up positions in the hallway. Keep everyone confined to their rooms. The rest of you come with me!"

As two nurses monitored the long hallways on either side of the floor, Derek directed everyone else toward the farthest point in the maternity ward. "We start at this end and search for a Hispanic woman and a baby girl. Look in every room, every closet, everywhere!" he shouted.

The hospital staff nodded their heads and headed out in various directions. Unknown to Derek, the staff practiced a similar drill twice a year. Even though child abductions from a hospital were extremely rare, the employees knew it wasn't completely out of the realm of possibilities. That was the exact reason for the security sensors on the all the babies' ankles.

The search went on for several minutes as the hospital employees and FBI agents efficiently worked their way down the first hall. Startled patients were ordered back into their rooms by the two nurses monitoring the hallways. A few minutes later, four cops from the local police department arrived and took up positions on every exit. With the entire floor securely locked down, Derek felt it was only a matter of time before they found Reina.

Moving slightly ahead of the rest of search party, Derek came to the laundry room for the maternity ward. He opened the door and stepped inside. It was much larger than he had expected, filled with piles of both clean and soiled linens. There were dozens of shelves with pressed laundry stacked in place. It was a perfect landscape for hiding.

Derek quietly worked his way around the hampers of towels and sheets, recognizing that any noise in the room was effectively muffled by all the laundry. Straining to listen, he heard a faint sound. It was cry of a baby. He stopped in his tracks and attempted to get a bearing on the direction of the noise. Suddenly, out of nowhere, a broom handle struck Derek on the back of the head. He lunged forward and collided with a shelf of clean towels, cutting his forehead on an edge of the cabinet in the process. He reached out for something to steady himself, but he ungracefully fell over and landed on his back with a thud. Searching for his unknown assailant, Derek saw someone step out from behind a rack of white lab coats.

It was Reina.

The assassin was dressed in green hospital scrubs. She held a baby wrapped in a pink blanket in one arm, and a broomstick in the other. Skillfully swinging the wooden pole with one arm, she lunged at the FBI agent on the ground. Derek raised his forearm to shield himself against the blow, but he only managed to slightly slow down the velocity of the weapon. The broomstick still smashed on top of his head and broke in half. Derek fell on his back again, but he managed to raise his foot just in time to catch Reina in her knee as she attacked. She recoiled back in surprise and smiled.

Reina decided that she needed both of her hands free to finish off the giant law enforcement official. She placed the baby into a hamper full of laundry and took up a martial arts position. Derek staggered to his feet and prepared for the upcoming sparring match. Reina did a quick roundhouse kick, catching the tall FBI agent in his left side. With her victim off balance, Reina moved in for a series of punches. Derek turned and brought his right arm around in a sweeping motion. Reina quickly ducked under his wild swing and skillfully landed two punches squarely in his stomach. Derek grabbed his abdomen and fell back against the wall. The petite woman was taking him to the cleaners.

Derek decided that he had enough and reached for his Glock 22 handgun, but the weapon wasn't in its holster. Somehow it had fallen out, and Derek figured it was probably buried in a pile of laundry somewhere. Out in the hall, he heard men shouting and banging on the locked door.

"You hear that?" Derek asked. He squared off against his assailant. "The cops are here. You'll never get away."

Reina flashed an evil smile, silently communicating that she had securely locked the entrance after Derek came in. This would be a one-on-one fight.

Derek primed himself for more action. Getting into a fighting stance, he prepared for an attack. Reina leaped forward. While she was definitely more skilled in combat than Derek, the FBI agent was a lot bigger. At six feet eight inches tall, Derek's reach was almost twice that of the smaller woman's. He jabbed at Reina with his right hand, catching her squarely on the cheek. Reina fell sideways and into a pile of linens. Derek reached down to grab her, but she began throwing all sorts of laundry, attempting to disorient him.

With towels and sheets flying all over the room, Derek blindly lunged forward at Reina. He wasn't expecting how quickly she would recover from his punch. She caught Derek right under the chin with a powerful kick that rattled though his jaw and into his teeth. He fell backward onto the ground in a daze. Reina bounded up and landed on her prey, clawing his face and gouging his eyes. Derek fought back mightily, using all his strength to throw Reina off his chest. He pushed her backward over a stack of towels.

The pounding on the door grew louder as Derek again staggered to his feet. Reina was hiding under a large pile of dirty laundry. He prepared for the assassin's next attack, but he was caught off guard by a muffled gunshot. The door to the laundry room flew open, and two police officers rushed in. One of the cops was holding a fireman's axe, and Derek quickly realized that the policeman hadn't shot the lock. He had broken the handle off with the axe.

A sickening realization came to Derek as he lunged forward into the pile of towels. Frantically throwing linens all about, he uncovered Reina's hiding spot. She was dead. In her hand was Derek's Glock 22 pistol.

"Search the room!" a cop shouted.

"Forget it. She was the only one in here," Derek said.

He sat back on the ground in tired exasperation. His primary suspect was gone, along with the chance of getting any information from her. In a defeated gesture, Derek grabbed a towel and held it to the cut above his eye.

"She must have realized there was no way out," an FBI agent said.

Several of the hospital staff rushed into the room. "Where's the baby?" one of them asked.

"The baby!" Derek shouted. He jumped up and started removing blankets from a large industrial hamper. "She's in one of these bins!" he yelled to the others. They all began frantically searching for the infant.

Derek didn't hear any crying, and he was worried that something had happened to the baby during the fight. Pulling back a large white sheet, Derek saw a pink blanket. He reached down and gently lifted the baby out of the hamper. A large smile broke out across his bloody face.

"It's okay," he said with relief. "She's asleep."

APRIL 28, SALT LAKE CITY, UTAH

Word quickly spread about the miraculous recovery of the Stones' baby, and soon the entire maternity department at Intermountain Medical Center was buzzing with excitement. Derek had become an instant celebrity in the eyes of the hospital staff. People patted his back and congratulated him for a job well done. The FBI agent took the celebration in stride, realizing that his work was far from over.

"That's a nasty cut. Let me have a look at it," Dr. Tappen said. Derek had just returned the baby to nursery when Cassandra saw his injury. She escorted Derek back to the nurse's station where he patiently waited as she stitched closed the cut above his eye.

An FBI agent and a local cop approached Derek during his small procedure. "We found this on her," the agent said. He handed Derek a cell phone.

"That's it?" Derek asked. He examined the device and saw that it was password locked.

"There wasn't anything else. No ID, no car keys, nothing," the cop added.

Derek popped off the phone's back cover and found the Mobile Equipment Identifier or MEID. It was a unique, hexadecimal number that corresponded to a specific cell phone. "Call the office and have them track this number. See if we can get a call history from the phone carrier," he said.

"I think two stitches will do it," Cassandra interrupted. She put a bandage over the wound. "You're a great man." She gave Derek a quick kiss on the cheek before packing her stuff and heading off to help check on the baby.

Derek turned in time to see a smile on the faces of the two other law enforcement agents. "Looks like you have a new admirer." The police officer laughed.

Derek didn't counter the taunt, but issued an order to the cop instead. "Have the staff review the security tapes for the hospital. Maybe we can see how and when Reina got here." The police officer acknowledged the request and quickly left to find the security room.

"Did we get her prints?" Derek asked the junior FBI agent.

"Yes, I've already sent them over." The FBI had a paperless technology that allowed them to digitally scan a suspect's fingerprints with a wireless, handheld device. It dramatically reduced the time required to identify a suspect.

"I want you to stay here and manage the investigation," Derek said. "I've got to track down Agent Payne and see what he knows about Tanner." Standing up, Derek felt the bruises from his fight. Even though she was much smaller, Reina had surely packed a punch.

Derek grabbed the other FBI agent from the laundry room, and they quickly walked out to their Suburban in the parking lot. Once inside the vehicle, Derek made a call to the Secret Service.

"Todd, this is Derek," he said after the call was answered. "We found Reina, but she killed herself before we could take her into custody."

"What about Tanner's baby? Is she okay?" Todd asked.

"Yes, both the mother and baby are fine. This hospital is crawling with cops now, so I'm confident that nobody else will disturb them," Derek said. "Where are you?"

"I'm at a hotel just off State Street," Todd said. He gave directions to Derek.

"Okay, we're on our way right now. We'll be there shortly."

"Adam is dead. I shot him," Todd announced dryly.

"What?"

Todd spent the next several minutes explaining everything that had happened.

After hearing the update, Derek replied by telling Todd what had occurred at the hospital. Using the information they had each discovered, Todd and Derek started filling in the gaps in the investigation.

"How did you know where to find Tanner?" Derek asked.

"It was a hunch. The Secret Service uses this hotel for protecting witnesses. I was hoping that Adam would naturally choose this one for his hideout," Todd said.

"Where is Tanner now?"

"He's on the way to the hospital. He's pretty banged up," Todd said. "I'm surprised he didn't talk."

"What about Sara?" Derek anxiously asked.

"Sorry, she's not here. Tanner doesn't know where she is either," Todd said. Then he offered surprising news. "But I've got the creator of the virus in custody. He's talking like crazy. We're getting all sorts of good stuff from him. He doesn't want to go back to China, and he's already requested immunity."

Derek took the news with renewed optimism. Even though Rey and Reina were dead, Tang Ju-Long was a significant lead. "We just pulled into the hotel parking lot. We're on our way up, right now," Derek said. He ended the call and sprinted up the stairs with the other FBI agent in tow. When they arrived, the hallway was blocked by a local police officer.

"FBI," Derek said. He flashed his badge to cop.

"It's okay. They're with me," Todd called out from down the hallway. He escorted the two FBI agents past the crime scene tape and into the hotel room. Derek immediately recognized Adam's body against the far wall.

"One shot in the chest, and one shot in the head," Derek observed.

"I was on the Vice President's protective detail for ten years. I learned how to handle a gun during that time," Todd said.

"I didn't know that," Derek said. "Why did you change jobs?"

"I was transferred out of protective detail because of my bad attitude," Todd said. He didn't offer any other details.

Derek looked around the room. "Where's Tang Ju-Long?" he asked.

"He's waiting in the next room," Todd said. He escorted the FBI agents to the computer programmer.

Derek could see that Tang Ju-Long was still shaken by the recent events. Walking up to the man sitting on the bed, Derek introduced himself. "I'm Special Agent Derek Cannon of the FBI."

"I didn't want any of this to happen. I was only following orders," Tang Ju-Long said. "Don't send me back to China."

"I guess that's an option if you're willing to cooperate," Derek said. "But you've got to tell me everything you know about this computer virus, and what we can do to stop it."

Tang Ju-Long nodded his head in agreement. With his intimate knowledge of the entire Chinese operation, he knew the FBI would have no problem keeping him around.

APRIL 28, FBI FIELD OFFICE, UTAH

Tang Ju-Long told Agent Cannon everything during the thirty–minute drive back to the FBI field office. In return for asylum in the United States, Tang Ju–Long detailed exactly how the computer virus worked and who was the mastermind behind the entire program. Derek took copious notes of the conversation but only as a backup pre–caution. The FBI vehicle was equipped with a hidden micro–phone that recorded Tang Ju–Long's entire confession for legal purposes.

Every investigation seemed to have its tipping point—a time when the dam holding back the facts broke under the pressure of good detective work. Derek felt like that barrier had just crashed down, and he was now flooded with new information and leads. When the FBI Suburban pulled into the parking lot at 10:00 a.m., Derek had gotten his second wind. He ran upstairs to the confer–ence room while the other FBI agent took Tang Ju-Long down–stairs for formal processing.

Derek burst through the door of the makeshift command center. "Attention, everyone!" he shouted "I've got a dozen different leads that we need to track down simultaneously."

He quickly divided the work among the team. One crew focused on the information about Reina, while the other group continued the search for Sara. After a few minutes, everyone was busy with their assigned tasks. Derek then excused himself for a moment. He went back to the quiet of his office to call Helen at the data center. He knew she would be blown away with what he had discovered.

"This is Helen," a familiar voice answered.

"This is Derek. You won't believe what I'm going to tell you," he said.

"Wait," Helen said. "I'm putting this call on speakerphone so the rest of my team can hear." She sensed something important was coming.

Derek spoke uninterrupted for ten minutes. He highlighted the story behind Tanner's kidnapping, and how Todd had tracked down and killed Adam before rescuing Tanner. Moving on to the story at the hospital, Derek recalled his search for Tanner's baby and his deadly fight with Reina. He concluded by reassuring Helen and her team that Tanner, Megan, and their baby were all safe. Helen was the first one to reply when Derek finished his unbelievable update. "That's unbelievable. Adam was the traitor the entire time." Like Helen, the rest of the NSA analysts were stunned.

After a few seconds, Sydney entered the conversation. "That explains how the Chinese knew so much about our efforts to stop the virus. They had inside information."

Derek dropped another bombshell. "That's not the entire story. We have Tang Ju-Long in custody. He flew in last night to change the computer virus. We captured him at the hotel where Tanner and Adam were."

"Is the virus still scheduled to launch in two hours?" Helen asked.

"Yes, that's what Tang Ju-Long said," Derek confirmed. "Do you guys think you'll be able to stop it?"

"If the Chinese didn't alter their program, then our counter-measures will hold," Rachel said.

"Tang Ju-Long said the virus was embedded in a computer chip on the motherboard. Does that make sense?" Derek asked.

"Absolutely," Mel said into the speakerphone. "It's brilliant, actually. Even if we find a way to remove the virus, the computer would re-infect itself as soon as it was rebooted. The only way to guarantee that the virus is completely off the computer is to physically remove the chip."

"But how do we know which computers have the infected chip?" Sydney asked.

"I can probably help with that," Derek answered. "Tang Ju-Long said that every computer system made at the Fengconn factory in Shenzhen in the last three years had the chip hidden on the motherboard. According to a report from the Secret Service, all the computer systems that control the stock market were made at that factory."

"There's a lot more computers than just those systems at the stock exchange. All the major PC manufactures in the US get their motherboards from Fengconn," Mel said, adding salt to their wounds. "I guess that's what happens when we ship all our manufacturing overseas."

"I've got an agent working with Tang Ju-Long to get a copy of the actual virus code. I'll send that over as soon as I can," Derek said.

"That would be great," Helen said. "I'll get our folks at the MART to analyze it, and see if they can find an easy way to identify which computers are infected. In the meantime, we'll just have to keep our fingers crossed and hope that the blocking program will keep the virus from launching."

"I've got one more thing here," Derek said before ending the call. "Does the name Yang Dao mean anything to you?"

There was silence on the line for a few seconds before Helen spoke up. "Yes, that name is code word classified here at the NSA."

"Well, who is he?" Derek asked.

"Let's just say if there was one man in China that ran all their cyber-warfare operations, that would probably be him," Helen said.

"Tang Ju-Long gave us that name. He said Yang Dao was the mastermind behind the entire virus program."

"We've suspected for a while that he was a major player in China's computer espionage program," Helen said. "I'll pass that name onto our folks at headquarters. In the meantime, I suggest you let the CIA know about Yang Dao."

Derek understood Helen's subtle suggestion. If someone had the ability to go after Yang Dao, it was the CIA. "I'll do that," he said. "I need you to do whatever you can to isolate and remove that virus. I guess that's what you guys at the NSA do best."

"And we'll leave the Reina investigation to you," Helen said. "Hopefully you'll be able to find Sara."

"I hope so," Derek said. He still held out hope that he'd find Sara alive, but the odds weren't in his favor. Statistically, after more than twenty-four hours, missing people were often dead.

APRIL 28, FBI FIELD OFFICE, UTAH

When Derek Cannon returned to the command room, he found his peers busting with excitement.

"Great news, Derek," an FBI staffer said. "We got the call log from Reina's cell phone. It appears that she called and rented a car from the Salt Lake Airport. It's a black Dodge Charger."

Another agent entered the conversation. "We forwarded that information to the team at the hospital, and they found a vehicle in the parking lot that matches the license plate. They're going over the car with a fine-tooth comb right now."

Derek nodded his head. "Can we get a copy of the rental agreement from the car company? Maybe we can get her name and address from that."

"I'm on it," a junior agent said. He picked up the phone to make a call.

Another FBI agent hung up her phone and spoke to Derek. "We've got positive confirmation. Basic DNA evidence shows that

Reina and Rey are definitely siblings," she said. The facts were coming in fast now.

"That's good news, but we had suspected that," Derek said. "Do we have anything new about Reina?"

"We're still working on it. The Secret Service is sending us over all the information they have on Adam Crawford. They were shocked to learn that one of their own was behind all of this," she said.

"I bet," Derek said. He took a drink of lukewarm water from a bottle. "What about Sara? Do we have anything on where she is?"

A third agent at the end of the table spoke up. "Nothing yet. We're still looking for her and our missing Suburban."

"Yes!" shouted the junior agent on the phone. He was speaking with the rental car agency. "Will you fax that over to us?" he said before hanging up. "We've got an ID on Reina! She goes by the name Maria Lopez. They're faxing over a copy of her driver's license and credit card."

"I'm sure they're both fakes, but it's a decent starting point. Good job, everyone," Derek said.

———•—•———

The conclusive evidence of a cyber-attack against the United States presented more than just a technical problem. It was also a political fiasco. Passive spying against an adversary was commonplace, but launching an active, aggressive computer virus against a nation was considered an act of war. While her analysts worked on the technical nuts and bolts of the virus, Helen discussed the political impact of the virus with the admiral over the NSA. He reassured Helen that he would deliver all the information to the President of the United States in a special meeting at noon. It would then be up to the President to decide how to respond to China.

As Helen discussed politics with the NSA's head officer, the rest of the QC team was on a conference call with Slammer and Viper, examining the exact payload of the virus. It was only then that the true destructive nature of the malware was known.

"We better hope and pray that Tanner's blocking routine works, because this virus is super-lethal," Slammer said over the phone. Except for Tanner, the other analysts on Helen's team weren't very skilled in understanding malware. They had to rely on the MART team for the specific details on how the virus worked.

"How lethal?" Rachel asked.

"Just imagine every bit of financial data that you have is suddenly wiped out. All your bank accounts, credit cards, 401(k), everything. It's all gone in minutes!" Slammer said.

Viper jumped into the conversation. "Until you physically remove the computer chip that has this malware, it will keep infecting the system. You could restore the data a thousand times, but it still wouldn't make a difference."

"So the only realistic way to deal with this virus is to physically crack open every computer system and visually inspect to see if it has the bad chip?" Mel asked.

"That's why it's so nasty. We've never seen anything like this. I mean, there's always been talk of a ROM-embedded virus, but nobody here has ever seen it," Viper said.

"It would take years to go through all our computers," Rachel said. "We're talking about millions of infected systems. It would be impossible to completely remove the virus."

"I guess we could start with the high-profile servers, like the computers that control the stock exchange and major banks," Sydney said. "Maybe that would help."

"Look, this virus is supposed to launch in less than two hours. When the Chinese see that nothing has happened, they'll immediately try to fix it. We have to assume that they will eventually be able to launch the virus, even without Tang Ju-Long's help," Viper said. "Although we have Tanner's blocking routine, I bet we only have a few days to find all the chips and disable them before the Chinese discover a method to get around our antidote."

It was then that the NSA analysts realized the daunting task before them. The remedy to the computer virus required physically interacting with every infected computer system in the

United States. No government agency in the world had the time or resources to do that.

"Dude, wait a sec," Slammer said. He was examining the print-out for the virus program. "What's this 'put' statement for?"

"What do you mean, like an update routine?" Sydney asked.

"Yeah. It's way down in the virus code on line 1451. It's just a small function. I missed it the first time I glanced through this, but it looks like the virus is expecting an update of some sort," Slammer said. He was onto something. "Wait! This could be an EEPROM chip, not a ROM chip, we're talking about."

The NSA analysts understood the significance of Slammer's revelation. A ROM, or read-only memory chip, was hardcoded with a programming routine. It was permanent and couldn't be changed, but an EEPROM chip (Electrically Erasable Programmable Read-Only Memory) had the ability to be reprogrammed. If the virus code was stored on an EEPROM chip, there might be a way to reprogram the chip and disable the virus all together.

"I think we might be able to write some code to knock out this virus. Even better, we could fry the EEPROM when we're done so it would never be reactivated," Slammer said with renewed confidence. "Do we have the code for the master server in China that is sending out the ping request?" he asked.

"No, but maybe Tang Ju-Long could give us that info," Rachel said.

"Well, where is he? I could figure this out in ten minutes if I could just ask him a few questions."

APRIL 28, FBI FIELD OFFICE, UTAH

Agent Cannon thanked his lucky stars for the geniuses at the NSA. He had just finished speaking with someone named Slammer on the MART team. While Derek had to restrain his laughter at the silly alias, Slammer obviously knew what he was talking about when it came to computer viruses. Right now, Tang Ju−Long was on another phone line with Slammer, explaining exactly how the master server in China worked. With a lot of luck and some cyber−magic, Derek hoped the NSA might be able to perma− nently defeat this Dragon Virus.

While Derek had been awake for thirty-two hours, he didn't feel tired. There was more good news with the FBI's investigation on Reina. The driver's license and credit card that she had used to rent the car were indeed forgeries, but they proved to be valuable resources. The same credit card was used to rent a hotel room in Boise the night that Jeff Kessler had been murdered.

The FBI's investigation hit the jackpot a short time later when a rookie agent called from the hospital. He had been searching the black Dodge Charger for clues. "We know Reina's residence," he said excitedly. "We found a parking tag for an apartment complex called Wasatch Apartments in the glove box."

"One second," Derek said.

The FBI agents in the surveillance van had previously sent Derek a list of all the apartments within one mile of where they had last seen Reina. Searching down the list, Derek found it—Wasatch Apartments, 8350 South Redwood Road. He couldn't believe how quickly things were moving now.

"Great work. I'm going to send our surveillance team over there with a picture of Reina. Maybe the landlord or whoever rented the apartment can identify her," Derek said.

———•———•———

The charcoal-gray Ford van pulled up to the rental office for Wasatch Apartments. It was a massive complex with over five hundred units, covering a full city block. Agents McMahon and Skidmore walked into the rental office, while the electronics technician remained in the back of the surveillance van.

"Good morning. I'm Special Agent Lloyd McMahon of the FBI," the seasoned law enforcement officer said. He flashed the manager his FBI badge. "This is my partner, but don't mind his scraggly appearance. He's been on vacation," Lloyd said with a smile. "We're looking for someone in an investigation. Have you seen this woman?" he said. Lloyd handed over a picture of Reina to the office manager.

"Yes, that's the woman in 325, I believe," said the manager.

"How long has she lived here?"

"She started renting back in February, so I'd say just over two months. She's very quiet," the manager said.

"Her name is Maria Lopez. We believe that she is involved in a crime, and we need to examine her apartment. Can you show us where it is?" Lloyd asked.

The manager showed the FBI agents to apartment 325. Lloyd

knocked loudly on the door while Cameron stood off to the side. Nobody answered.

"Open the door, and then step back," Lloyd said. Using a master key to all the apartments, the manager opened the door and quickly stood aside as Lloyd took out his gun. He stepped through the door, followed closely behind by Cameron with his Glock 22 in hand.

The apartment didn't seem unusual. The lights were off, but the shades were partly opened, allowing daylight to fill the main living area. A couch and TV occupied the front part of the two-bedroom apartment, and an oak table stood off in the corner of the kitchen. Lloyd noticed a black laptop on the table.

Walking down the hall, Lloyd peered into a large bathroom that had a washer and dryer hidden behind a set of closet doors. He checked behind the door, but nobody was there. He let down his guard.

Cameron came into the room. "Nobody's here. I checked everywhere and there's no sign of Sara."

"Let's call Derek and give him an update. Maybe we can get something off that laptop we saw on the table," Lloyd said.

———•———•———

It was just before noon when Derek heard from the FBI agents at Reina's apartment. Unfortunately, there was still no sign of Sara, but they did find a critical piece of evidence—the laptop that Reina had presumably used for all of her secret communications. For the second time in twenty-four hours, Derek called upon the services of Ricky Hawes to provide forensics analysis on the computer. Ricky was on his way to Reina's apartment, and he promised to have all the information off the laptop by the end of the day.

The surveillance team also found an official Mexican passport at the apartment. Reina's picture was on the document, along with the alias of Maria Lopez. While it was moderately easy to get a fake driver's license and credit card, forging a passport was extremely complicated. Derek knew the best counterfeits were always made by a nation-state, and China was at the top of the list for exceedingly high-quality forgeries. Derek passed on the information to the Department of Homeland Security, hoping to have them track down when and where Reina had entered the United States.

Derek leaned back in his chair and closed his eyes, blocking out the sights and sounds of the hectic conference room around him. For some reason, it always seemed like the ending of an investigation was exponentially faster than the beginning. He couldn't believe that it had only been five days since he was called out to investigate the crash of Flight 2512. It seemed like it was over a year ago that he had found the discarded SAM container at the golf course. While the facts about Reina were coming together, they had still hadn't learned anything of Sara's whereabouts. Derek swallowed hard. He worried that she wouldn't be found alive.

"Here's the report from the NSA," a young woman said, interrupting Derek from his thoughts. She handed him a folder with the word "secret" across the top. It was the complete bio of Bryan Morrison. Unknown to Helen and her team, Derek had requested all the information the NSA had on Bryan through the Attorney General over at the Justice Department.

"What's it say?" Derek asked.

"I haven't read though the whole thing, but I think he's clean," the agent concluded.

Derek took a couple of minutes to flip through the report. Bryan had passed every polygraph test in his six years of service with the NSA. Before joining the NSA, he had served as an intelligence officer in the US Air Force. Then something caught Derek's attention, and he took a second glance at Bryan's military history. Bryan had once served with an airman named Adam while at the Pentagon. The connection between Bryan and Rey was made.

"It says here that Bryan served with Adam Crawford at the Pentagon. Check out this connection," Derek ordered. "Find out how well they knew each other, and if they kept in contact over the years."

APRIL 28, SALT LAKE CITY, UTAH

Noon came and went with little fanfare for almost every American. They continued with-drawing money out of their checking accounts, buying groceries with their credit cards, and updating their 401(k) retirement plans. Except for the stock market being shut down because of the presidential order, the rest of the banking system in the United States appeared to function normally.

Unknown to the rest of the nation, a handful of analysts at the NSA data center in Utah watched as the virus blocking routine performed brilliantly. The master server in China stopped sending its ping signal at precisely 12:00 p.m., and QC immediately picked up with the duplicate ping traffic. The computer virus embedded in millions of computers across the United States didn't launch.

SHAOXING, CHINA

Halfway across the world in China, the operations center for the First Technical Reconnaissance Bureau was filled with energy. Over thirty programmers sat at their computer workstations, providing real-time feedback on the launch of the computer virus. The layout of the room was very similar to mission control for NASA, with a shift manager coordinating everything from a central desk.

Yang Dao stood next to the manager, waiting impatiently for a status update. "How come nothing has happened yet?" he asked.

"I guess it takes some time for the virus to completely erase all the financial data," the shift manager said. He had issued the command to stop the ping request over fifteen minutes ago.

An assistant seated next to the manager spoke up. "Sir, I don't see any network traffic coming from our master server."

"Is it possible that the ping signals didn't stop?" Yang Dao asked.

"No, I don't think so, but we can physically power off the server to make sure it's completely offline," the manager said.

"Do it," Yang Dao commanded.

The assistant got up and walked out of the control room and down a long hallway. He entered the climate-controlled computer room with thousands of servers, and quickly found the main system responsible for the ping signal. He powered off the computer and physically removed the network cable as well for good measure.

"The system is completely down," he said as he returned to the command center.

Yang Dao looked at the clock on the wall. It was now 2:20 a.m. in Shaoxing. The virus had launched twenty minutes ago. "Shouldn't we be seeing signs of a panic forming in America?" he asked.

"Yes, we should have seen something by now. It's just not making any sense," the duty manager said.

Someone at the front of the room stood up and shouted. "It hasn't launched yet! The virus hasn't launched yet." He ran past the rows of computer desks and up to the major general before saluting. "Sir, we set up a test system at our embassy in Washington. It doesn't contain any real data, but it's infected with the virus just like all the other computers in America," he said. "I just logged into that dummy system and verified the virus hasn't launched. Someone is spoofing our ping requests."

"How is that even possible?" asked the operations manager. He was sincerely confused.

Yang Dao immediately thought of Tang Ju-Long. "I know how," he said with frustration. He pointed to the telephone on the operation manager's desk. "Give me that phone." Yang Dao didn't want to do this, but he was left with no choice. He dialed a direct number to a private cell phone in the United States.

———•———

SALT LAKE CITY, UTAH

Todd was helping the local cops wrap up the crime scene at the hotel. He was just about to leave when he heard a faint chirping sound.

"Someone's phone is ringing," he said.

All the law enforcement officers in the room checked their personal phones, but none of the devices were ringing. The chirping continued. Todd slowly walked around the room, listening for the sound. It was coming from beneath the mattress. He put his hand under the bed and pulled out a cell phone.

Todd immediately recognized the device. It was Adam's personal phone. He answered the call with a cautious "Hello."

"What's the situation there? The virus didn't launch," Yang Dao said in English. It didn't even occur to the caller that Adam might not be the one who answered the call.

Todd quickly guessed that the man calling on the phone was likely part of the spy cell operating in the United States. He motioned for the other police officers in the room to be quiet. "Uh, we've had a problem," Todd said. He disguised his voice in an attempt to keep the mysterious man talking.

Unfortunately, Todd's facade wasn't good enough, and Yang Dao realized that it wasn't his nephew on the phone. "Who is this?" he demanded.

Todd decided it was time to change his approach. "This is Agent Todd Payne of the United States Secret Service. Who is this?"

The phone call quickly disconnected.

FBI FIELD OFFICE, UTAH

The mood had turned somber at the FBI field office. Twenty minutes ago, the local cops found the missing FBI Suburban. It was stashed in a parking garage by the hotel where Tanner had been taken. A quick search of the vehicle revealed a dead body hidden in the back under a blanket. It was Sara. She had been strangled to death.

"I wonder how Reina managed to get to Sara?" a female FBI agent asked. She, like the rest of the staff, was numb from the news of Sara's murder.

Derek took a deep breath. He knew from his own experience that Reina had lethal hands. "I guess Reina somehow intercepted Sara on her way to pick up Tanner at the data center. If that's the case, Sara never had a chance."

APRIL 28, FBI FIELD OFFICE, UTAH

Derek checked the clock on the wall of his office. It was 4:00 p.m., and all indications showed that the NSA's blocking program was working perfectly. He had just spoken to Helen, and she verified that the super–computer was successfully keeping the Dragon Virus at bay. She also informed Derek that the guys on the MART team were currently working on a long–term antidote, and they said it would be ready later that evening. Helen didn't explain how the remedy would be applied to the millions of infected computer systems across the United States, but Derek figured that the NSA had a secret way to do it without the public's knowledge. Some things were best left unsaid when dealing with the NSA.

A knock on the door startled Derek. "Come in," he said.

A junior FBI agent came into the room. She had a folder in her hand. "I've got the initial details on what happened to Sara," she said.

Derek still had a hard time accepting Sara's death. It stung like a nasty cut. "Okay. What do you have?"

"We traced all the inbound calls to Sara's phone. It looks like Adam called her just after she left to go pick up Tanner. We think that he convinced her to stop on her way to the data center. He probably ambushed her and stole the car," the agent said.

"That makes sense. Tanner told us that Reina was wearing Sara's clothes and a wig when Adam picked him up at the data center," Derek said. "They probably killed Sara just before that."

There was an awkward silence as both agents thought about Sara. She had been a favorite among the FBI staff. "I have some other information too," the agent said. "You'll like this." She handed two sheets of paper to Derek, hoping the positive information would dispel the gloom of the quiet office.

The first paper contained a report from Ricky Hawes, the IT specialist who did the forensic analysis on Reina's laptop. He had positively verified that the laptop was the same computer used to send the encrypted emails. Ricky also discovered documentation on several bank accounts registered to Maria Lopez, each with at least $5000. The laptop had accessed the online bank accounts, providing further evidence of Reina's illegal activities.

"So that was her laptop?" Derek asked.

"Definitely, there's no doubt about it," the other FBI agent said.

Flipping to the second sheet of paper, Derek looked at the final fingerprint report. The document positively matched the fingerprints found on the SAM container at the golf course with fingerprints all over Reina's apartment.

"The evidence linking Reina to the attack on Flight 2512 is overwhelming. She was definitely the one who did it," the agent said. "Unfortunately, she's dead, and we don't have anyone to prosecute," Derek said.

The State Department verified that Reina, a.k.a. Maria Lopez, had come into the United States via a flight from Mexico City to San Francisco. The Mexican authorities, however, had no information about this Maria Lopez. Her passport was a fake, and the trail to Reina ended with the flight from Mexico City.

"I know," the other agent said, "but at least we have good information on Rey. That really helped us fill in the gaps."

Since Adam had worked for the government and served in the military, the FBI had significant amounts of information on him. After graduating from high school, Adam had joined the Air Force, where he quickly achieved the rank of E-4 senior airman. It was during his time in the military that Adam had met Bryan Morrison. Bryan was also an enlisted Air Force serviceman, and the two had become friends while serving together at intelligence specialists at the Pentagon.

A search of Bryan's work computer showed that he had corresponded with Adam via email. Bryan had casually mentioned the discovery of an unusual computer virus to Adam who, undoubtedly, had forwarded that information back to China. While Bryan's actions weren't necessarily considered treason, he had definitely broken some rules by carelessly sharing classified information with Adam.

Derek handed the papers back to the FBI agent. "Good work on this," he said. "I'll be back down in a minute." The FBI agent nodded her head and left the room, closing the door quietly behind her.

Alone in his office, Derek let out a big, long sigh. His crazy day had capped off an insane week. Unfortunately, his work was far from over. He was flying to Washington, DC, to attend a formal hearing with several members of Congress and the National Security Council. It seemed that every person of political importance wanted a private briefing on what had happened in Utah. Derek's thoughts turned to Tanner. He was about to go into surgery. Tanner's fibula would heal on its own, but the doctors said they needed to put a plate on his tibia to make sure it mended correctly. Despite the broken leg and rib, Derek knew that Tanner was glad to be at the hospital. His wife was now conscious, and Tanner had been able to see her and his newborn before going into surgery.

Despite the death of his partner, Derek was optimistic about the direction of the investigation. Everything pointed back to China, but it still wasn't clear how Reina and her brother had gotten involved with Yang Dao in the first place. Unfortunately, Derek couldn't do anything about the Chinese general, but he knew that the CIA would find the information useful. He just hoped that the folks at Langley would be able to do something to keep Yang Dao from launching another cyber-attack against the United States.

APRIL 28, FORT MEADE, MARYLAND

With music from the heavy-metal band Metallica bouncing off the walls of their office, Slammer and Viper diligently finished up the remedy for the Dragon Virus. Tang Ju—Long had confirmed that the virus was embedded on an EEPROM chip, and that it could be reprogrammed using a secret code sequence. With that bit of information, the two brothers quickly developed a new rou—tine that would completely erase the computer chip, replacing the virus's code with an alternate set of instructions. The new directions were simple, yet sinister.

The reprogrammed chip would cause the infected computer to send a continuous string of random network packets to every known IP address in China. When the modified virus launched, millions of computers in America would simultaneously flood the major Internet gateways in China, creating a condition called a Distributed Denial of Service, or DDOS, attack. The Chinese Internet would slow to a crawl, unable to process the billions of new connection requests. The infected computers would relentlessly spam the Chinese Internet for two hours and then suddenly stop. At that point, the last function of the brother's program would erase the EEPROM chip, permanently disabling it from running anything in the future.

Slammer and Viper weren't sure why they had been ordered to create a DDOS for two hours against China, but they didn't question their instructions because they came directly from the admiral over all the NSA. He had personally visited the brothers after attending a special meeting with the President of the United States. The admiral explicitly instructed Slammer and Viper to turn the computer virus back on China. Of course, it would be obvious to the Chinese that the DDOS came from United States, but Slammer and Viper realized that was the brilliance behind the retaliation. The Chinese couldn't acknowledge the counterattack because doing so would be an admission of guilt that they had put the virus on the computers in the first place.

While Slammer and Viper weren't sure how this scenario would all play out, they couldn't have been more excited. They would be creating the largest DDOS in history. Taking down the Internet of an entire nation was hard-core, and it would instantly earn the brothers the respect of hackers all over the world. Unfortunately, their accolades would never be officially recognized. The admiral told Slammer and Viper that, if they ever mentioned a word of the DDOS to anyone, he would personally and permanently assign both of them to the NSA's Arctic Listening Post in Fairbanks, Alaska.

———•—————•———

At 8:00 p.m. on Friday evening, exactly eight hours after the Dragon Virus had been scheduled to launch, the members of the QC team prepared to execute the long-term antidote created by Slammer and Viper. The analysts were gathered around the console to QC, unsure if the mysterious code was safe.

"Are you sure this is going to work?" Helen asked. She was on a conference call with the rest of her team.

"Absolutely," Slammer replied. "But make sure you know your bank account balance before we kick it off," he said with a laugh.

"What exactly does this code do?" Rachel asked.

Viper gave an answer. "It's simple. It uses your supercomputer to quickly distribute an updated program to the EEPROM chips on all the infected systems. It will blow away the virus and disable the chip from running anything in the future." Viper intentionally left out the part about the Chinese DDOS attack that would occur for two hours after the update got pushed out.

"I guess that's okay, or at least the admiral thinks it is," Helen said. She had recently spoken to the NSA's director, and he informed Helen that the brothers would be sending her some new code to execute. "Do it," Helen told her analysts.

Sydney pushed the enter key on the keyboard interface to QC, and the supercomputer sprang to life. Using the spoofed IP address of the master server in China, QC magically pushed out a code update to every infected computer system in the United States. It was a feat that could only be accomplished by the NSA, with their supercomputer and their secret backdoors into many of America's data networks. The infected computers across the country quickly executed the code, willingly receiving their update from the masquerading quantum computer. Ten minutes later, the DDOS attack began.

Millions of computers in the United States simultaneously began sending network packets to the primary Internet routers in China. Using some specialized computer equipment at the NSA's Fort Meade complex, the brothers were able to see the increasing latency in network responses from China. Their code was working, but Slammer and Viper were disappointed not to be in China at that exact moment. They wanted to witness their handiwork first-hand. Anything that used an Internet connection, from an ATM to a website, was getting thumped. But that wasn't all. Computer systems running assembly lines at manufacturing plants or servers running subway trains were also frozen, unable to process any information. Computers controlling the cellular phone networks and the power grid also ceased to function. For the next two hours, the Chinese society would grind to a halt as they experienced life in a non-digital world.

—•———•—

SHAOXING, CHINA

At the First Technical Reconnaissance Bureau's facility, panic turned into utter chaos. It was after 10:00 a.m. local time, and all the monitors in the data center were all flashing red, warning of massive network congestion across China. The DDOS attack was well underway, and the Chinese hackers were effectively locked out of their own systems.

Major General Yang Dao was in his office, stewing over the fact that the virus had failed to wipe out America's financial systems as planned. He was also in serious trouble because many of his covert actions over the past week were unsanctioned. While he had authority to conduct an active cyber-espionage program against the United States, Yang Dao acted on his own when ordering Reina to shoot down the American airliner. The manipulation of the American stock market was also unauthorized, and it cost the Chinese government billions of dollars in US investments. Yang Dao was hoping that his illegal actions would have been lost in the economic ruin of America. But the virus didn't do its job, and now the major general's secret acts of war were available for anyone to discover.

Yang Dao was thinking about his awful predicament when his intercom blared out. "General, please come down. We have a serious issue," the operations manager said.

Yang Dao quickly grabbed his gray army jacket before heading down to the ground floor. When he stormed into the operations center, he walked into pandemonium.

"What's happening?" the general asked tersely. The room was in complete disarray.

"Sir, we're being attacked! Our network is totally down. We're completely locked out of our own systems," the manager said.

"How is that possible? I thought we were on a secure network," the general said. Even though Yang Dao wasn't a technician, he understood that the data center was located behind several layers of firewalls. The local network was specifically designed to limit unapproved access from the outside.

"Yes, General, but somehow the attack tunneled back through a single, open network port. It was the exact port that we had opened up in our firewall to allow us to communicate with all the infected computer systems in America," the manager said.

Yang Dao quickly filled in the missing connection. "Tang Ju-Long has told the Americans how to change the virus! They are using it against us!" he shouted.

"What do you want us to do? We cannot log into our systems," the operations manager said. He voice relayed complete hopelessness.

"Shut it down! Pull the plug on everything!" Yang Dao ordered.

Immediately, dozens of analysts who staffed the twenty-four-hour operations center leaped out of their seats and ran toward the door like a herd of cattle, squeezing through an open gate. The mob stormed down the hall, but stopped suddenly at the entrance to the server room. They couldn't get in through the secure door because the computer system that controlled the access card reader was also frozen by the DDOS attack.

"Get security over here!" the operations manager shouted. "We need this door opened now!"

The analysts waited ten precious minutes for the security guards to force their way in. It wasn't until the door was physically broken off the hinges with a crowbar that the programmers finally spilled into the data center. They quickly started pulling out all the power cables and network cords, but it was too late.

Slammer and Viper had coded one particular function in their retaliation program. Knowing the exact computer system in China that was coordinating the virus, the brothers instructed that server to log in to other computers on its same network and begin erasing data. When the computers at the Chinese facility were finally shut down, over 80 percent of the data used by Yang Dao's specialized hacking unit had been deleted.

Yang Dao entered the server room. "What's the damage?" he asked.

"We won't know until the attack is over and we can power everything back on. Fortunately, we have all our data saved off-site. We can restore it from our backup facility in Zhengzhou if needed," the operations manager said confidently.

He was wrong.

———•———

While the First Technical Reconnaissance Bureau was dealing with the virus attack on their primary data center, a suspicious fire started at a unique warehouse in the industrial city of Zhengzhou. Located about twelve hours northwest of Shaoxing, the citizens of Zhengzhou had never paid much attention to the unmanned facility with razor wire and security cameras. But the CIA knew about the secret building, and they had instructed one of their deep cover agents to burn the facility to the ground.

The fire started on the south side of the warehouse, and it quickly spread until it consumed the entire structure. Since the DDOS attack across China had effectively crippled local phone communication, the fire department didn't learn about the blaze until it was well underway. When the fire trucks finally arrived, the warehouse was a complete loss.

Unknown to the local authorities, the burned-out building was the secret disaster recovery site for the computer programmers in the First Technical Reconnaissance Bureau. In less than an hour, Yang Dao's division of army hackers had lost practically all of their data. It would be years before they could recreate their cyber-warfare program.

APRIL 29, WASHINGTON, DC

Saturday morning was normally a quiet time in Washington, DC. Most of the politicians had gone home for the weekend, allowing large groups of tourist to enjoy the millions of pink cherry blossoms out in full bloom without any partisan rhetoric. However, the visitors in the nation's capital were surprised to see a black limousine speeding down the road with a police escort.

If the sightseers could have seen inside the limousine, they would have recognized the Secretary of State. She was on her way to an emergency meeting with the Chinese ambassador. Riding in the car with the US diplomat was a top-secret folder. The contents contained the details of the FBI's investigation into the attack on Flight 2512, the Chinese manipulation of the stock market, and the destructive Dragon Virus. Most important, the report contained evidence pointing to Major General Yang Dao as the ringleader. It was time for the Chinese to come clean about their rogue major general and his cyber-espionage program.

Riding in the silence of her limousine, the Secretary of State envisioned how she would play out her political game with the Chinese ambassador. After exchanging pleasantries, she would present her evidence of the Chinese conspiracy, along with the not-so-subtle hint that the United States was responsible for the DDOS attack that brought China to its knees for two hours. Because of the overwhelming evidence, the Secretary of State knew that the Chinese ambassador would have no choice but to accept the "tit-for-tat," or the equivalent retaliation from the United States. The Secretary of State would then ask for a high-level meeting with the Chinese president to discuss economic matters between the two countries. In an attempt to save face, the Secretary of State knew the Chinese ambassador would have to agree her request. Then the two diplomats would exchange plastic smiles and insincere pleas-antries before ending their meeting. On her way out the door, the Secretary of State would take one last political jab. She would tact-fully explain that, if the Chinese couldn't take care of Yang Dao, the United States would be forced to deal with the rouge general to prevent future complications between the two nations.

APRIL 30, SALT LAKE CITY, UTAH

The morning sun came through the window, illumining the private hospital suite. Tanner stirred in response to the sudden light and tried to turn over to get away from the offending source. Unfortunately, his leg was securely restrained in an upright position, preventing him from moving more than a few degrees in either direction.

"Good morning, Sweetie," Megan said. She was sitting in a separate hospital bed next to Tanner. "We tried to be quiet and not wake you." Megan was in her pink hospital gown, holding their baby. With a beam of light shining directly on his wife, Tanner thought she looked like an angel.

"Oh, it's okay," Tanner said with a yawn. He stretched out his right hand and took Megan's hand in a tight squeeze.

The hospital staff was kind enough to put the Stones in the largest suite they had, but Tanner and Megan were still separated by their individual beds. Tanner blew his wife a kiss before reaching up and scratching his toes. They itched like crazy. His left leg was in a cast and held up by a pulley system, ensuring that his tibia and fibula would heal properly. The surgery to screw a plate in Tanner's shin was a success, but he would still need to do a couple of months of physical therapy to get his strength back to normal. Unfortunately, there wasn't much the doctors could about the broken rib. Tanner would just have to live with it for the next month while it slowly healed.

Megan glanced at the clock on the wall. It was 11:00 a.m. on Sunday morning. "I can't believe you slept in this late, but I guess you deserve it."

She gingerly got out of bed. Her abdomen was still sore from the C-section three days ago, but she was feeling surprisingly well. With the baby beginning to fuss in her arms, Megan leaned over and gave her husband a long kiss, making sure that she didn't bump his suspended leg in the process.

"I love you," Tanner said with a tired smile.

"I love you too," Megan replied. She closed the curtains to block the sun in her husband's eyes, and then sat down in a recliner in the corner of the large room to feed their baby. "Nicole sent us some flowers," she said, referring to their friend back in Albuquerque.

Tanner looked at the direction that Megan was pointing. He noticed a large flower bouquet on the table. Next to the flowers was a small box. "What's in the box?" he asked.

"Derek stopped by on his way to the airport. He didn't want to wake you up, but he left a box of gourmet cookies for you."

"That was nice of him," Tanner said. He stifled a protracted yawn. "But I'm still shocked about Sara. I feel so bad."

Derek had visited Tanner last night, filling him in on the details of the investigation. Reina and Rey were both adopted by their uncle, Yang Dao, over ten years ago. Reina was the assassin while Rey was the spy. Adam was planted in the US government to feed classified information back to China. The entire operation was part of an unsanctioned plan by Yang Dao to destabilize the American economy.

Tanner also learned that his feelings about Bryan had been

wrong. Bryan wasn't a spy. He was guilty of sharing classified information with another member of the intelligence community, but it definitely wasn't anything close to treason.

A loud knock came from the door. "Come in," he said.

"Hey, there you are!" Mel said. He came through the door followed by the rest of the QC team. "We didn't think the cops would let us in. We had to go through three separate checkpoints to get up here."

"How are you doing?" Helen asked, holding a pink teddy bear she had brought as a gift for the baby.

"Doing well, I guess," Tanner said. He gave his boss a simple hug.

"Don't listen to him. We're doing great," Megan said. She held up the newborn for everyone to see. "This is Sara Nicole Stone. We named her after two very brave women."

"Sara is for Sara Heywood, right?" Rachel asked. A quiet fell over the room as everyone thought about what had happened to the FBI agent.

"We felt it was a good way to remember her," Tanner said.

"Who is Nicole for?" Sydney asked.

Tanner shook his head. "That's a story that Helen will have to tell you."

Rachel and her teammates looked confused.

"There's more to Tanner's background than just what he's done at the NSA. I'll tell you when we get back to work," Helen said.

"Look at that," Mel said. He gestured toward the news report on the muted television. "Turn it up so we can hear what happened today."

"What do you mean?" Tanner asked. He'd been out of the news loop for almost two days.

"The Secretary of State had an emergency meeting with the Chinese president this morning. Nobody in the media is quite sure what it was about, but rumor is that China is trying to save face after we announced evidence of their secret cyber-warfare program," Mel said.

"Yeah, the Chinese Internet went down for two hours on Friday. It was the worst DDOS attack ever recorded," Sydney said.

"I wonder who was responsible for that," Tanner said with a wink. The rest of the QC team immediately broke out in laughter.

"What are you all talking about?" Megan asked.

Tanner turned to his wife and gave her a "I love you, but I can't say" smile. He was back to his clandestine ways. He turned up the television so everyone could hear the news report.

"The Secretary of State completed her four-hour meeting with the Chinese president just a few moments ago," the TV reporter said. "Representatives from either party declined to comment on the specifics of the talks, but it appears that the leaders agreed a strong US economy is essential for both countries. In a sign of good faith, China has approved to purchase a half-trillion dollars of US Treasuries when the stock market opens back up tomorrow. The Chinese move should buoy-up the US economy and prevent an almost certain economic recession."

"Yeah, I bet they agreed," Rachel said. "They didn't want to have their Internet go offline permanently."

Once again laughter broke out among the NSA analysts, except for Mel. Being the pessimist of the group, he didn't see anything funny about the announcement. "This doesn't solve anything," he said. "We're back to the same old problem. We keep piling up the debt, and China keeps buying it."

"I guess you're right," Helen said. "But at least the Chinese finally owned up to their cyber-warfare program."

"Do you really think they'll change?" Sydney asked.

"As long as I have you guys around, I'm confident that we'll keep one step ahead of them," Helen said.

It was good to have her team all together again.

EPILOGUE

MAY 5, CHONGWU PENINSULA, CHINA

Yang Dao told himself to relax. It had been five days since the computer virus failed to launch, and he was still alive. Nobody had found him yet, even though he suspected that he was now wanted by both the American and Chinese governments.

The major general fled out of Shaoxing toward the South China Sea immediately after the denial of service attack had ended. Taking a combination of high-speed trains, buses, and taxis, Yang Dao blended into the anonymous crowds of his fellow countrymen. After several days of sporadic travel to elude any followers, he eventually took refuge at his secret villa on the Chongwu Peninsula.

Yang Dao pondered his failure. He had lost everything. Somehow, the NSA had managed to get the best of him and his elite computer hackers. In his solace, the general concluded that it wasn't his fault. The Americans had a supercomputer that trumped everything the Chinese did. Until they either destroyed the quantum computer or developed one of their own, the Americans would maintain the advantage in cyberspace.

Yang Dao decided he needed some fresh air. Walking out on the balcony of his small villa, he watched the beachgoers in the sunny weather. The sound of the waves crashing on the beach was therapeutic for his troubled mind.

The major general knew his brilliant career was over. He'd never be able to show his face again in a military uniform, but that wasn't all. He also knew that he would likely have to leave China to avoid prosecution. Yang Dao wasn't sure if his children were dead or alive, but both Rey and Reina understood the contingency plan. If the operation failed, they were to clandestinely work their way back to the family's villa and regroup with their father.

Leaning on the edge of the balcony, the general noticed a white sailboat as it calmly floated on the water. Taking off his glasses for a better look, he detected the faint images of two people on the vessel. Something flashed in the general's eyes. It was a signal from the sailboat. *Had Rey and Reina returned home?* Yang Dao optimistically waved both his hands, just before a bullet shot through his skull, killing him instantly.

Out on the sailboat, a Chinese military sniper put down his high-powered rifle. "Who was he waving at?"

"Beats me," the spotter said. He continued looking through his field scope for any sign of movement. The major general's body lay motionless.

Confident of his shot, the sniper disassembled his rifle. "Well, he's dead now. Beijing will be glad to know that Yang Dao won't be around to cause any more problems," he said.

The loose ends were all tied off. The major general's botched operation against the Americans was officially over.

ABOUT THE AUTHOR

Few people understand the terrifying, yet realistic, threat of computer hacking like Denver Acey. Denver has spent his entire professional career in the information technology industry where he has witnessed and even thwarted actual cybercrime. From his top–secret job working for the US government to securing computer networks at Fortune 500 companies, Denver is personally familiar with hackers and their unscrupulous activities.

But over the years, Denver has become increasingly frustrated with Hollywood's inaccurate portrayal of cybercrime. Hackers are more intelligent and more sophisticated than simple teenagers who guzzle down Mountain Dew while playing video games. Cybercrime is a billion-dollar business that encompasses organized crime and foreign governments. For these elite hackers, the fruits of success are iconic trademarks, innovative patents, and government secrets.

Because of his unique background, Denver decided to write a book to dispel hacking myths while highlighting the tenacity of cybercriminals. Utilizing actual computer hacking concepts and scenarios that he has experienced firsthand, Denver illustrates—in a simple way for even the non-techie to understand—how vulnerable we all are to cybercrime.